SLAYING PARADISE

The Second Edition

By:

T.V. Holiday

Open Eyes to Infinity

Clear eyes
Sight beyond sight,
No longer the center
For others is my light.

Tender my soul
A magnificent calling awaits,
A legacy that lasts
Engraved in time and space.

Heavyweight blueprints in my mind
For a vision utterly divine,
For those who are lost
It is you I'm set to find.

See with me
Live with me
Cry with me
Ride with me.

God is forever
Love is the message,
Establish that connection
I'll guide you through the wreckage.

Souls free to witness
Ever present in this journey,
For the pathways we trek
To live a life so heavenly.

Contents

T.V. HOLIDAY

Travis Holiday transported his latest prisoner to the Las Colebras Women's Detention Facility. He arrested Chelsea Turner for punching her girlfriend. While driving, she tossed and turned in the backseat. She rambled incoherent sentences and banged her head against the window. She was visibly irritated. Her forehead swelled after banging her head. The sting from the forming bruise momentarily settled her down.

"I hate going to jail. I'm gonna' have to get my vajayjay looked at all because I hit my stupid girlfriend," Chelsea stated. The more she thought about her impending visit, the angrier she became. She frustratingly kicked the backseat divider, which caught Travis' attention again.

"I get you're upset, but stop banging and kicking back there. Don't make this worse than it is," Travis firmly told her. He didn't want Chelsea to hurt herself. Any injury would mean a trip to the hospital, not jail. It had already been a busy shift. He was on his second trip to jail and had multiple reports to finish. Nothing was going to prevent her from going. A hospital visit would only be an extension of his night.

She caught a glimpse of him in the rearview mirror. Chelsea could see his firmness. He had an athletic build and was of average height. She didn't want to test his patience. She nodded to acknowledge his request and leaned back. She didn't mean to be disrespectful. She had been to jail multiple times and wanted to get it over with.

"I'm sorry you're going through this," Travis sincerely replied. He sensed her frustration and empathized with her. "Do your time and move on. Hopefully, you don't go back."

"I wish. Knowing my girlfriend, I'll be back here after the next argument," she sighed.

"If that's the case, why go back to her?" Travis inquired.

Chelsea disappointingly hung her head. He heard her sniffling in the backseat. She wiped her nose with her knee and used her shoulder to wipe her tears. "I don't know," she whimpered.

"Yes, you do," Travis kindly insisted. Although she was a prisoner, he wanted to help her understand what she was feeling. He hated domestic violence incidents. They could be the most violent radio calls an officer could go to. Despite the extremely violent occurrences, they usually involved people who were in an emotional situation that took one step too far. Anybody could've been in his backseat for the same reason.

"No, seriously, I don't. If you've got the answer, then tell, 'cause I'm lost?" she desperately asked.

"You love her," he replied.

His answer brought her emotions to the surface and she sobbed. Travis sat quietly. Although she was under arrest, he saw her as a regular person. He didn't see everyone as a criminal. Travis believed bad people who wanted to hurt others existed. But he also remembered that people made mistakes. His perspective helped him treat his prisoners with respect.

"I hope you aren't beating yourself up about it. It's quite normal, y'know. When we love someone, sometimes we accept more than we should. Love can be blinding," said Travis.

Chelsea felt foolish. She had been arrested multiple times as a result of her relationship. She couldn't imagine other people making similar decisions. "What about you? You ever been blinded by love?" she asked.

Travis hesitated to respond. His mind ventured elsewhere. Her question was one he grappled with from time to time. Memories flooded his mind of incidents where he could've been blinded by love. He knew the answer. He didn't like it either. She noticed his silence, which struck her as odd. It stoked her curiosity. She asked if he had heard her. Her question reeled him back to the moment. He looked in the mirror, where his eyes suddenly looked sorrowful.

"...I have," Travis solemnly answered.

His transparency surprised her. She could tell he was thinking about something. She didn't think he would be honest about it. "Care to share?" she asked.

Travis split his eyes between the road and Chelsea. He contemplated whether to answer her. She seemed desperate to hear what he would say. There were times when he kept parts of his life private. For others, he shared his experiences when he felt it would benefit him and the other person.

He remained silent, and Chelsea, disappointingly, slouched in her seat. She had hoped he would say more. She never met an officer who spoke more to her than was necessary. Travis felt her sadness. She was in a low place. He didn't want to leave her hanging. He could tell this would be one of those times when it would be beneficial to share. If not for him, for Chelsea.

"I'm married," he told her.

Her eyes perked up. She was surprised to hear his response. "How long?" she asked.

"A long time. Like seventeen years long," he gently smiled.

Chelsea excitedly unbuckled her seatbelt and leaned forward. She could hear despite the noise from the freeway and the radios playing in the background. She was anxious to have a conversation with him. "You happily married?"

Travis heard her unbuckle the seatbelt and glanced into the backseat. Her closeness to the window startled him. "Wait, did you take your seatbelt off?"

"What? We're talking! I want to hear you," she nonchalantly pleaded. Chelsea didn't see it as a big deal.

"I appreciate that, but it didn't mean take off your seatbelt. Come on, Chelsea. How the heck did you do that anyway?" he sighed. He couldn't believe she was able to unbuckle herself. He had made sure her handcuffs were secured before they left the police station.

"I got talents. So what, you were about to answer my question…" she giggled. She didn't care about the seatbelt. Their conversation was more important to her.

"Talents, huh? I'll answer that question after you put your seatbelt back on," he responded. It wasn't the first time he had a prisoner unbuckle themselves. He didn't want to pull over forcefully to put her seatbelt back on. He knew that he had her full attention. He believed she would cooperate with him if he simply asked.

"Really?"

He sternly looked into the mirror. Chelsea saw his face and exhaled, "Okay, okay."

She slipped her hand out of the handcuffs and put her seatbelt back on. Travis watched, unbelievably, as she did it. He couldn't believe she was able to slip her handcuffs easily. She slid her hand back into them and smiled in the mirror. She cleared her throat for him to notice she complied with his request. He couldn't help but chuckle at the nature of the situation.

"Now, can you answer my question already?" she mockingly interrupted.

Her sarcasm amused him, and he was glad that she wasn't crying anymore. "I get asked that question a lot. Happiness comes and goes. If we always base things on our happiness, we'd never stick with anything."

Chelsea couldn't believe him. She thought her question was straightforward. His answer seemed contrived. "Are you serious? Who in the world told you that?" she jokingly retorted.

"I read it somewhere," he laughed.

She focused on his eyes through the mirror. She wanted to get a better read of him. Chelsea appreciated his apparent willingness to speak. She was determined to have a real conversation with him. "It sounds like you're lying to yourself," she cynically said.

Her refusal to accept his response confounded him. He thought she might've rejected the idea solely because of the concept. He didn't expect her to turn it around on him. "What? No, I'm not."

"Yeah, you are," she insisted.

"No, I'm not!" Travis became defensive. He wondered what impression he gave to make her think he lied. He replayed his response and examined his tone. In his mind, there was no way he didn't believe what he said.

"You got a girlfriend?" Chelsea asked. His insistence that he was wrong strengthened her confidence. Chelsea believed she was right. He had been nice to her. She wanted to return the favor.

Travis confusingly shook his head. He was bewildered about how the conversation flipped on him. "A girlfriend? I told you I'm married."

"I know. The question still stands. Do you have a girlfriend?"

"No, I got a wife," he persisted. He hoped his answer would stop her insistence.

Chelsea enjoyed the back-and-forth they were having. She didn't want to be disrespectful. She felt he was on the verge of cracking and didn't want to let up. "A girlfriend's more fun. Do you want one?"

"Why you offerin'?" he humorously responded.

His question made her laugh. She had never laughed in the backseat of a police car. She hoped the ride wouldn't end. "Hey, your wife can share. Sharing is caring, right?" she smirked.

Despite the nature of their conversation, he was entertained. "You're funny, Chelsea. Thanks, but I don't think my wife would be okay with that type of sharing."

They arrived at Las Colebras. She was processed and cleared for entry. Travis walked Chelsea to the holding cell where the deputies were set to take custody of her. She tried to reread him. Her time with him was the most positive interaction she had with a police officer, considering the circumstances. He wasn't like the other officers she met.

"You're pretty cool, Officer Holiday. Thanks for being nice. I hope you stop lying to yourself. You're a good guy. Good guys deserve to be happy," Chelsea told him.

Travis appreciated her tenderness toward him. He took her to jail, yet she wished him well. He couldn't help but laugh as well. The deputies came and walked her into the jail. She smiled and waved goodbye before she went out of sight. His interaction with Chelsea was what he enjoyed most about being a police officer. He met people who made him feel a range of emotions. He felt grateful to be a light for people in their lowest moments. His career brought him fulfillment and allowed him to live a life of service, as he had always desired. He couldn't imagine doing anything else.

Chapter
2

Travis finished his shift at midnight without making another arrest. A heavy fog filled the air. The fog in San Diego typically sets in very thick late in the evening. It made driving extremely difficult. Travis got on the freeway to go home. The traffic was light. Despite the fog, people still drove fast and recklessly. Travis lived north of San Diego, and the freeway was under construction.

As he drove home, traffic became busy near the construction. There were more drivers on the road than normal. Travis neared his exit but couldn't merge into the next lane. Cars boxed him out, which frustrated him. He honked his horn at the car next to him. He motioned to an old lady if he could move over. She wore large coke-bottle glasses and could barely see over the steering wheel. She inched forward as they got closer to his exit. Travis honked his horn again and rolled down his passenger window.

The woman looked at him, confused, as he motioned for her to get into the next lane. She waved her hand in response. He asked if she would let him over, but she inched forward and did not respond. Travis motioned to her again, but she drove in front of him. More cars passed as his exit was two car lengths away.

Another car passed and left an opening in the lane big enough for him to enter. He tried to merge into it but was cut off by an F-350. Travis swerved out of the lane to prevent a collision. The truck pulled up to Travis, and the driver looked at him. The driver was a bald man with an eerie smile. The driver smiled and motioned for Travis to move in front of him. Travis waved for him to keep driving, but he didn't move. The man only smiled. Travis gave up and irritably drove in front of him. He missed his exit.

Traffic began to clear, but the fog remained thick. The area surrounding the freeway became mountainous. There weren't any railings along the road, which had a large drop-off on the other side. Travis sped up to 80 miles an hour. No one else was around. The F-350 was elevated and its lights shone through Travis' rear window.

The light reflected off every mirror. The glare made it difficult for him to see.

Travis sped up to 100 miles an hour, but the truck stayed behind him. The driver turned on his bright lights and blinded Travis even more. He passed the exit where he planned to turn around. He couldn't see anything in front of him due to the light and fog. Travis squinted his eyes as the truck moved alongside him. The driver had the same eerie smile on his face and pointed forward. Travis looked back at the road and saw red flares ahead. He saw faint, flashing yellow lights. A broken-down car was in his lane. He slowed, but the F-350 swerved into his car. Travis turned to the right and dodged the vehicle in front of him. The road had no barrier, and he drove off the cliff.

Travis' car flew into the air. The vehicle slammed into the mountain and rolled down the mountain. His head split open after it struck the car ceiling. His ribs cracked when his chest smashed against the steering wheel. His knees fractured as they smacked the bottom of the steering column. The car rolled uncontrollably down the hill until it crashed into a set of trees. The car was turned on its side. The airbags deployed and knocked him unconscious.

After an hour, Travis blinked his eyes as he slowly regained consciousness. He looked around and noticed he was hanging from his seat. He survived the crash and couldn't be more grateful. Pain shot through his body as he woke up. He wanted to undo the seatbelt but couldn't move his arms. They were broken. Travis was stuck. He wondered how he would free himself when he unexpectedly heard footsteps approaching the car.

The footsteps stopped and the car moved. It was slowly lowered back to the ground on all four wheels. As Travis sat in the car, a blinding light cut through the fog. It was similar to the F-350 that ran him off the road. A sudden chill trickled down his back. He thought the bald man had returned to kill him. The light revealed it was a man. But it wasn't the bald man. It was a man in a white gown. He had a full beard

     T. V. HOLIDAY

and long, curly brown hair. His skin was fair and his eyes were blue. He approached Travis with a smile and offered to help.

He pulled Travis out of the car. He had feeling in his arms and legs, but couldn't move. His body was covered in blood and glass. The man gently laid him on the ground and stood over him.

"Stand up, Travis," the man gently told him.

"What?" Travis mumbled. He was disoriented but had enough wits left to comprehend what was happening. He realized the man said his first name. The pain wrecked his body and made it difficult for him to respond.

"Stand."

The pain in his body withered away. His bones snapped back into place. His ribs were mended. The blood and glass fell off him. He rapidly felt vigorous. A moment ago, he was overtaken by paralyzing pain. Now he had strength. Travis was astonished at the disappearance of his pain and stood without difficulty. He looked at the man, surprised and bewildered, as the glow around him dimmed. He wondered where he came from. He knew of no mortal man, aside from Jesus, who had the power to heal someone with only a word. Something was extraordinary about him.

"Who are you?" Travis nervously asked.

"Someone who has been watching you. My name is Mark. I was sent here to find you," he answered.

"What are you talking about? Who sent you?" asked Travis. Mark's answer was unsettling. Travis immediately thought about Mark watching him while he was with his family. He wondered if it was true. Nobody could have responded to his crash so quickly. Neither could anybody give him the strength to stand on command. Nothing about the moment made sense.

Mark pointed to the sky and another chill overcame Travis. He couldn't believe his answer. He imagined seeing a heavenly figure, but never believed he would see the day. He still wasn't sure if that day had arrived.

Travis looked at the cliff he swerved from. He didn't believe there was any way he could have survived the crash. His body was broken before Mark arrived. His life didn't flash before his eyes. That was always supposed to be a sign that one's life was about to end. He didn't see a bright light either. Without those signs, there was only one question he had to ask.

"Am I… am I… d-d-dead?" Travis stuttered.

"No, you're not. You've been chosen to defend others in God's name."

Travis was greatly relieved to know he survived the crash. He wasn't ready to leave his family behind. There was much more he wanted to do in his life. He wasn't ready to die.

"Why me? What have I been chosen for?" Travis shockingly replied. He felt a heavy weight land on his shoulders. He was fearful to hear Mark's next words. His presence brought a level of significance. Anything he was bound to say would have the potential to change his life. Thoughts raced through Travis's head. He pondered what Mark's statement meant. He felt there were many ways to interpret its meaning.

"For years, you always had the feeling that you were preparing for something. I'm here to tell you that you were right. The time you were preparing for is here. It's time for you to fight for others on behalf of God. Your life here is over. Your new life is waiting for you in a place named Carnage Coast. It's a place where only I can show you. You will have to follow me," instructed Mark.

Mark's revelation paralyzed Travis. He felt like he was dreaming. He looked at his car and realized it was not a dream. It was real. Very real. "What is my new life supposed to be in Carnage Coast?" he asked.

"You will become someone to fight against evil in its purest form. You will bring back lost souls. You will become the light in the darkness.

You will become God's fist in his war against Lucifer. God needs you to embrace the mantle of The Iron Warrior," said Mark.

Travis was speechless and baffled by his disclosure. If Mark was right, any doubts he had about the Bible would be erased. For God to exist meant evil existed as well. It would mean the parts of the Bible he chose to ignore, the Ten Commandments, God's words, all of it would be real. He spent his life choosing to believe what was written because he had to choose to believe something. He felt that the other religions contained fragments of truth. All of it would be wiped away with Mark's revelation.

"What is The Iron Warrior?" he fearfully asked.

"The Iron Warrior is the one who is strong, hardened, and dedicated to serving others. Iron signifies hardness and strength. It doesn't bend or yield under pressure. Warriors, fight for something greater than themselves. They develop themselves so they can be strong enough for others. The highest honor a warrior can have is to serve and show love to others. Isn't that the way you live your life? How can The Iron Warrior be anyone else but you?" explained Mark.

Travis couldn't believe what he was hearing. Travis didn't feel he was strong enough to be The Iron Warrior. He didn't feel he could be who God wanted him to be. He struggled with it daily. "I'm sure there are others who would be more qualified than me," Travis responded.

"Others weren't chosen. Someone who had the approval of the Lord saw something in you," Mark revealed.

Travis was stunned by Mark's response. He expected him to say God, but he didn't. He wondered who Mark referred to. Since it wasn't God, he didn't feel the same obligation as if it were.

"Why are you reluctant to answer God's call?" asked Mark.

"Who says I'm reluctant? You said that someone who had God's approval chose me. I'm not refusing God. If I say no, I'm refusing the person who chose me." Travis countered.

"To refuse that person is no different than refusing God. If you tell God no, you will be no different than anyone else he has called upon," Mark told him.

Travis' eyes watered. Mark was right. "I'm not telling God no. I'm just trying to go home. I go to church, I pay my tithe, I lead small groups. I try to live a good life. I'm already doing everything I can. I can't do more," Travis explained. He wanted to be a man after God's heart. He divided his time among his responsibilities to be the man whom he felt God wanted him to be. The thought that God wanted more was unbelievable.

"Those things don't constitute all of God's work. God has plans for everyone who chooses to do his will. Those things may be everything for someone else… but not for you. More is required from you. Deep down inside, you know it. That is why you have been able to do everything you mentioned. You can handle those things. You can do that because your true job is much greater," Mark revealed.

Travis broke down. Mark was right again. Every time he felt he wouldn't be able to answer God's calls, he was proven wrong. God gave him the strength to continually do more.

"When you run from the battles you must fight, your path will always bring you back to them. There are battles you must fight. Running only delays the inevitable. Don't run from this," said Mark.

Sadness filled Travis. He had a family to go home to. A family he loved more than life itself. He believed it was his life's purpose to raise his son to manhood and grow old with his wife. "What about my family? Will I ever see them again?" asked Travis.

"I am not allowed to answer that. Understand that your choice carries a great weight. Many things will happen no matter what you choose. But if you refuse, you may never see them again," Mark informed him.

"Why can't you answer that?" Travis begrudgingly asked. He was faced with the biggest decision of his life. He wanted more clarity. He wanted more answers if he had to possibly walk away from his family. He never wanted to be in a position to choose between God and his family. Yet there he was.

Travis leaned back and looked up to the sky. He couldn't see through the fog. He thought about his faith. He heard his older brother's voice say, "I walk by faith and not by sight." He couldn't see God, but he had to make his decision based on faith. Faith that it was the right decision. He looked at Mark and wondered. Travis knew Mark was a heavenly person. He didn't question it. Travis could feel God's presence through Mark's words.

"Are you sure you have the right guy? I mean, I curse, I fight… I'm not perfect. I mean, straight up… I can be an asshole. Even my wife has called me one. Are you sure those are the qualities for someone who is supposed to be The Iron Warrior?" asked Travis. He couldn't help but question Mark. To be The Iron Warrior seemed much bigger than him. He wanted Mark to realize who he was talking to. Travis didn't want Mark to make a mistake for something of such great importance.

Mark laughed at his comments. He could sense his nervousness. "Travis, I believe that is why you were chosen. God does not look for those who are perfect to serve him. He looks for those who are willing and able."

Travis looked at Mark and felt righteousness in him. The feeling assured him that the moment was not an accident. Travis badly wanted to see his family. They were his world, and he didn't want to live without them. The only light in his choice was the possibility of seeing them again. For him, any choice that involved seeing them again was the right choice.

"Alright …I'll do it. I'll become The Iron Warrior," said Travis. "Now what am I supposed to do about my family? How are they going to find out about me? What are they going to be told?"

"There is nothing for you to do. That will be taken care of," said Mark.

"Why did I have a feeling you were going to say something like that?" asked Travis.

"Don't worry, Travis, God will provide for those you leave behind and the future before you. Now come with me. Trust me, Travis. Trust God," Mark instructed.

Travis followed Mark into the fog. Fear and trepidation crept into his heart as he followed Mark. He wasn't sure what he was getting himself into. He was leaving everything he knew behind. He was chosen to become The Iron Warrior. To put his mind at ease, he tried to focus on the possibility of seeing his family in the future.

Chapter
3

eanwhile, in Carnage Coast, a woman named Lynda Lynch walked down the street. She wore a short, shoulderless red leather dress with three-inch red high-heeled boots. Her lips were bright red. Her long brunette hair stopped at her shoulders. Black eyeliner outlined her hazel eyes. Red blush highlighted her cheeks.

She stopped at the corner of Third and Broadway Avenue. It was a slow night for Lynda. It was cold and no one was out. She desperately needed money. The rent was due on her 500-square-foot apartment, which wasn't worth the money she paid. Any money she earned wasn't hers to keep. Lynda worked for the biggest pimp and drug pusher in Carnage Coast, Lazarus.

Lazarus controlled 30 women. He pimped them to local political figures and his business associates. He pushed narcotics through his women and created a stranglehold over the streets. He gave his political friends and business associates percentages of his profits and women to buy their cooperation. Lazarus was the most powerful man in the city. He offered the ultimate good time to anyone willing to pay.

Lynda was an alcoholic. She had difficulty keeping a job. One night, she was drunk and smashed a beer bottle across a woman's face, which led to a bar fight. She was arrested for assault. While in jail, she was noticed by a woman named Kym. Kym and the woman Lynda injured worked for Lazarus. He paid her bail and made Lynda one of his prostitutes as punishment for injuring one of his women. She worked for Lazarus for six years. Lynda was at rock bottom and didn't know any way out. Her hatred for life and Lazarus grew every night she was on the street. Every date was the worst night of her life.

"YO!" a voice blared from down the street.

Lynda turned and saw two men approaching her. Their arms were covered with tattoos and bandanas covered their bald heads. There was a Hispanic man named Hector and a white man named Slim, who paid large sums of money to do whatever they wanted to Lynda. Lazarus never allowed Lynda to go to the hospital. If she did, Lynda paid with the little bit of money she had. She couldn't afford it. If she spent money that was supposed to go to Lazarus, he called Hector and Slim to punish her.

Lynda did not acknowledge them. She did not look forward to seeing them again. They cornered her against a light pole. Hector glared at her while Slim bit his lip and looked her up and down. She gave them their drugs and hoped they'd leave her alone, but she knew better. She knew what was coming. Her silence angered them. They promised to make it quick since they had prior engagements. Their promise didn't bring relief.

Hector grabbed Lynda's hair and pushed her in front of him. Her body went numb as she thought about the hours ahead of her. During her time with them, Lynda never thought she would make it to the morning. Her body was beaten and ravaged. Slim sped up and pushed her down. Hector grabbed her hair and dragged Lynda into a dimly lit alley before she could stand. Her legs scraped along the concrete. They were out of sight of everyone.

An hour passed, and Lynda lay motionless on the ground. Hector and Slim were gone. She was in pain. Her eyes swelled from the impact of their fists. Her neck had imprints of Slim's hands around it. Her hair was filled with trash. Her dress was torn across the stomach. The bottom of it was hiked up. She felt where they rammed her head into a dumpster. Her hand was wet from the blood that trickled from the wound. Lynda tried to move her legs but cringed at the slightest movement. She was torn on the inside. Lynda could not feel all of her teeth. Her lips were cut and swollen. Blood flowed from her broken nose onto her mouth. Somehow, though, she was still alive.

Lynda lay on the ground until she could move. Footsteps could be heard nearby. She hoped no one would see her. She couldn't defend herself. She hoped it wasn't Hector and Slim. Lynda lay as still as possible. She breathed slowly as she leaned against the building. The footsteps stopped in front of her. She looked up but could barely see through her swollen eyes. She saw a faint figure of a man standing above her. The light in the alley was too dim to see anything else.

"How could those animals do such a thing?" he asked softly. He knelt in front of Lynda, who remained still. She hoped her silence would convince him to leave.

"Lynda, I know you can hear me. I can understand why you're so quiet. You don't know who I am. I could be another guy like those two animals who have been doing this to you," said the man.

Lynda tried to look at him again, but her vision was blurry. "H-h-how do you k-know me?" she stuttered.

"Lynda, I've watched you walk these streets. No one has been taking care of you. A woman like you deserves someone to treat her properly. You should have someone who wants you. Someone who wants you for who you are. I've been wanting you for a while now, Lynda. Your life doesn't have to be this way," he explained.

She tried to sit up but was in too much pain to move. She wanted to see who was talking to her. "Who are you?" asked Lynda.

"My name is Luc. There is no need to be embarrassed. I want to help. You don't deserve what's happening to you," said Luc. He gently grabbed Lynda's arms and leaned her against a building. His hands were warm to the touch as if they had been hanging over a fire. They left a burning, tingling sensation on her body.

"You're not one of those religious crusaders, are you?" she asked. She kept her guard up as much as possible. Lynda met numerous religious men and women while she walked the streets. They cursed and condemned her to hell. People whom she had never met called her a sinner. They were hypocrites in Lynda's eyes, and she didn't want anything to do with them.

"Not at all."

"Good 'cause I don't believe in that shit anyway. God doesn't care about me, and I don't care about him. I hate him," she said. Luc smiled. Her anger and hatred toward God were genuine. He could feel it.

She tried to pull herself up but couldn't. She didn't have enough strength to stand or pull herself up. Lynda gave up and sat back against the wall. Trying to stand up took a lot out of her. She scanned the ground and reached for her money. She couldn't afford to lose it.

"You don't need that money, Lynda. If you give me what I want, you'll never need money again," said Luc.

Lynda was able to come back to her senses. His response intrigued her. To Lynda, he sounded weird. But there was something about him that strangely moved her. His words were alluring.

"Look, Luc… you sound like a pretty nice guy. You really sound like a stalker, but no thanks. I really need to go. I need my money. I have to get more, or that's really gonna be my ass. So, can you please just leave me alone?" Lynda told him.

"Is this really the life you want to go back to? I can give you something different, Lynda. All you have to do is give me one thing. Why don't you let me make your dreams of fame and fortune a reality? Let me give you the life you dreamed of?" Luc asked.

Lynda was shocked. Luc spoke of things that only her family knew. She abandoned those dreams once she became stuck to Lazarus.

"How could you know that?" she asked curiously.

"I know a lot of things, Lynda. I can share them with you if you let me," Luc slyly suggested. "I can free you if you let me."

Lynda was silent. She didn't know what to make of Luc. She still couldn't see him. He asked to show her something and slowly stood her up. She was limp in his arms. She tried to use his arms to balance herself, but had difficulty standing. Luc lowered his hand and touched Lynda's left leg, and slowly raised it. She felt the tingling, burning sensation again. It intensified the longer his hands touched her body. Lynda suddenly felt strength return to her leg. The blood and bruises from her legs healed as Luc's hands passed over them. He healed the tears inside. The sensation felt like the climax of a great sexual experience. He traced his hands over her eyes and allowed her to see again. He traced his fingers along her lips, reducing the swelling. Lynda moved her tongue and felt her teeth again.

She felt alive. Lynda never felt a sensation like that in her life. Her heart beat stronger and faster. The burning and tingling sensation faded when Luc removed his hands. Lynda was mesmerized by Luc's appearance. His complexion was light. His ethnicity couldn't be determined by looking at him. A black, clean-cut goatee surrounded his mouth and was the only hair on his head. He wore an all-red suit with a black shirt and red tie. Luc also wore sunglasses.

"That's only a taste of what I'm willing to offer. All you have to do is give me one thing. If you give me this one thing, I'll give you everything you want. I won't treat you like you've been treated. I want you to become a woman who burns with a fire that will bring men and women to their knees. One who has the power to bring others to me willingly. All you have to do is give me this one thing," Luc explained.

Lynda's eyes closed as she listened to his proposal. He spoke of everything she ever wanted. All she had to do was give him the one thing he asked for.

"What do you want from me?" she asked softly. She was in a state of ecstasy while in his arms.

"I want you, Lynda… I want your soul," Luc stated.

Lynda opened her eyes after hearing Luc's request. She thought it was strange. Lynda never thought about her soul. She wasn't even really sure she had one to give.

"My soul? Why?"

Luc smiled. He spoke softly into her ear, "It's who you are. It's the essence of you. You're nothing without it. I want you, Lynda. I want everything about you… everything that makes you who you are. I've wanted it ever since I saw you. It's so rich and beautiful… I don't want to go without. No man on this earth wants you like I do. Not even God was willing enough to do for you like I have. I care about you, Lynda.

Give me your soul. Be mine. Belong to me and I will take care of you forever."

Lynda closed her eyes again. Luc's words were sweet and tender. He was a dream come true. He was a man who expressed a desire to have her. No man ever spoke to Lynda with such passion. Lynda lost herself in his words. "Yes," she said.

A burning, tingling sensation seized her body. She felt a newfound strength surge through her. She hugged him tightly. A man finally stepped into her life and offered her light. She felt there was a chance to finally close a dark chapter in her life.

T.V. HOLIDAY

Two days passed while Travis traveled to Carnage Coast. Mark had a vehicle waiting for them. It was a 1979 Ford F-150. It was the same truck Travis' grandfather used to drive, the one he called The White Ghost. It was white with blue trim. It had silver metal running boards underneath the doors with white wheels and lettered tires. The front bumper guards reflected everything. The motor roared as Mark cranked the Ghost. It sounded as if the truck was alive.

As he passed through the City of Angels, Mark had him take a road west. It was long and straight. Travis was exhausted by the drive. He wanted to stop, but there was no place to rest. He was hungry. The mirrors showed nothing but fog and darkness.

"Can you tell me about Carnage Coast? You haven't said anything about it since we left. Is it some large warzone or something? Is there any form of civilization? Or is it just rubble?" he asked.

"Carnage Coast is the key to the war between God and Lucifer. It is a chosen battleground. If he can overtake Carnage Coast, he'll have the freedom to fully express his will throughout the world. The evil you know is only a hint of his power. If he wins, he will be able to exert his will without God's resistance. Darkness will envelop the earth. Anyone who is not his follower will burn. Pain and misery will be all that there is. There will be no light. There will be no hope. God will not step in to stop it. The rapture will never come," Mark told Travis.

"What's stopping Lucifer now? Why doesn't he simply take over like he wants to?" Travis asked.

"God will not let Lucifer create mere chaos and destruction. Besides, Lucifer doesn't want that anyway," said Mark.

"What does he want?" Travis asked curiously.

"Lucifer wants to erase God from existence. He wants to have others defy God like him," said Mark. "If he can win over the city, then he'll have proven his point. He has to rid the presence of God in Carnage Coast by getting them to condemn and deny God. If he can cause others to lose faith and outright denounce God, he will show that humans value their will above all else. Carnage Coast will be proof that he can drive God out of the world. To do this, Lucifer has been allowed to do whatever he can to win. He has opened the door to his home, Brimstone, on the Southside of town. It is accessible through a sandpit. It's where his demons and monsters come through to terrorize Carnage Coast," Mark explained.

Travis wondered how he was supposed to make a difference with the fate of the world at stake. He wondered how he was supposed to fight against Lucifer.

"For all of the demons and monsters Lucifer can use, God has had champions to fight on his behalf. At this point, The Iron Warrior is the only one left. He is the only one standing in the way of hell on earth. The Iron Warrior is powered by his faith. As God's Champion, you'll have special abilities to fight the battles that lie ahead of you. You will only be able to use those gifts through your faith. The stronger your faith in God, the stronger your abilities will become. Without faith in God, you will be powerless. You will become a mere man. There will be nothing to protect you from Lucifer's attacks. Anything from a knife to the chest, gunshot wound, or cancer will kill you," Mark revealed.

Travis paused. Mark's words carried a lot of weight. He was driving into a literal battlefield between heaven and hell. He felt overwhelmed and, rapidly, fearful. The burden of responsibility hit him in the chest. He didn't want to believe Mark. Travis didn't want to run away from what God called him to do. He never imagined it would be something of such great magnitude. He was now faced with the challenge of believing in God or dying.

"What about the people there. What are they doing?" Travis asked.

"The people who live there are called to it. Only those who are called to Carnage Coast can find it. They serve a purpose. Some are merely witnesses while others are part of the war. Others will also have their fates decided. The power of human choice is tested daily there. It is a city unlike any other," Mark continued to explain.

His mind and body grew weary. Mark's statements weighed on Travis' mind. The drive weighed on Travis' body. The gas gauge on the Ghost never lowered from full. There were no signs of him stopping on his way to Carnage Coast. He did not have a reason to stop, even though he wanted to. He was speeding toward his future with the burden of the world on his shoulders and no way to stop it.

Travis and Mark continued on the uncharted road. Shapes and silhouettes of large buildings materialized in the distance. The desert slowly faded and gave way to crop fields. The air smelled of smog and dirt as they got closer. Travis passed a sign that stated, "Welcome to Carnage Coast: The Seventh City." An eerie feeling crept up Travis' spine as he realized he had finally arrived in his new home.

Travis entered the city and finally saw cars. The skyscrapers housed local businesses and politicians. Downtown Carnage Coast was similar to the downtown of a major city. The sidewalks were overcrowded and cars were lined up at every intersection. Homeless people stood on the corners and center islands asking for money. It didn't look like the battlefield Travis imagined. He felt relieved at the sight of so many people.

Mark directed them to a large arena surrounded by glass windows. Staggered spotlights illuminated the building. Large banners hung from the top, featuring athletes. It had a dome-like roof that let sunlight in. It also allowed for fireworks to be fired into the sky. The arena was highlighted at the top with the letters "The Pavilion."

Travis was amazed by the enormity of the building. Mark stated that Carnage Coast didn't have a sports team. The Pavilion was home to the Carnage Coast Wrestling Association, the city's only form of entertainment. The display of good versus evil was essential in a city with so much at stake. Mark, to his shock, revealed that Travis was the owner of the CCWA. Travis was speechless. Mark told him God would provide, but he didn't expect anything like what Mark showed him. In a span of three days, he saw God's work move at a rapid rate.

Travis parked The Ghost and walked up to the arena with Mark. They went inside and walked through the curtains. A professional wrestling ring was staged in the center of the arena. The stage was massive. It took up an entire side of the arena. There were enough seats to fit 30,000 people. Mark tapped on Travis' shoulder and motioned for him to follow. They took an elevator to the top floor, where the day-to-day business operations were conducted. They went to a large office at the end of the hallway. The people who saw them did not speak.

There was a desk outside the office. It was neat and clean, but it was empty. Travis walked inside the office. It was a large suite with windows along the western wall, looking out over the ocean. A woman in her early twenties walked into the office. She was African American with short black hair. Her thin eyebrows highlighted her brown eyes. She wore dark-framed glasses and a black pinstripe suit. Her skirt was cut above the knee, showing off her smooth legs and dark skin.

"Mr. Holiday, it's nice to finally meet you. My name is Cheryl Smith. I'm sorry I wasn't at my desk. I had some things to handle. I wanted to make sure everything was ready for your arrival," she joyfully said.

Travis was unsure of how to respond. "You've been waiting for my arrival?"

"Of course, Mr. Holiday. We were informed you would be coming here personally. I understand you won't be here very much. I wanted to make sure everything was set, so you're aware of everything," she said.

"Wow! I don't know what to say. Um… thank you," Travis responded.

"You're welcome, Mr. Holiday. The information for the mayor's fundraiser is on your desk," she said.

"Wait a minute… mayor's fundraiser?"

"Yes, the mayor's proposal to host a campaign fundraiser here. It's in three weeks. I thought that was what you came in for?" she asked.

Travis was still caught off guard. He looked at Mark for guidance. Mark stood by silently as Travis tried to find another response. He felt everyone knew what was happening except for him. "Thank you,

Cheryl. Thanks for everything. I'll look at the stuff on my desk and call you if I have any questions," Travis told her.

"Okay, Mr. Holiday. It's nice to finally have you here. We've been waiting for you," Cheryl replied.

Travis nodded his head and forced a slight smile onto his face. Cheryl left and closed the door behind her.

"Can you please explain that?" Travis asked, frustrated.

"You have an important role here aside from being The Iron Warrior. As the CCWA president, you have to work with the local businesses and politicians. Since this is the only venue in town, everybody wants a piece of your business. It's the best way for businesses to get their messages out. Whether it's through commercials or sponsoring one of your events, they want the publicity," explained Mark.

Travis thought to himself for a moment and spoke, "How am I supposed to do all of this? How am I supposed to be The Iron Warrior and this businessman?"

"You really need to listen. Cheryl gave you the answer. They don't expect you to be here daily. You'll be able to balance both," said Mark.

Travis sighed and shook his head with a smirk on his face. "It's nice to know you believe I can do it. I'm not sure I can."

Travis walked toward the window and looked out into the ocean. His body was numb. Nothing in his life was small anymore. He had a large role in everything that he did. He longed to be only a husband and father.

Chapter
5

After meeting Luc, Lynda stayed in her apartment. She didn't want to speak to anyone but Luc. Lazarus constantly called, but she ignored him. Lynda never gave him the money she made the other night. For the first time in a long time, she kept it. She sat in a T-shirt and sweatpants, watching TV. The ecstasy kept her on a constant high. It was addictive. Luc promised to visit her in a few days. She thought about him daily and dreamed of him every night. His words replayed in her mind. He swept her heart away. Lynda was at peace until she heard the doorknob rattle. She heard familiar voices on the other side. The door was kicked open, revealing Hector and Slim.

"We're baaaaaaaaack!" Slim smirked with his arms stretched open. He and Hector reeked of alcohol.

Lynda hadn't thought about them since the alley. The two men who beat her within an inch of her life returned. As her emotions rose, the ecstasy overtook her. Her fear became a rush of excitement. Hector and Slim were awe-stricken by her beauty. They could tell she was different, but weren't sure why. They belittled her and demanded to know why she hadn't answered Lazarus' calls. She was too overwhelmed with the feeling in her body to answer them.

Hector slapped Lynda. But to her surprise, it didn't hurt her. She felt a surge of excitement rush through her body. The ecstasy became intense. Her heartbeat increased. Her nails stretched into claws.

Slim pulled Lynda's hair. "Maybe I need to stick something back in her mouth and make her remember when to talk again," he snickered.

"I think you're right, Slim. She forgot her manners," said Hector. He snatched Lynda's face and looked into her eyes. "You ain't gonna' heal this time. We'll tell Lazarus we found your body in the dumpster. He won't give a damn anyway."

Her excitement rose while they laughed. Hector shoved Lynda face-first to the floor. Slim reached to pick her up, but she quickly clawed his face. He wailed and stumbled backward. The scratches on his face burned. He uncontrollably shook his head. The burns were agonizing.

Lynda was dumbfounded. She examined her hand and was disturbed by what had become of it. Before she could think any further, Hector rushed toward Lynda and rammed her against the wall. He held her there with his hand on her throat and tried to punch her, but she moved. He punched a hole in the wall and hollered. He backed away and waved the drywall off his hand. It immediately swelled. It was broken.

Lynda was astonished by their inability to hurt her. She didn't want to give them a chance. She ran up to Hector and scratched his face. The scratches burned and forced him to step back. She followed him but was stopped when Slim smashed a glass cup over her head. The impact knocked her down. She quickly sat up and felt blood start to ooze down her face. Slim ran toward Hector to see if he was okay. Lynda stood and wiped the blood away. She looked at her hand and watched the blood absorb into her skin. The wound on her head shut. Slim was puzzled, but Hector was livid.

Hector reached into his waistband and removed a black handgun. He cocked it and aimed at Lynda. Although she hadn't felt pain from their hits, a gun removed any hope she had of preventing the inevitable. Despair quelled the ecstasy in her body. She dreaded what was to come.

"You just signed your death warrant. This is the last night you'll ever walk this earth. You're gonna' suffer ya' hear me," Hector threatened.

He snatched Lynda by her hair and forcibly kissed her while Slim laughed. He shoved her back to the floor and kept her at gunpoint. Sweat trickled from the top of his head and down his face. Hector coughed as his body burned inside, unlike anything he had ever experienced. He loosened his neck collar and fanned himself. He was visibly uncomfortable. His discomfort caught Lynda and Slim's attention. They didn't know what was wrong with him.

"Hec, you okay?" asked Slim. He checked on his friend while Lynda backed away.

Hector tried to speak but could only cough. Smoke billowed out of his neck collar. He instantaneously erupted in flames. Hector wailed while Lynda and Slim shrieked in horror. Slim jumped back while Hector tried to walk toward Lynda. His body buckled after two steps. He dropped the gun and collapsed.

Lynda and Slim made eye contact and eyed the handgun. They raced for it. She grabbed it first, but Slim kicked her in the face. The blow forced her back and allowed Slim to get it. Once again, she didn't feel the blow. Before he could stand, Lynda clawed his groin. Slim shrieked and crumpled while blood filled his pants.

She delighted in his misery. Lynda remembered all of the torture she suffered at their hands. For all of the tears she shed, she was happy to see tears in his eyes. She grabbed his face and kissed him. He tried to keep his mouth closed, but she forced her tongue inside. She retreated as his body incinerated before her. She joyfully watched his body turn to ash and the pungent smell spread throughout the apartment.

Her happiness disappeared when she heard footsteps approach her door. She panicked. Lynda looked through the flames and saw three figures standing in the doorway. A familiar voice called her name and said, "It's okay." Lynda instantly recognized it was Luc. He had finally returned. He stood between two large black men. They were imposing figures, forming a wall behind Luc as they stood next to one another.

Luc stuck his hand out and motioned for her to come over. Lynda ran over and jumped into his arms. She was beyond excited to see him. Her uncertainty vanished in his presence. He held her hand and surveyed Hector and Slim's remnants. He was pleased with what he saw.

"Luc, something is wrong. These guys came in and tried to attack me. My hands turned into claws. The craziest part is that I kissed them and they caught on fire. What's happening?" she nervously asked.

Luc patted Lynda's face and tenderly kissed her forehead. Her anxiety amused him. "I made you more special than you already are. I gave you… special gifts. Because of what you did for me, I'm giving you the world. You're a living sensation. The ultimate ecstasy. They couldn't handle you. No man can handle you anymore," Luc explained.

Lynda couldn't remember what she gave him. She thought back to the alley and could only remember his nice words and soothing hands. His presence and compassion were all she chose to remember. As she thought of their encounter, Lynda realized what he was talking about. All Luc wanted was her soul. Ever since she said yes, things were different. She felt the ecstasy every day. She could feel an energy surrounding him that sent her body into overdrive. She realized Luc was the reason for her change.

"Who are you?" she suspiciously asked.

"My name is Lucifer. Ever since you gave me your soul… you've been my woman. All the teachings about heaven and hell are real. The only difference is that hell ain't such a bad place to be when you choose to come with me," he revealed.

Lynda backed away from Luc. She tripped over Hector and Slim's ashes but caught herself. She backpedaled until her back smacked against the wall. She was startled. She couldn't believe the Devil was in front of her. She dreamed about him hours ago. Lynda never imagined she would be in love with him.

"It can't be true," Lynda panicked. She breathed rapidly but couldn't control it. His mere presence made her shiver. Her fear fed the ecstasy inside. It intensified as he got closer.

Luc slowly approached her, "Of course it's true, Lynda. You don't have to be afraid of me. I'd never hurt you. I want to give you everything that you want," Luc calmly said.

"Why?" Lynda asked.

"Because you deserve it. Think about it, Lynda. I've been the nicest man to you in your whole life. I was the one with you in that alley after those animals tore you apart. I was the one who brought you back from death, not God. You don't deserve to be punished like God has allowed. You deserve to finally be the one with power. God was going to let you suffer. I couldn't stand by and watch it happen anymore. I couldn't stand by any longer after what Hector and Slim did. I stepped in to make a difference. I stepped in to make sure God wouldn't hurt such a beautiful, gorgeous creature like you again," Luc told her.

Tears dripped down her cheeks. She had been bitter and angry toward God for the way her life turned out. She didn't want anything to do with God or his followers. The man who delivered her from her misery was Luc. That meant the world to Lynda.

Lynda remembered how she felt in the alley. He was right. He was the only one there for her. The warm feelings she felt when he reached out erased her fear. She was conflicted. She always hoped God would be the one to save her, but it was Luc. The same one who stood in front of her that very moment. He extended his hand and told her to trust him. She hesitated to raise her arm. His smile was unchanging. She put her hand into his and slowly stepped away from the wall. Luc stood still as she walked toward him.

"How am I supposed to repay you? All I gave you was my soul. That can't be enough," she cried.

Luc pulled Lynda and held her. "Don't worry, Lynda. Your sweet soul was more than enough. Because of you, I'm closer to taking over this world. I wish more people were like you. This world would be such a better place. Are you willing to be my woman and carry out my work?" asked Lucifer.

She felt just as willing as she did in the alley. "Yes," she said.

Luc grinned from ear to ear. He was satisfied to hear Lynda's answer. He could feel her commitment to him. She was his now. Lynda asked what he wanted her to do. Luc wanted to know what she desired.

She saw how men like Lazarus had astonishing power. Men like Lazarus did whatever they wanted. They had everything. Lynda wanted that power. As much power as Lazarus had, she wanted more. She learned how powerful sex could be during her years on the street. She believed it was the most powerful drug on earth. Sex brought down all kinds of men in power.

"I want power. Power is more than fame and fortune. I want what Lazarus has. I want to become the most powerful woman in Carnage Coast. With that type of power, I can spread my name throughout the world. I've been living off sex for the last six years. Sex drives this world and mine will be the sweetest and most powerful," Lynda exclaimed.

Luc nodded his head. "I like that, Lynda. I like that a lot. Your sex is powerful. Hector and Slim were prime examples. The ecstasy inside you will consume any man. I need you to share it with the world," said Luc.

"Why?"

"Lynda, I want more souls. I need souls. The more I have, the closer I get to taking over this world. Bring me more. You bring me souls through your sex. As long as the ecstasy inside you rises to its peak during sexual contact, you bring me another soul," Luc revealed.

"Do I take souls every time I kiss someone?" she asked.

Luc answered her with a single nod. Lynda thought about her future. She became concerned about the rest of her life. She didn't want to be alone. She didn't want to kill every man she encountered. A flurry of new questions raced through her head. She wondered whether she would ever have a man in her life. Luc felt her growing concern.

"Lynda. Don't think that I would leave you with no one," Luc reassured her.

He motioned toward the men in the doorway. They never moved.

"I want you to meet Sidious Craig and Coldred Black. They are for you. I picked them personally. They are not going to leave your side. They'll protect you and do whatever you need. If anyone messes with you, they will have to get through them first. They've been faithful servants to me, and I'm giving them to you. Exert your will, Lynda. Become the most powerful woman in Carnage Coast. With Sidious Craig and Coldred Black, no one will be able to stop you," said Luc.

Lynda was excited. Luc's assurance eased her worries. She walked toward Sidious Craig and looked him up and down. He wore a black muscular shirt and black jeans. His black boots had spikes for soles. His hair was tapered into a nice fade. His skin was smooth and clean. There were no blemishes on his face.

Coldred Black was the taller of the two. His appearance was distinct from Sidious's. Coldred sported a mullet-style haircut and had a scraggly goatee. He wore a long, brown trench coat over a pair of loose-fitted blue jeans. Coldred wore an untucked black button-up shirt. The only similarity between them was their sunglasses, which hid their eyes.

"Do you guys talk or what?" Lynda asked curiously.

"Yes, Ms. Lynch. We were waiting on Luc to introduce us," said Sidious.

"Yeah, the only problem is to make sure that one doesn't talk too much," Coldred quipped.

"Kiss my ass, Black," Sidious snapped back.

Lynda bizarrely looked at Lucifer. She was surprised to hear them bicker.

"Lynda dear," Luc started. "I'm going to leave you all to get acquainted. I'll be back later to see how things are going."

Lynda thanked Luc and promised to make him happy. He smiled and kissed her cheek before leaving. She began to devise a plan that would allow her to use her sex and bring Luc more souls. She wanted to become the woman he envisioned her to be. She knew her dreams of power could become a reality.

Chapter
6

Travis and Mark left the CCWA Headquarters after a few hours. Mark directed him to the city's outskirts. He showed him a house atop an isolated hill overlooking the ocean. The house was in the middle of nowhere. There wasn't another house nearby for miles. It was a one-story ranch-style house with two bedrooms and 1.5 bathrooms. A two-car garage was also attached to the house. There was a "Just Sold" sign in the front yard.

Mark directed Travis to park in the garage. After learning of his new role, Travis stopped questioning Mark. He realized things were already set in place for him. He felt everything in his life led him to Carnage Coast. He had seen God's work, but never like the last few days. He started to come to grips with being God's champion.

Once inside, Travis noticed the house was already furnished. He smirked and remembered Mark's words, "God will provide." They walked through, and Travis stepped onto a patio connected to his room. He took in the sunset over the ocean and smelled the sea air. About 100 feet beneath him, he saw a road that ended at the bottom of the hill.

He wished his family was with him. He was in a new house by himself. It wouldn't have the sweet smell of his wife's home-cooked meals. There wouldn't be any noise of feet running throughout the house. His bed was empty. He was alone.

Travis looked for Mark and found him in the garage next to The White Ghost. He thought it was a little odd for Mark to be standing in the garage by himself.

"There are a few last things to show you before my work here is done," said Mark.

Mark walked toward the door. Next to it were three light switches. Mark flipped the third switch, and the rear wall of the garage shook. The center of it rattled and split in two. The two sides slowly retracted, revealing an elevator.

Mark walked in and motioned for Travis to follow. He pressed the down arrow, and the doors closed. The elevator's interior had mirrors on the walls. The elevator descended for what felt like three floors. The doors opened and revealed another basement—one unlike any he had ever seen.

A large surface lay out for a car sat in the center of the room. It marked the beginning of a tunnel that led outside the garage. The far side had a complete gym. A tool chest was on the other side. The garage was big enough to fit four cars. It had a kitchen and another living area with a television. He wondered whether it was supposed to look like a Batcave.

"Travis… my time with you is over. I've completed my job and brought you to Carnage Coast. I can't go any further," Mark solemnly said.

Travis was bewildered. His amazement quickly went away after he heard Mark. "What's going on? Why are you suddenly depressed?" asked Travis.

"Travis …you're going to face many obstacles. You're going to get attacked in every way imaginable. You're going to need your faith more than ever to complete your walk. There are a few things you'll have to help you figure it out. As you move forward, you will see things through Divine Eyes. Divine Eyes will help you see your next mission. It's like a vision, but it won't be clear. Sometimes, looking at someone, reading, or even hearing something can trigger them. Divine Eyes will only point you in the right direction. It'll be up to you to determine your mission.

When you become The Iron Warrior, you'll be equipped with The Armor of God. You'll become faster and jump higher. Your strength will be amplified, too. You'll become three times stronger than you already are. You'll be able to strike with maximum force. Everything you're being given is enough to fight the evil you will face.

You can still die. You must have faith in God. As long as you keep your faith, no bullet or disease can kill you. Don't ever renounce your faith or denounce God. That is the main way to your destruction. The White Ghost was a gift from your grandfather. When he learned you had been chosen, he wanted you to have it, as he had promised. The fate of the world lies on your shoulders, Travis. The world needs your faith," Mark explained.

Mark turned away from Travis and walked down the tunnel. Travis stood humbly as he left. Mark's words repeated in his head. The more he thought about them, Travis realized something. He wondered what Mark meant about the main way to his destruction. Travis ran after him to get more clarification.

Travis ran toward Mark and yelled for him to stop. He did, but didn't turn around. He faced the end of the tunnel as Travis caught up. Travis asked for clarity about the main way to his destruction. Mark hesitated to speak. He was unsure of what to say.

"Your faith is not the only…" Mark started but became quiet. He tried to say another word, but there was no sound. It was as if his voice left him. He began to fade away. Mark disappeared before he could say another word.

Chapter 7

T. V. HOLIDAY

Lynda wore a long, black, elegant, sleeveless dress she bought years ago, along with designer sunglasses. She dreamed of wearing it on a date when she met a great guy. That night never came. She didn't need to wait for an occasion anymore. She was going to see Lazarus. Lynda wanted to appear as magnificent as she felt.

It was Friday night, and people were out partying. Lazarus' building was eight blocks from her apartment. The walk used to be taxing after standing all night. Lynda left with Sidious and Coldred, and they caught everyone's attention. Coldred carried a black garbage bag that had gifts for Lazarus. They walked by some Lazarus' hoes, and she heard them mumble under their breath. They weren't her friends. Their jealousy was sweet to her ears. She beamed with confidence. In a matter of three days, men who tormented Lynda for months and years were now dead by her hands.

They arrived at The Pit, which was Lazarus' base of operations. The Pit was a legalized casino and hotel. It was the only casino in town. Since there were no tourists, the rooms were used by Lazarus' high-end women. Everyone in Carnage Coast knew what happened at The Pit. The price was high, and Lazarus' women were the comps.

Lynda was never allowed inside for a long time. She typically entered through the backdoor at the end of the night to give Lazarus her money. She entered through the main entrance for the first time. Once inside, everyone stopped what they were doing. Men made cat cowls when she walked by. For Lynda, it was only a matter of time before she would become the center of attention everywhere.

They walked up to the elevator that led directly to Lazarus' office, but were cut off by Honey. Honey stood watch and only allowed people who had business with Lazarus to enter. Honey was a lightweight but very skilled in martial arts. She had a nasty attitude and a reputation for hurting those who ignored her. She always gave Lynda a hard time. Honey harassed her every time she came by.

Honey refused to let her enter with Sidious and Coldred. Sensation was impatient and didn't want to deal with her. Honey tried to punch her, but Coldred grabbed Honey's fist. He squeezed it and crushed her hand. She crumpled to her knees and cried out in agony. Coldred knelt and whispered into her ear.

"We're going in. Don't say anything else. Press the button and leave," he calmly ordered.

Honey tried to punch him with her free hand. He grabbed it and bent her arm backward. He broke Honey's forearm. She wailed while Lynda mocked her.

A woman leaped on Sidious's back. Coldred tried to help, but another woman jumped on his back. As Sidious and Coldred fought with them, Tracy ran toward Lynda. All of Lazarus' women made their way toward the elevator to stop Lynda, Sidious, and Coldred.

Lynda sidestepped Tracy and rammed her head against the elevator door. She grabbed Tracy's hair and clawed her face from her forehead to her cheekbone. Tracy hollered as Lynda had a devilish grin. She raked her nails across Tracy's chest. Blood seeped out as Lynda tossed her into a slot machine. She turned around and saw Janice and Bonita running at her, but they were cut off. Sidious flipped the woman off his back onto Janice and Bonita. The women fell while Sidious threw his arms up and yelled, "And the field goal is goooood!" He turned around to find Coldred still wrestling with the woman on his back.

Coldred grabbed her arm from around his throat and whipped her off him. She fell to the floor, and Coldred punched her in the face. The impact broke her jaw. Lynda, Sidious and Coldred stood in front of the elevator and laughed. They waited for another woman to come near them, but no one did. The elevator opened and everyone backed away from them. Lynda, Sidious and Coldred backed into it and waved goodbye while the doors closed.

Lazarus' office was enormous. It was surrounded by windows that overlooked the casino and city. His rear wall was lined with surveillance cameras. It allowed him to keep a watchful eye on everything inside and outside of his casino. No one would be able to sneak up on him. He had a gun case alongside his surveillance monitors. Lazarus also had a large conference table for his meetings. On the opposite side of the table was a large jacuzzi, where he lounged when he wasn't conducting business. He always had his favorite women sitting in it.

Lazarus was at his desk, a few feet from the elevator. He puffed his cigar and blew a smoke ring into the air. Lazarus was a black man in his early forties. He wore a baby blue three-piece suit. His beard and haircut were neatly trimmed. He wore gold rings on every finger and a large gold Jesus chain. Jasmine and Bella were naked in the jacuzzi when the elevator opened.

Lazarus shouted at her to come in. Lynda took the black bag from Coldred and swaggered toward Lazarus' desk. She motioned for Sidious and Coldred to stand back and keep Jasmine and Bella company.

"You two don't touch those bitches unless you pay," Lazarus yelled.

Coldred stepped toward Lazarus' desk, but Sidious held him back. He encouraged Coldred to ignore the comment and suggested they get cozy with Jasmine and Bella. Sidious lightened his temper. Coldred glanced at Jasmine and Bella and then back at Sidious. He nodded in agreement and they hung back.

"You two deaf or what? I said don't go near them unless you pay! Take another step and I'll blow your motherfuckin' balls off," threatened Lazarus.

They ignored his threat and stood over Jasmine and Bella, who were quiet. Lazarus stood and went for his gun case but stopped by Lynda's words.

"Calm down, Laz. They ain't gonna' do nothin' none of your regular customers wouldn't do. Chill out. Didn't you wanna' speak to me anyway?" Lynda coolly said.

"That's right, I do wanna' talk to you! Where you been? You been out for almost a week! You know how much money you owe me? Where is it?" Lazarus yelled. Lazarus went back and sat at his desk.

Lazarus yelled at Lynda often. Over the years, she learned to ignore it.

"Is that all you have to say to me? Where is your money?" she joked.

Lazarus was not impressed by her nonchalant demeanor. Lynda never talked back to him. "Check it bitch, first thing is that I ask the motherfuckin' questions. Don't talk back or I'ma slap the shit outta you in front of ya boys back there. Second, that ass belongs to me. When it's not on the street, it's costin' me money," said Lazarus.

"I been home," said Lynda as she sat down. She crossed her legs and relaxed. She wasn't worried about anything.

"Home? Who said you could be home all motherfuckin' day? I know I didn't say no bullshit like that," Lazarus heatedly asked. "And hold up. Where you think you at? You walk up in here with motherfuckers I don't know. Wearing some high-dollar dress and lookin' like you a bitch wit class or somethin'. You forgettin' who you talkin' to? You actin' real cool like I won't fuck yo shit up. You betta get some act right in you!" he interrupted.

Lynda laughed and looked up to the ceiling. She took pleasure in hearing his anger. Her demeanor infuriated him and she loved it. "I stayed home because I wanted to. I'm a grown woman. I can do whatever I want," she told him.

Lazarus frustratingly threw his hands up, "I'll be goddamned! Who you been fuckin' wit! Tell me cuz I wanna' know who put the confidence in yo' voice. It's all good though. I'ma get Hector and Slim to pay ya ass a visit. Them boys been lookin' for you. I woulda thought they caught you by now. I see they didn't. They'll straighten yo ass out. Then we can talk about my money," Lazarus arrogantly snapped.

He looked through his cell phone for Hector's number. He thought her demeanor would change once he mentioned them, but it didn't.

She was unfazed. Lynda snickered as she reached into the black bag. She pulled out a black round object and threw it onto his desk.

"How 'bout you ask him?" Lynda stated while she wiped black residue off her hands.

"What the fuck!" shouted Lazarus. He jumped back in surprise and examined the object. It had a burning stench. It was wet, with charred flesh and singed hairs on top. It was a human head burned beyond recognition.

"Y'know, while we're at it, how 'bout you ask Slim too. I don't think Hector is gonna' be sayin' anything," said Lynda. She reached into the bag and threw another round black object onto the table. It was another human skull. "There you go. Ask them if they've been by to see me."

Lazarus didn't want to believe it was Slim and Hector. He looked at Lynda's grin and was enraged. His blood boiled. He took a second to collect himself. Lynda was calm. Lazarus could tell she was different.

Lazarus sat and tried to play cool. The stench from the heads sickened him, but he kept himself together. He grabbed a bottle of Jack Daniel's and poured a shot for Lynda. She took it and waited for his response.

"Alright …what's the deal, Lynda? What you want? Wassup, you wanna keep your money or somethin'? You wanna' work outta The Pit? Why you walk up in here wit' these cat's heads in a bag?" Lazarus slyly asked.

Lynda sipped her Jack Daniel's and made him wait. She glanced back at Sidious and Coldred, who stood by the pool. Coldred was silent while Sidious made small talk with Jasmine and Bella. Coldred made eye contact with Lynda and nodded. She looked back at Lazarus and sipped more of her Jack Daniels.

"I want everything," Lynda frankly told him.

"Whaaaaaaat! You ain't never lie 'bout that. I want everything too… but I wanna' know what you want from me," Lazarus coolly said.

Lynda smirked. "No, Laz. I want everything. I want money, power, and, not to sound too cliché, respect. I want what you have."

"I feel that Lynda. I don't know what happened to you over the last week. I'm impressed. I mean, I'm really fuckin' impressed. I didn't know you had this type of bitch in you. I can really use that and get you everything you want. Just give me some time. I'll hook all this shit up for you. You ain't said nothin' but a word, girl," he promised.

Lynda smiled, "Yeah… right. Y'know, Laz, that's going to be a problem for me."

"How so?" he asked. He played like he was confused.

"I know you're full of shit," Lynda started. "You're going to have me sit around until you find a way to off me. That's cool, but you still don't understand what I want. I want The Pit and the business. Like I said… I want everything."

Lazarus laughed a little but stopped when he sensed her earnestness. A coat of disbelief covered him again. He could tell she was serious. He didn't believe she could actually overtake him. Even with Sidious and Coldred in the room, Lazarus still felt like he had the upper hand. He scooted closer to the desk and slowly reached under the desk for the .44 Smith & Wesson Model 29 he called Dirty Harry.

"You weren't lying about everything. But you really don't think I'ma just hand over my shit like that, do you? Cuz you come in here and throw some heads on my desk makes you think I'ma fold my shit up. I'm a real nigga ho. You can't play me like that. I ain't no bitch. You betta get an army if you want my shit," Lazarus responded.

"I don't have time for that, Laz. Sign it over to me and leave here alive. Or I'll kill you and take it anyway," she coldly told him.

"It's like that, huh? That's wassup," said Lazarus. He quickly stood and shot Lynda in the head. The impact knocked her out of the chair. "It's like that bitch!"

Lazarus fired two rounds at Coldred. The impact forced him through the windows into the casino. Sidious ran after Lazarus but was shot as well. The impact forced Sidious back, but he stayed on his feet. He walked toward Lazarus but was shot again. Sidious remained upright but was now close to the window. Lazarus fired another round that propelled him through a different window and onto the casino floor.

Jasmine and Bella screamed as the blood splattered them. He yelled for them to shut up and walked around his desk. He looked at Lynda while blood oozed from her head. She lay motionless. Lazarus spat on her lifeless body. He couldn't get over their conversation. The longer he stared at her body, his disdain grew deeper. He planned to make an example out of her for anyone who wanted to test him. A ring came from the elevator that signaled it was back at his office while Lazarus reloaded his revolver. He waited for the doors to open. He didn't know who would be coming out.

The doors opened, and a woman stepped out. She screamed and stayed inside when she saw Lazarus with the gun. "Lazarus, it's me, Kym! I was coming to see if you were okay. They raised a ruckus downstairs. We didn't know if you were gonna' be able to handle them. What happened?" she yelled.

Kym slowly poked her head out. Lazarus lowered his gun when he realized it was her. He gestured for her to enter while the elevator closed behind her. Kym saw Lynda's body and the busted windows. Kym wasn't shocked by what she saw. During her years working for Lazarus, she saw crazy things. Dead bodies didn't bother her.

"This bitch rolled up in here throwin' motherfuckers heads around. She was talkin' 'bout takin' my shit like she somebody all of a sudden. I killed that ho. That'll teach motherfuckers to walk up in here on some brave shit," Lazarus said.

He felt good about himself as he told her what happened. Killing one of his own women would only make his reputation tougher. While they spoke, the elevator door rang again. Lazarus didn't pay it any attention. He figured it was another one of his women checking on him.

"What happened to the window?" asked Kym.

"Oh yeah, right. I shot those assholes who were with her. They fell through the window. Where you think those bodies downstairs came from?" Lazarus laughed.

Kym stopped laughing and was confused. "What bodies?"

Kym's question stymied Lazarus. The elevator opened. He heard a male's voice inside it.

"I hope Lynda lets us rip this asshole apart," said the voice.

He was startled at the mention of Lynda's name. Lazarus looked wildly and aimed his gun at Sidious and Coldred. The same men he shot. His heart dropped as Sidious and Coldred stepped out of the elevator. Jasmine and Bella screamed at the sight of them.

"What do you want us to do, Lynda?" Sidious yelled.

Lazarus turned around and felt his body go numb. He couldn't believe his eyes. Lynda stood behind him. She brushed herself and shook off the blood. Lazarus' hands trembled. He could hardly hold onto the revolver.

"Grab him," ordered Lynda.

Before Lazarus could turn around, Sidious and Coldred grabbed him. Lazarus couldn't budge. He was stuck. Kym stood in awe. Lynda wiped the spit from her face and onto Lazarus's blue suit.

"H-h-ho…" stuttered Lazarus.

"How? As you said, somebody put some confidence in me," she answered. Lynda gripped his mouth. Lazarus bellowed when she squeezed with the strength to crush his jaw. "I want to kiss you so bad right now. One more time, Laz. I want everything. Either give it to me now or…."

Before Lynda finished, she had an idea and grabbed Kym's hair. Kym tried to push herself away, but Lynda slapped her. Kym cried out from the slap. Lynda was going to use her as an example. While she looked at Kym, Lynda remembered her misery had started because of her. If it wasn't for Kym, Lynda may have never met Lazarus. She finally had the opportunity to give Kym the payback she always desired. Lynda forced herself onto Kym and kissed her. She threw Kym to the floor and stepped to the side as she exploded into flames.

Lazarus shrieked in horror as he watched Kym burn. Jasmine and Bella screamed. Lynda removed Kym's hair from her nails and wiped her mouth. She stepped around her body and moved toward Lazarus, whose eyes were fixed on Kym.

"What's it going to be? Everything? Or a kiss?" Lynda calmly asked.

Lazarus broke down and shed tears. He wished he were dreaming. Lynda traced her finger around his mouth and kissed his neck, which burned. Lynda continually kissed him. He moaned in agony.

"Answer me, asshole!" she whispered.

Lazarus weakly nodded, "Everything. It's all yours."

Lynda was overjoyed. The first part of her plan went as she had imagined.

"You're going to arrange a meeting with all of your friends. You're gonna' tell them I'm running things now," instructed Lynda.

Lazarus didn't have anything to say. He was overtaken by fear. He didn't want to do anything to upset her. He witnessed what she was capable of and didn't want any part of it.

"In the meantime, you're going to spend time with my friends here. I know they're dying to return the favor for shooting them. Think of them as Hector and Slim minus all the sex stuff. You're gonna' have just as much fun with them as I had with your homeboys," she laughed.

Lynda looked around and walked toward the windows that overlooked the casino. She remembered all the times Lazarus beat her in front of others. She remembered the embarrassment and pain. It was time to return the favor. Coldred punched Lazarus in the abdomen and broke one of his ribs. Lazarus fell and groveled in pain. Sidious kicked the other side of his chest and cracked another rib. They dragged Lazarus to the window and beat him while people watched.

Lynda walked toward Jasmine and Bella, who were still in the jacuzzi. They backed away as she got closer. She instructed them to inform the other women of a meeting she planned to hold later. Lynda threatened that they would be like Kim if they didn't show up. They quickly jumped out and ran to the table to retrieve their clothes. Lynda stripped down and stepped into it. She sat back and watched Sidious and Coldred pummel Lazarus.

Before leaving, Jasmine asked who they were supposed to say was hosting the meeting. Lynda thought about it. The sensation that pulsed through her body was the ultimate ecstasy. Lynda didn't want to go by her name anymore. She wanted to be known as the embodiment of ecstasy realized. She was sensation itself. That was how she would be referred to from that point on.

"Sensation," Lynda answered.

Jasmine and Bella ran into the elevator and left. Lazarus' moans and groans pleased her ears. She waited years to see him flinch. Now she could watch him quiver. Sidious and Coldred beat Lazarus within an inch of his life. She wanted to be the one to kill Lazarus. She had a kiss waiting for him. It was all part of her plan.

T.V. HOLIDAY

A week has passed since Mark disappeared. Travis went to work and tried to get adjusted to his new job. Every day was difficult. He sat alone, thinking about his family. He imagined seeing his son in one of the spare bedrooms. In bed, he reached over for his wife, but she wasn't there. Going home was an unavoidable misery.

At work, he partnered with Cheryl to organize the mayor's fundraiser. It was a major event for his company. Every key businessperson and politician in Carnage Coast planned to attend. Cheryl reminded him of its critical value to the company daily. Working with her helped him realize that he was out of his league running the company. Cheryl knew every fundamental aspect of the CCWA. In recognition of her work, Travis promoted her to Executive Vice President and gave her an office next to his.

Aside from work and home, Travis waited for a sign. Mark told him that he would know what to do, but Travis was lost. He wasn't sure if he had received a sign and ignored it. He didn't know how to start his role as The Iron Warrior. He searched the house for something Mark could've left behind. He was in desperate need of guidance.

Travis went home in his 1967 Shelby GT500. It was his everyday vehicle. The White Ghost was reserved for The Iron Warrior. Travis always dreamed of having a mustang. His father, brother, and great-uncle had mustangs. After he decided to go to Carnage Coast, Mark had one waiting for him.

He arrived home, and the silence shifted his mood. Travis felt good at work because he was around people. He had been in Carnage Coast for almost two weeks and didn't know anyone. No one lived next to him for miles. The emptiness inside the house angered him. He didn't want to spend another night alone. He was isolated.

Travis stood in the doorway looking inside. He was tired of waiting for a sign. He flipped the garage switch and took the elevator to the basement garage. The White Ghost was parked in front of the tunnel.

He wore a black T-shirt with jeans. He didn't care about wearing anything specific. He only wanted to leave. It was time to do something.

Travis cranked the Ghost and its engine roared. He stepped on the gas pedal and sped out of the garage. The tunnel led to a black wall that retracted, revealing the road beneath his patio. The road was blocked by a barricade that opened once he got closer. He sped through without slowing down and headed into the city.

Travis wasn't worried about anyone seeing him. He didn't know anyone, and no one knew him. He was an average guy with an old truck. He didn't know where anything was. Everything about Downtown Carnage Coast was new and unfamiliar.

It was a Thursday night and downtown was packed. Many people were out, which seemed unusual for 9 p.m. Of all the places Travis lived, he never knew Thursday was a night to party. Downtown was filled with nightclubs, restaurants, and hotels. It also had a mall and a movie theater. As Travis drove down the street, he saw several alleyways. They were dimly lit. They seemed like perfect places for predators to hide. The air smelled of trash with a mix of alcohol and marijuana from the nightclubs. Carnage Coast came alive at night despite the supposed trouble it was home to.

Travis stopped at a four-way intersection when a Hispanic female went by. She was a beautiful woman with a caramel complexion, long dark brown hair, brown lipstick, hazel eyes, and trimmed eyebrows. She wore a gold necklace, a strap leopard tank top, and a black mini skirt with open-toe black heels. Her smile had a welcoming aura. She blew a kiss at him and crossed the intersection.

Travis was mesmerized by her beauty but felt something in his eyes. They became itchy. The feeling came from out of nowhere. He tried to rub his eyes, but his finger was shocked. Electricity blitzed from them. His eyes became focused on her. Something about her triggered a feeling he had never experienced. He felt an abrupt urge to follow her. Travis realized he was looking through Divine Eyes. He finally had a sign.

The light turned green, and Travis slowly followed her down the street. She glanced back and noticed him again. She knew what she was doing. She captured him with only a look. The woman stopped walking and winked at him while he drove by.

He looked for a parking spot and pulled into a nearby alley. The key had a button that read "Lock." Travis pressed it and heard clanking noises from underneath The Ghost. He bent down and saw a metal sheet extended across the bottom. It formed a layer of protection against anyone who would tamper with The Ghost. Another noise came from his tires. He leaned back and watched the bolts tighten on the wheels. A sheet of plexiglass covered the windows. The Ghost was secured.

He went back to the street to find her. People cluttered the sidewalk, but none like the woman he saw. Travis was desperate to know why his eyes blitz. He found her leaning against a wall and staring at him. She was alluring. Like a skilled fisherman, she reeled him in. The weather was hot and humid. Her skin glistened in the streetlights. She stood next to three other women who were just as beautiful. They talked amongst themselves, all while her eyes stayed fixed on him. His eyes blitzed again and the electricity became stronger. Something about her wasn't right. He could feel it.

Travis took another step but stopped when a large black man walked up to them. He took her attention away from Travis. Her demeanor slightly changed. She remained cool, but her flirtatious nature disappeared. The others seemed annoyed with the man's presence. She waved them off and motioned for him to follow her. They disappeared into a nearby alley while the other women walked by. He overheard them say, "She betta' be okay."

He walked toward the alley and poked his head around the corner. He could barely see anything. They disappeared into the darkness of the alley. The electricity in his body surged. He didn't have any weapons. Travis was defenseless. He had no idea what he was stepping into. He felt trepidatious and uneasy. "I walk by faith and not by sight," echoed in his mind. The words no longer had a distinct voice. The urge to go into the alley overtook his fear and trepidation.

"I guess this is it," Travis quietly said to himself and entered.

He stayed close to a concrete building. Sweat dripped down his face. His heart felt like it was going to burst. Trash and body odor permeated throughout the alley. Walking down a dark alley wasn't anything new to Travis. He did it hundreds of times when he was a police officer. He no longer had body armor or weapons to protect him. There was no one to call in case he needed help. All he had was his wits and faith. He kept walking and slowly came to a halt when he heard voices.

"What do you mean, this is the last time?" the man argued.

Travis heard a sigh. "I told you, Danny, I'm not gonna' be on the streets anymore. I got a new boss. I'm gonna' be doing movies now. I'm gonna' miss you though," she said.

"I don't want you to be with anyone else! You my girl. I been faithful to you. I took care of you more than anybody and you know it. That's why you never been with anybody but me. Don't do this, don't leave!" Danny heatedly responded.

Travis' eyes adjusted to the low light. He moved closer and saw the woman from the street hug Danny. She leaned back, slowly backed out of his arms, and wiped a tear from his face.

"Like I said Danny, this the last time. If you can't make it nice, then I'm leavin'," she said.

Danny snatched her arm and brought her closer. "You ain't goin' nowhere, Domino. If I can't have you, nobody will," Danny snapped.

"Danny, you're crazy! What you gonna' do?" Domino nervously asked.

Travis heard the sound of a switchblade flip open. Domino screamed seconds after.

"Let her go!" Travis yelled nervously. He stepped away from the wall and slowly walked toward them.

Danny looked toward Travis' voice and saw him get closer. "Who are you?"

"Help me, please," cried Domino.

Danny pushed Domino down and focused on Travis. Travis grabbed a nearby trashcan lid and held it at his side. He felt silly holding a garbage can. He felt like a poor version of his favorite hero, Captain America. He tried to keep it out of Danny's sight. Travis hoped he wasn't too obvious when he picked it up. Danny's knife shone in the moonlight when he raised it to his face.

"Alright, hero! I let her go! You want some?" yelled Danny.

Travis hesitated before responding. He couldn't believe he actually said something. Part of him wished he had stayed quiet. Travis didn't want to get stabbed. All he had was a measly trashcan lid. He started to regret his decision to follow them into the alley. He became resentful of Divine Eyes. If he had ignored it, he wouldn't have ended up in his current predicament.

"Not really," Travis jokingly responded. The humor helped contain the anxiety rushing through him. "I didn't want you to hurt her …or me. Y'know what, my dude, how about we just leave it be and walk away. I won't call the cops and nobody gets hurt. Cool?"

"Fuck that!" Danny countered.

"Uhhh, great," Travis groaned. As a police officer, he prided himself on talking his way through situations. A bad feeling crept inside his body as Danny stood with the knife. He didn't think he would be able to talk his way out of it.

"Y'know uhhh… Danny, right? Listen man, I really don't know what the hell I'm doin'. I saw her walk back here and I been wantin' to talk to her since she walked past my truck. Now you're about to hurt her and I may never get a chance to talk to her. As good-looking as she is, you can't stab her. Then neither one of us may ever talk to her y'know what I'm sayin'?" Travis reasoned.

Danny pointed to Domino and looked back at Travis, "That's my girl. Ain't nobody else gonna' have her but me. Her ass is mine."

Travis nervously laughed and shrugged. "Dude, I'd feel the same way. If I had a badass chick like talkin' about leavin' me, I'd be upset too."

Danny paused and eyed Domino again. Still on the ground, she was bewildered. She was surprised by Travis as much as by Danny. He returned his gaze to Travis and raised his knife again.

"This has nothing to do with you. I don't know you, and I don't give a damn about you. You shoulda' left us alone. Now I'ma gut you," threatened Danny.

Danny charged toward him with the knife. Travis threw the lid like a boomerang and nailed him in the face. Danny grunted and stumbled backward. Travis searched for another object to serve as a weapon while he had the chance. He couldn't find anything. Danny shook off the hit and ran at him again. Travis jumped on top of a garbage dumpster. Danny wildly swiped at his ankles. Travis jumped over the knife and landed back on the dumpster. He created a large dent in the dumpster lid. He tried to balance himself but jumped again to avoid another wild swipe from Danny. He landed on the dumpster and kicked Danny in the nose.

Danny fell, which allowed Travis to climb off the dumpster. Blood flowed from Danny's nose. Danny pounded his fist on the ground out of frustration and stood. Travis grabbed a nearby trashcan and slammed it on Danny's head. The blow put him back down and severely dented the can. Danny was still conscious and started to get back up.

Travis slammed the garbage can over his head again. Danny fell back down and didn't move. Travis quickly snatched the knife out of his hand. He checked Danny's pulse to make sure he was still alive. It took a second, but Travis felt Danny's pulse. He didn't want to hurt him. He only wanted to stop Danny from hurting Domino.

Travis walked over to Domino and helped her up. Domino brushed herself off and smiled at him. He experienced Divine Eyes, which led him to save someone. His new instincts proved to be correct.

"Wow! You really kicked his ass!" she said excitedly.

Travis took a second to breathe. He was out of breath. "Get outta' here. I didn't do anything but try to stay alive."

"Yeah, well, you did a pretty good job," said Domino.

"Thanks," Travis muttered.

His eyes became electric again. He closed them to shield himself from Domino. He didn't want her to see him.

"You okay?" Domino asked.

"Yea…." Travis started, but was cut off by arms bearhugging. It was Danny. He tightened his grip and tried to squeeze the air out of Travis' lungs. His power forced the knife out of Travis' hand. He heard the knife fall and slammed Travis on the concrete.

"Alright, hero, you asked for it," said Danny.

He grabbed Travis' throat and stated, "Now, you're gonna' pay for sticking your nose in my business."

Danny punched him in the stomach. The wind was knocked out of Travis. He fell, gasping for air as Danny picked up the knife. Domino stood against the wall. She was too afraid to leave or interfere. Travis tried to find something to pull himself up while Danny slowly stalked him. He stepped on Travis with both feet. His 280 pounds kept him from moving. While he struggled for air, Danny humorously watched. Danny stepped off and Travis tried to catch his breath. Danny reached back and stabbed him in the back.

Travis wailed in pain as Domino screamed. Travis' body went into shock. Thoughts raced through his mind as blood seeped out. He started to lose feeling in his right side. His body began to feel cold.

Resentment flooded his mind as he remembered all of Mark's promises. He left his life behind to go to a city he had never heard of. He left his family to become who God wanted him to be. Everything led to that moment. It led to him being stabbed in the back while a large man hysterically attacked Domino.

"I'm supposed to be the light in the darkness, right?" Travis said aloud. He didn't care if Danny or Domino heard him. He was upset with God for everything that happened to him. "I'm your fist in the war, right? A warrior powered by faith, huh! I'm The Iron Warrior, right? Prove it! Prove it to me!" Travis cried out.

The feeling in his right side swiftly returned. He felt a surge of adrenaline race through him. The knife handle broke on his back. The blade fell out and his wound healed. His eyes blitzed as he felt a new power lift him to his feet. Light emanated from inside of him as white and silver metal shards appeared. Metal plates surrounded his forearms, legs, and chest. The metal traveled up and covered his face like a helmet. The metal formed boots to cover his feet. He became The Iron Warrior.

Danny and Domino watched in amazement. The Iron Warrior looked at himself in astonishment. He felt power vibrate through his hands. He could crush anything he put his hands on. His body was more alive than it had ever been.

"What the…?" said Danny. "I don't know what the hell is going on, but I'm about to put your ass back down!"

Danny reached back and punched The Iron Warrior in the stomach, but he didn't flinch. Danny groaned and held his fist. His knuckles swelled. He punched The Warrior again, but it didn't have an effect. Danny winced and tried to shake it off. The Warrior grabbed his shirt and lifted him with one arm. The Iron Warrior had the strength of 10 men. He flung Danny against the dumpster. He glanced at Domino, who was in shock. He approached Danny, who deceptively pulled out another knife. He tried to pick him up, but Danny swiped the knife. The blade broke against his abdomen. Danny shuddered as he held the broken end of the knife. He never saw a knife break on someone. The

Warrior stood him up by his shirt collar and headbutted him. The blow knocked Danny out. The Warrior threw him in the dumpster.

"And there goes the trash," commented The Warrior.

Domino slowly moved toward The Warrior after he closed the dumpster lid.

"He'll be fine for tonight. He'll at least be able to stay out of trouble for a while. You can get out of here, Domino," The Iron Warrior confidently said.

He faced Domino, who was still in awe. She touched him and felt the cold metal that covered him. She was fascinated by the shining man in front of her.

"That was the first time anyone has done that to Danny. He usually has his way with people," she said.

"His first, huh? That's funny, he was my first, too," The Warrior smirked.

Domino laughed lightly at The Warrior's comment. She flirtatiously batted her eyelashes and moved closer. "To the winner goes the spoils, right?" Domino smiled.

The Warrior thought about his emotions. He was frustrated. He wanted proof and it was finally realized. God proved him wrong. The Warrior felt wrong and ungrateful for challenging God's power.

"That's usually the case, but you're not looking at a winner tonight. How about you call the police and go home?" he suggested.

She sensed his sadness and was confused. "The police? Forget the police. Come with me. Let's party! You deserve it," she said.

The Iron Warrior grabbed Domino's arms and held her still as he stepped away from her. He had to figure out everything that happened.

"No thanks, Domino, maybe next time," The Warrior respectfully said.

He stepped around her and ran toward the street. He had to get back to The Ghost. The Iron Warrior had a lot on his mind. His job was done for the night… at least, he hoped. He asked God to help him leave unnoticed and he changed back into Travis. The metal retracted into him. His light diminished and revealed Travis once again. He ran back to The Ghost and sped off. He had questions, but didn't know how to get any answers. On the way home, he prayed for someone or something to help him.

T.V. HOLIDAY

Travis returned home. He needed someone to talk to. He wanted Mark. Mark brought him to Carnage Coast and explained everything. Without Mark, Travis felt like he was wandering aimlessly. He went to the living area in the garage, where there were couches and a television. He found a neatly folded note on the table. Nobody could've been inside his house. Travis opened the note and noticed it was from Mark. The note read:

Dear Travis,

I can imagine you have a million questions. My job was to only bring you to Carnage Coast. Now that you are there, you must meet with Mike. He will help you throughout your time in Carnage Coast. His address is 1401 Broadway Street. Good luck and Godspeed, warrior. Your mission has only begun.

-Mark

Travis felt relieved and headed to Mike's address. He didn't care that it was almost midnight. There was someone to speak with. Someone who could help him understand everything. On the way to Mike's, Travis thought about Mark. He was about to tell him something before he disappeared. It seemed like Mark was taken against his will. Travis wished Mark had the chance to finish whatever he was going to say.

Travis arrived at 1401 Broadway and was shocked to see a rundown church. Shingles were missing from the roof. Many of the windows were busted. Wooden 2x4s covered holes in the walls that kept trespassers out. The church looked like it was on its last legs. The sign on the door read: "Welcome to Last Hope." A faint light could be seen through the remaining stained-glass windows.

He pushed open the rickety doors. The inside was humid and musty. Candles barely lit the hallway. Tables with pamphlets and flyers lined the hallway. The stairways led to the second floor, which housed additional pews and classrooms. Travis entered the sanctuary, which was huge. Multiple pews lined the inside. The room smelled clean and was completely different from the outside of the church. Purple drapes hung from the balcony. Large lights hung low from the ceiling. Everything led toward a stage with a microphone. It seemed like the church regularly held weekly services.

"I've been waiting for you to show up. If you waited any longer, I'd have been asleep," a calm voice echoed from the front.

The voice stopped Travis from moving further. "Mike?" he asked.

A man walked out from the far-right corner and onto the stage. He was dressed in a dark blue T-shirt and jeans. He was a skinny, bald, white man who appeared to be in his 50s. He nodded his head to reveal he was indeed Mike. He sat in the front pew and motioned for Travis to join him.

"How long have you been waiting?" Travis asked. He sat in the pew behind him. Mike adjusted himself so he could face him.

"Uh … maybe an hour or two. I take it you had quite the experience tonight?" Mike pleasantly said.

Travis was shocked by his knowledge of the evening. "Let me guess, Mark told you, right?"

Mike chuckled at Travis's question. "Who else?"

Travis felt at ease around him. "Yeah, I have. How did that happen, man? One moment, I'm stabbed, and then all this metal stuff comes out of me. It's tripping me out?"

"As you probably guessed, you became The Iron Warrior for the first time. I take it you looked through Divine Eyes, too?" said Mike.

Travis witlessly looked at Mike, "Um…yeah."

Mike continued to laugh at Travis's wonder. He knew Travis didn't understand what was going on. "I've been assigned to watch after you here. You can come to me for questions, guidance, prayer, or anything you need. I've been watching over God's champions for many years. Tell me about tonight."

"I got tired of sitting at home. I decided to go out. I was looking for something to happen. I got downtown and saw this woman walk by me. My eyes started to feel funny. They felt electric. I wanted to talk to her. She went down an alley with this big guy. I followed them and he was about to kill her. I tried to stop him, but got stabbed. After I got stabbed, I turned into the Iron Warrior and put him down," Travis explained.

"Did you say something before you turned into The Iron Warrior?"

Travis remembered when he got stabbed. He was hesitant to tell Mike that part. He didn't want to tell a pastor of all people that he angrily challenged God.

Travis sighed and embarrassingly lowered his head. "Ummm… I called out God in a not-so-appreciative way. I said… uh… I'm supposed to be the light in the darkness, right? I'm your fist in the war. Supposed to be powered by faith… ummm… and I'm The Iron Warrior. Then I told him to prove it to me."

Mike smiled. "Travis, I'm not going to judge you for that. Mark told me you have been having difficulty with all of this. Especially being without your family, it's not easy. Not everyone whom God has called upon has accepted graciously and freely. You have time to settle into this. What happened tonight was something special. You invoked The Iron Warrior. That is how you change and harness your power. You have to invoke him. Say those words in complete faith and your transformation will be complete. To be you, simply say the opposite," Mike revealed.

Travis felt guilty. He didn't want to have a difficult time doing what God wanted him to do. But he was human. He had moments when he was able to manage his emotions. Those moments dwindled the longer he was away from his family. "Thanks," he said.

"One more thing. Did you look through Divine Eyes again?" Mike asked.

"Uh… yeah. They kept blitzing when I spoke to Domino. Why?"

Mike thought more about the incident. He listened intently to help Travis see things clearly. "Your eyes light up whenever somebody or something is connected to a source of evil. That person or thing doesn't necessarily have to be evil themselves; they only need to have some connection to it. Believe it or not, but you may have gone after the wrong person."

"I think you're wrong on that one. This guy was definitely who I was supposed to go after," Travis responded reassuringly.

Mike shook his head in disagreement. "No. You wouldn't look through Divine Eyes again if you completed your task. If they were blitzing, maybe she was the one you were supposed to focus on."

He thought about Domino. Her appearance was very revealing. At first, he believed it was because of the temperature. Everything he saw tonight in Carnage Coast involved women in little to no clothing. He was so distracted by the nightlife that he stopped seeing things like a cop. Travis reflected on how he followed Danny and Domino into the alley. She only had a small purse with her. He overheard her say that she wasn't going to be on the streets anymore either. He realized Domino was a prostitute. He looked through Divine Eyes when she walked by his truck. Mike was right.

"Thanks, Mike. I finally have some work to do. I'll see you around," said Travis.

"Sunday, right?" asked Mike.

Travis stopped and faced Mike. "What?"

"Yeah, church on Sunday? Just because your family isn't here doesn't mean that you can't go to church anymore. How can one be God's warrior and not serve him outside of battle?" said Mike sarcastically.

Travis hadn't thought about church since he arrived in Carnage Coast. His family motivated him to regularly attend church. Without them, he was falling away from it.

"Yeah, sure, I'll see you Sunday," said Travis as he walked out.

T.V. HOLIDAY

Jasmine and Bella gathered all of Lazarus' women as Sensation requested. They were surprised to see the woman who Lynda had become. They remained strictly loyal to Lazarus until a demonstration of Sensation's power quickly changed their stance. Sensation disclosed her plan that detailed how they would no longer have to work the streets. Despite their fear, they jumped on board for the promise of a better life.

Before her meeting with Lazarus' business partners, Sensation met with his lawyers. She assumed ownership of his businesses and bank accounts. She legally owned the casino. Sensation took everything from him. When Lazarus wasn't signing things over to her, she had Sidious and Coldred beat him to pass the time. She hired a doctor to nurse his wounds and keep him alive. Her contempt for Lazarus knew no limits.

Sensation's women escorted the politicians and businesspeople into her office. The men were the most powerful figures in Carnage Coast. Mayor Raymond James sat across from the head of the table. Police Chief Lawrence Olson sat next to him while Chief Judge Thomas Brandon sat across from Olson. The manager of Carnage Coast's Citizen Bank, Charles Whaler, was among the dignitaries. Representatives from the Department of Motor Vehicles, local insurance companies and businesses lined the large table in the casino office. Two Hispanic men named Marco Salazar and Enrique Gonstaves, who supplied most of Lazarus' drugs, were present.

"Hey, Tom, why are we here?" asked Chief Olson.

Judge Brandon threw his hands up, "Hell if I know! How have you been, Larry? The wife still nagging you?"

"Of course!" Chief Olson laughed. "It doesn't matter how much money I give her; she keeps asking me to spend time with her. I can't stand her. She's been the biggest mistake of my life. The only thing that makes me smile is when I get to work, and Candy is on her knees waiting for me."

"Larry, you still go home?" Mayor James surprisingly asked. "I stopped going home a long time ago. Tina does so much for me that I feel like I'm at home when I'm at work."

"Gentlemen, Lazarus wasn't the one who called for this meeting," Whaler chimed in with his English accent.

They were surprised to hear him speak. Whaler rarely said anything. He never fraternized with them. He kept his business to himself. Whaler never had a girl to pay for his services. He only took money. His ways disturbed everyone else.

"Oh yeah… then who did? You know, Lazarus is the only one we get together for," said Salazar.

"To my knowledge, we were called by a lady," Whaler told them.

They all scoffed at his answer. While they spoke amongst themselves, Sidious and Coldred entered the room. They didn't say a word. Their appearance caught everyone's attention. Sidious and Coldred seemed out of place.

"Who the hell are you two?" Enrique Gonstaves rudely asked.

Sidious snapped and threateningly pointed to Enrique, "I'll be the fist in your mouth if you don't talk to me with some respect."

Enrique couldn't believe Sidious' response. He grabbed the gun from his waist and aimed it at Sidious, but Coldred quickly snatched it from him. Coldred crushed the gun with his hands and dropped it on the table. Everyone was impressed by his physical display.

"Shut up and listen!" Coldred callously ordered. He stood unflinchingly while they looked around to assess each other's reaction. The room temperature rose. The men became tense. They instantly realized it wouldn't be a regular meeting.

"You're here to meet Carnage Coast's newest Queenpin. Whatever power you had is gone. If you've got something to say, don't. If you can't keep your mouth shut, Coldred and I will shut it for you. Now, without further ado, please welcome the most beautiful and powerful woman to walk this earth. We give you… Sensation," said Sidious.

 T.V. HOLIDAY

Sensation entered wearing a dark blue dress. The top of it was split open down to the center of her navel. The bottom half was split on both sides, revealing both legs. Her hair was up in pristine fashion. Her perfume captivated them while it filled the room. She wore a looped gold belt with earrings to match. She sauntered to the table while Sidious prepared her seat. The men were taken away by her aura.

"Thank you for that introduction. You and Coldred are too sweet to me," Sensation seductively smiled.

"Anything for you," Sidious and Coldred replied.

Sensation turned her attention to the men at the table. They fought through the enchantment and gave her cold stares. Their disdain emerged while she made herself comfortable at the head of the table. They couldn't believe she called them to a meeting.

"You all look like a happy bunch. I called this meeting to introduce myself. As my wonderful man told you, my name is Sensation. I am the new owner of this casino and your new business partner. Lazarus is no longer in charge. You'll no longer contact him for anything. Your business with him is done. You'll only work with me. I can see by the look on your faces that it sounds terrible. I wanted to clear the air tonight so everyone knew their role as we move forward. Because, gentlemen, we are moving forward.

"You're not going to get the same services anymore. I'm keeping my profits. I'm not paying any of you for a free ride. For those who stay, you'll work for me. Your businesses will be my businesses. My ladies are no longer for sale to you. They're not hoes. They're my Diabolical Donnas. You can call them The Double Ds. We're the new powerbrokers in Carnage Coast and we're going in a different direction.

"The Double Ds aren't working the streets anymore. You get your own people to sell that shit. The Donnas are going into the porn business. We've been selling ourselves for years. My Donnas are not pieces of bargain basement meat to satisfy your sick fantasies. We're finally going to get paid what we're worth. The porn business is a billion-dollar industry. We'll bring in more money than all of you ever have. To play with us, you'll pay an extra 10 percent of the profits on top of the 45 percent you already pay. Make no mistake, gentlemen, this is my city now. If you don't want to pay, leave. The time for you to speak is now," Sensation explained.

The men remained quiet and were deadpan. They sat as if she never spoke. They looked at one another and pointed skeptically toward her. A snicker could be heard from one corner and slowly spread among the rest of them. They doubled over in belly laughter. All of them laughed except for Whaler.

"This must be some kind of a joke! Bitch you almost had me for a minute. Now for real, where is Lazarus?" Marco chuckled.

Their contempt entertained sensation. She sat undisturbed and crossed her legs. She wanted to let them have their moment. Sensation cut her eyes toward Marco. She cemented his gleeful image in her mind. It would be the last time he ever laughed at her again. She raised her finger toward Coldred. "Coldred," she said.

Coldred ran over and punched Marco's face. The impact knocked him out of his chair and the laughter came to a screeching halt. Everyone was surprised as Enrique reached into his pocket. Before he could make a move, Coldred kicked him in the face. The blow knocked out one of his teeth. Coldred turned his attention back to Marco, who tried to get up. He forcefully stomped on his right hand and broke it. Marco clasped his hand and wailed in agonizing pain. Sidious stood over Enrique while The Donnas surrounded the men. Sensation smirked as the men realized they were in a serious situation.

"Gentlemen, you will never refer to me as bitch again. I've been called a bitch for too long. I am a lady and you will respect that. My name is Sensation and my ladies are The Diabolical Donnas. If anyone ever calls us different, we'll break you," Sensation calmly warned.

"Okay… Sensation, what's really going on here? We're called to a meeting and told we're supposed to hand over the majority of our businesses to you. We don't know you. How do you expect us to react to such a demand?" asked Judge Brandon.

"That is for you to figure out. My demands are what they are," she arrogantly responded.

He rolled his eyes, "You're not getting a damn thing from any of us. You have nothing. I can give two shits about you and your Double Ds. This is a man's game. So, how about you get Lazarus in here and get back on your knees."

Sensation proudly laughed at their resistance. She didn't anticipate them rolling over and handing her everything at once. She knew it would take more than threats to change their minds. They were used to getting their way. They viewed women as insignificant. Sensation had a trump card waiting in the wings.

"For one, I have The Double Ds. They have all kinds of dirt on every one of you. If I wanted to ruin your lives, I could. The fact that you're all present here would raise a ton of eyebrows. None of you could use the negative publicity. Think about your families," said Sensation.

"Some of us may not want our families anymore. Trying to blackmail us isn't the answer you were hoping for, darling. As Tom said, you have nothing. If we wanted you to jerk us around, we would've paid for it. Now get Lazarus!" ordered Chief Olson.

The moment had arrived. She was ready to reveal her trump card. Sensation glanced at Sidious and nodded her head, "You heard the man… bring in Lazarus."

Sidious walked into the back room while Marco and Enrique crawled back into their chairs. Marco had a gash on his head, and Enrique held his limp hand. Sensation made eye contact with Mayor James, who remained silent. She believed his expression would soon change.

"Miss Sensation, blackmailing me is unnecessary. I would like to work with you. My bank is the largest in Carnage Coast. Let me know what you need, and we'll do what is necessary to make it happen," Whaler informed her.

"Why, thank you!" Sensation excitedly responded. She was happy to hear someone polite. "It's so nice to hear someone do the smart thing. All this anger is unnecessary. You all should be like Mr. Whaler."

"Fuck him!" Marco whimpered.

The sound of a door opening grabbed their attention. Sidious rolled Lazarus into the room and they watched in awe and disbelief. Lazarus sat slumped forward in a wheelchair, wrapped in bandages. His face was swollen. He was tired and miserable. Lazarus' eyes were glazed over. He was barely conscious. His weak state shocked them. He was a powerful man who ran roughshod over Carnage Coast. He was the one they feared. She reduced Lazarus to a shell of himself. Sidious wheeled him next to Sensation, whose eyes were focused on the mayor. His face finally showed the shared doubt among the men.

Coldred lightly slapped Lazarus' face to wake him. "Gentlemen, as you requested, here is Lazarus. Let him be your example should you continue to resist. He didn't want to go with the program. So, I showed him something that really changed his mind. Then Sidious and Coldred helped to produce what you see now. Any questions?" Sensation gleefully explained.

"I don't care what you do to Lazarus! I'm not giving in to this bullshit! I've got balls for a reason. I'm a man. We're all men. I'm not going to let everything we worked for go down the drain because a woman wanted to grow a pair. Fuck you, these two clowns and your Double Ds. Candy is staying with me as payment for this charade. You better hope I don't put all of my efforts into shutting you down," threatened Mayor James.

Sensation was appalled. She didn't expect him to have such a backbone. Coldred moved toward the mayor until Sensation snapped her fingers and motioned for him to return.

"D-d-d-don't fi-fight her? She will k-ki-kill you," Lazarus muttered.

"See, I knew you would be useful!" Sensation exclaimed.

"Fuck that, Lazarus! Sorry about what happened to you, but I'm not giving shit to her!" said Mayor James.

She remained unnerved by his defiance. Sensation noticed that he was the only one willing to challenge her. The rest anxiously watched. She recognized the importance of the moment. She wasn't going to let it slip through her fingers. Lazarus was there for a reason. It was time for him to play his part.

"Hey, Laz, let's show them why they should listen?" Sensation cheerfully asked.

Lazarus' eyes watered and his body was paralyzed with panic. She giggled as she moved closer and stroked his bandages. He tried to move away. His fear of her made the men concerned. They couldn't understand why he would react that way.

"Mr. Mayor. Before you go, Lazarus would like to show you why he gave in to me. He would like to show you all," she said.

Sensation forcefully grabbed Lazarus' face and clutched his jaw. She stared at his fright-filled eyes. "Laz, this is for everything. Every time you held me down and assaulted me. Every time you beat me. For all of the shame and dirtiness I've carried. Every ounce of pain you ever gave me. May your soul rot in hell, you miserable son of a bitch," she softly said.

Sensation kissed Lazarus and he shrieked. She pulled back and watched as smoke billowed from his bandages. She lightly slapped his cheek and said, "Bye bye baby."

Lazarus erupted into flames and screamed. The men jumped back from the table. They were horrified. Sensation calmly wiped her lips as Lazarus' body burned next to her. No one said a word. Mayor James tensely sat back in his seat. Their resistance dissipated at the sight of Lazarus' burning body and they agreed to her demands. Sensation officially took her place as Carnage Coast's Queenpin.

Chapter 11

Travis went out every night to find Domino again. Every prostitute triggered his Divine Eyes. He asked around for her, but she became out of reach. He was sure Domino told the others about what happened. He referred to himself as the one who fought with Danny. His belief was confirmed when they excitedly acknowledged who he was. The fight gave him credit with them. He hoped that credit would help him find Domino sooner rather than later.

Travis drove through the alleys within the heart of Downtown Carnage Coast. He saw two people by a garbage dumpster. It looked like they were in a heated argument. He turned off The Ghost and quietly stepped out. He walked along the wall and slowly approached them. As he got closer, the moonlight revealed them to be a man and a woman. Travis' eyes flickered. His Divine Eyes activated again.

"I told you that's it. We're The Diabolical Donnas. We ain't workin' out here anymore. You gon' have to pick up from somebody else now," she snapped. She was scantily clad and carried a small purse. Her arms were crossed, accentuating her agitation. She boldly stood before him without any fear.

Travis stood back and watched for a while before getting involved. He had been going in circles during his search. He hoped to get more information by surveilling them.

"Cut the bullshit! I ain't hearin' none of that. I don't care what y'all call yourselves now. Diabolical Donnas, Double Ds, I don't care. You still a ho. Stop actin' like you ain't holdin' and gimme what I need," the male argued. He was an average-sized man with a muscular build. He wore baggy jeans, an A-shirt, and gold chains hung from his neck. He was decidedly bigger than her.

"I said no! You betta' stop bein' disrespectful. There are consequences for callin' us anything but Donnas. Now get outta' here before you start makin' people nosey," she frustratingly responded.

"I should just slap you and take the shit anyway," he threatened.

She smacked her lips and stepped closer. "I'd like to see you do it. I guess you haven't heard, huh?"

"Heard what?" he arrogantly asked.

"You haven't heard? My guy doesn't like it when dumbasses try to hurt us," said another woman from a nearby shadow. She walked toward them and Travis' eyes fluttered again. She wore a brown leather jacket with a brown leather miniskirt. Her knee-high high-heeled boots allowed her to show off a fraction of her legs. He got closer and his eyes widened in shock when he recognized who she was. It was Domino. He had finally found her.

The man lightly chuckled, "Yeah, I heard about him. I think it's a bunch of bullshit you bitches made up to scare cats."

Domino's assured smile confused him. They usually backed down when he was aggressive. It wasn't working; they were different now. "As she said, we're not bitches. We're Donnas. Besides, you can always ask the last guy. He's still in the hospital. Or… you can hit us and find out."

He slapped Domino and pushed the other woman against the dumpster. "Let's find out!" he yelled.

"I hope you're happy," said Travis as he stepped from along the wall.

The man and Domino were surprised by Travis' sudden appearance. He wasn't as nervous as the last time he confronted someone. The man didn't appear to have any weapons. Travis was ready for a fight.

The man grinned at Domino. "You really weren't playin'. The Donnas got a protector. Let's see if he can hold up his end of the bargain."

He lunged at Travis, who ducked under his arm and grabbed him around the waist. Travis suplexed him onto the concrete. His body folded as he landed on his neck. Pain shot through his back and shoulders. He let out a painful growl. He looked at Travis, who was already upright and waiting for him. The man waved them off and stumbled away.

"Don't touch them again!" Travis yelled.

He turned to Domino and the other woman. She jumped up and ran toward him. Domino hugged him tightly, which surprised him. The other woman slowly picked herself up and approached Travis as well.

"I knew I'd see you again," Domino whispered. She stepped back with a joyful grin and gazed at him. Her demeanor softened. She felt safe knowing he was there. He saved her once and was there again when she needed someone.

"Hey, fly guy, this is Charity," said Domino. Travis tipped his head to greet her.

Charity looked him over and was impressed. She had heard Domino speak about him, but was skeptical. Her skepticism disappeared at the sight of him. "Damn D, you wasn't kiddin', he is nice," she chirped.

"I told you, girl! My guy ain't gonna' let anything happen to me!" said Domino. "I heard you been lookin' for me. That true?"

Travis was taken aback by their adulation. He appreciated it but was more focused on finally speaking to Domino. "Yeah," he quietly responded.

"You lookin' to cash in your credit?" Domino teased.

Travis lightly laughed, "No. I appreciate that, though. I need to talk to you about last time. Can we talk?"

"Anything for you, lover," she responded. Domino turned to Charity and reached into her pocket. She gave her a small, clear bag filled with a white powdery substance. Travis recognized it was cocaine. Although it was illegal, he ignored it. He wasn't a cop anymore. There was more to learn and figure out than to make an issue of her selling drugs. "Take care of this and I'll meet you back at The Pit."

Domino assured Charity of her safety before she left. Travis and Domino went to The Ghost and she marveled at the sight of it. Domino was impressed by how clean it was. Once inside, she noticed all of the features had been updated. She had been in many vehicles, but none like The White Ghost. She leaned over and lowered her zipper to give him a view of what he could have. "You finally got me. Now, wassup?" Domino flirtatiously said.

Travis was briefly shaken by her cleavage. He smacked his head to help him remember why he wanted to talk to her. "I see what you're doin' there. I like what you got. And you have definitely been blessed. I'm not gonna' tell you to stop, but I do have some serious stuff to talk about," Travis playfully admitted.

Domino rolled her eyes and sighed, "Fine! But why do you keep denying this? I mean, is there something wrong with me? Is it because of what I do? 'Cause I'm not going to be doin' this anymore."

"That's exactly what I wanna' talk to you about. I do know what you do. But there is something about it that… it's hard to explain. It's important for me to find out, though. And for the record, I'm married. If I wasn't, maybe I'd take you up on that. At the same time, I chose to help you. You don't owe me anything. I'm just glad I was able to be there before it got worse," he explained.

She was dumbfounded by his explanation. "I don't care if you're married. You obviously can't be happy. If you were, you wouldn't be in these alleys protecting us. I mean, be real, are you a cop?"

"I care that I'm married. It doesn't matter whether I'm happy. I'm not cheating on my wife. And I'm not a cop; I'm something else," he defensively answered.

Domino sensed he was hiding something. She felt sorry for him. "Y'know, I've been with enough guys to know an unhappy one when I see him. Married guys stay because it's safe. They stay miserable by choice. But at some point, they crack. That's when they come to find me. I get the best of them. I make them alive again. Eventually, their worlds collapse. You're holding on to something that was probably dead a long time ago. I'll back off for now. Just know I've got the medicine you need whenever you're ready to come and get it," she expounded.

Travis looked into her eyes. He believed eyes were the windows to one's soul. She read him like a book and was on the money. He was deflated that she had quickly assessed him. He was speechless.

Domino accepted his silence as confirmation of her assessment. She empathized with him. "You don't have to say anything about that. But you can tell me what you are. I've replayed that night in my head a lot lately. What was that?" she asked.

Travis pondered how to answer. She had already read through him. Domino saw him transform into The Iron Warrior. It didn't matter what she did for a living; to lie would be an insult to her intelligence. He didn't want to lose the little bit of confidence she had in him. He felt the only way to keep it would be to tell the truth.

"That's a tough one to answer. There's a lot I can tell you, but it may be too much. I don't know. I'm trying to figure this out myself. What you saw is…," he stammered.

She picked up on his hesitation. Domino felt he was honest. "Hey, I didn't tell people that you transformed. I don't know if that's gonna' make it easier for you to speak. I only said you kicked Danny's ass. I didn't think it was a good idea to say more. I've seen some crazy things, especially lately. Things I never could've imagined," she disclosed. Domino turned away before she finished speaking. Travis noticed the minor change in her demeanor.

"What kind of things?" he curiously asked.

She closed her eyes and took a deep breath. Domino unconsciously fiddled with her jacket zipper. Travis could tell she was wrestling with something, too. Her distress freed him to be more transparent.

"It seems like both of us are trying to make sense of things. In that case, I'll level with you. I was sent here to fight against evil. I know that sounds like something straight out of a comic book, but it's true. There's some real serious stuff going on in Carnage Coast. You saw what I become when it's time for me to fight it. That was the first time, too," he revealed.

She was shocked. She leaned toward him again and looked into his eyes. Domino wanted to see if he was telling the truth. Travis remained unflinching during her examination. His staunch expression confirmed he was sincere. His honesty frightened her.

"If that's true, then why did you follow me that night? Did you know what was going to happen?" she cautiously questioned.

"I'm glad you asked. I get a feeling that comes when I see somebody or something. It's not a vision. It's only a sign. It comes because whatever I'm seeing is associated with something evil. Either something bad is about to happen, or, from what I understand, the person may be evil. I had it when I saw you," he described.

Her eyes fearfully widened as she tilted her head. She had heard weird proclamations in her time, but none ever came true. Domino believed he had told the truth because she had seen him fight Danny. She became dreadfully anxious.

"Is that why you've been looking for me. You think I'm evil?" she asked.

"I've been looking for you because I don't know. I could be wrong, but you don't seem like an evil person. Not to mention, I've been getting this feeling when I see a lot more women. I had it earlier. Can you help me out with this?" he answered.

Domino was relieved and exhaled. She was glad he didn't think she was evil. She had the answers to his questions but was afraid to speak. She unconsciously fiddled with her zipper again because of her nervousness.

"Look, Boy Scout. I'm really thankful you were there last time and tonight. I know you keep gettin' this feelin'. But I think you outta' let this one go. You're askin' 'bout somebody who even scares me. Danny was one thing. But the person you askin' 'bout ain't no regular person," she mercifully warned.

Travis gently grabbed her hand to comfort her. He sensed her fear. Domino glanced at him with tearful eyes that she fought against.

     T.V. HOLIDAY

"Domino, I'm not a regular person either. Not anymore. Please, who is this person? What are you connected to?"

Domino squeezed his hand and took another deep breath. "Her name is Sensation…."

Travis' Divine Eyes electrified at the sound of her name. Domino snatched her hand back and braced herself against the door. Travis raised his hand and motioned for her to calm down. He tried to put her at ease.

"I'm sorry Domino. My eyes do that without warning. I guess this Sensation is the answer I was lookin' for," he said.

"Did your eyes do that the night you saw me?" she frantically asked.

"Yeah! That's what I'm sayin'. This happens whenever I see you or any of the other girls on the street. What is it about her?" he pleaded.

Domino calmed down and situated herself again. "I ain't sure either. She used to be one of us. Then something happened to her. She changed. She took over everything from Lazarus. She's about to take over the city."

"How?"

"I don't know. But she has everything Lazarus had. In some ways, she ain't so bad for us. She's takin' all the girls off the street. We're gonna' get a small number to replace us. But all of us are her Diabolical Donnas. That's why your eyes keep lightin' up. You keep seein' The Double Ds. Ain't nobody steppin' to us or her. If you do, she'll…" Domino trailed off. She became choked up over her next words.

"What is it, Domino? She'll kill you or somethin'?" he anxiously asked.

A tear rolled down her cheek. Her foot nervously tapped the truck floor. "I can't tell you. Just know she's a walking kiss of death. I've seen her do it. One of the girls fought back when she took over. Sensation killed her right in front of us. I'll never be able to unsee that. She let us know then. Don't step to her. I like you, Boy Scout. I don't want that to happen to you. That's why I'm tellin' you to leave her alone."

Travis listened to Domino's pleas and remained steadfast in his desire. "I can't Domino. I have to go after her. Remember, I'm not from here. I want to go home. The only way is through her."

"You're already unhappy. Is it really worth it?" she asked.

Her question reminded him of his family. He chose to go to Carnage Coast with the hope of seeing them again. That hope pushed him forward.

"I love my family, Domino. When you love someone, it's always worth it," he answered.

Domino glared into his eyes again and sensed his commitment to them. She felt happy to be around an honest man. "Why're all the good guys taken?" she smirked.

"Thanks for telling me all of this. I really appreciate it," he said.

Domino shook her head and opened the door. She eyed him one more time, "Don't thank me for nothing. If I had it my way, we wouldn't a' been talkin'. I still got that medicine whenever you need it," Domino stated as she stepped out of The Ghost.

"How about we just leave it as a favor you owe?"

"I'd rather not. But since you won't let me do it any other way, that'll have to do. Hopefully, I can answer it before you do something stupid," said Domino.

She closed the door and walked away. As Travis watched her leave, he thought about Sensation. Whoever she was, she was powerful. Whatever she did instilled the right amount of fear in those around her. He had never been involved in anything on such a grand scale. Sensation was larger than life. He needed to find a way to meet her.

Chapter
12

Days passed before the mayor's fundraiser arrived. Travis met with Cheryl in The Pavilion. They went to a banquet room on the second floor. It was a spacious skybox normally used for parties of that magnitude. A stage was located near the front with two large flat-screen televisions. Servers floated about with luxurious appetizers. It was a sophisticated affair. As they entered, Travis's eyes pulsated. He felt the electricity surge and realized his Divine Eyes had been activated. He quickly covered them with his hands.

Cheryl noticed his movement and was concerned. "Travis, are you okay?" she asked.

"Umm… yeah. The light in here is pretty bright. Uh… I'll… be alright. I could use some sunglasses, though," lied Travis. There was a strong presence of evil in the room that concerned him. "Cheryl, who are these people?"

She had one of the servers find a pair of sunglasses before she answered. "Many of them are small business owners, local city officials, and community leaders. Why?"

The server returned with a pair, and Travis quickly put them on. "Uh …just curious. Trying to get a lay of the land y'know," he said.

Cheryl introduced him to everyone. Most of them triggered his Divine Eyes. Travis felt like he was having an anxiety attack. The electric surges made his hands twitch. He subtly took deep breaths to control himself. Travis placed his hands in his pockets and followed Cheryl around. He observed how easily she worked the room. From watching her interactions, he realized she would be a great asset.

"Is this the man I need to thank for letting us use this great building?" a voice sounded a few feet away.

Travis and Cheryl turned to notice a man approaching them. He wore a dark gray three-piece suit with polished black shoes. It was Mayor James. As he got closer, Travis' eyes continued to blitz. He sensed the mayor had a strong connection to something evil.

"Good evening, Mr. Mayor! How are you?" Cheryl exclaimed.

Mayor James extended his hand for a handshake. "I'm fine, young lady. I wanted to come by and meet our host. We haven't been formally introduced yet. I'm Mayor James," he beamed.

Travis was hesitant to shake his hand. He had to remind himself of where he was. He didn't want to be awkward. Anything could damage a potential relationship with the mayor. He knew how important his standing was in the city. Travis understood he had to maintain it and shook his hand.

"Travis, Travis Holiday," he responded.

"Thank you for allowing my staff to use your facility. I really appreciate it."

"Uh … yeah, no problem," Travis coolly responded while his eyes continued to spark. He struggled to remain calm. Something wasn't right about Mayor James. The banquet wasn't the time or place to engage in anything more than formalities.

"I understand you're new in town, right? What do you say we get together sometime? I'll give you the rundown about Carnage Coast?" Mayor James generously offered. His welcoming demeanor was kind enough to disarm a defensive person. Travis' Divine Eyes helped him see through the mayor's facade.

"That sounds like a good idea. I'm still getting adjusted. I'll let you know," Travis answered.

"Great." Mayor James turned toward Cheryl and smiled, "Did you get that young lady?"

Cheryl was insulted by his assumption. Her once amiable disposition became cheerless.

"Mayor James, this isn't my secretary," Travis interrupted. "This is Cheryl Smith. She's our executive vice president of operations. You'll be speaking with her more than me."

Mayor James was appalled by Travis's insertion. "I apologize for the assumption, Ms. Smith. It's not every day that you see a beautiful young lady like yourself in such a powerful position. I'm still getting used to the idea myself lately."

"No worries, Mr. Mayor," Cheryl sarcastically grinned.

A male approached the mayor and whispered to him. Mayor James nodded and the man walked away. "Well, it's time to get this show on the road. Travis, it was nice to meet you. Don't go anywhere. I have someone I want you to meet in a little while."

"Sure," Travis responded by shrugging his shoulders.

Mayor James walked away as Travis rubbed his eyes underneath his glasses. Rubbing his eyes eased the electricity while he spoke with everyone.

"Thanks, Travis. I appreciated that," said Cheryl. She tried to keep a positive look on her face. Her humble tone revealed the offense she felt from the mayor's disrespect.

Travis picked up on her sadness. He wanted her to know he had her back. "Don't mention it. He's a dick," Travis remarked, which made her laugh.

They stood together and got glasses of water as Mayor James walked on stage. The crowd sat at dinner tables interspersed throughout the room.

"Good evening, ladies and gentlemen. Thank you for coming out tonight. You all mean so much to this city. Your importance and value are unquestioned. It goes without saying. You, along with the people, are who make this city what it is. Carnage Coast is a great city. We have outstanding city officials and prospering businesses. Since my time in office, we have created more jobs and become one of the most prosperous cities in America. This is a city where a person with bright ideas can turn them into reality.

"Many of you helped to make my dream a reality. My dream was to make this city bigger and more important than ever. Because of your gracious support, we've attracted more people to our great city. Carnage Coast is becoming one of the most powerful cities in the country. But my goal doesn't stop there. I want to make Carnage Coast one of the most powerful cities in the world. If you allow me to remain in office for another term, I will make that happen," explained Mayor James. He paused while the crowd applauded.

"Tonight, ladies and gentlemen, I am going to introduce you to a woman. She has the ability and a plan to make my new goal a reality. Through her vision, Carnage Coast will change the world as we know it. We will no longer be the best-kept secret in America. She has personally shown me the power and impact of her vision. It is groundbreaking, breathtaking, and life-changing. Ladies and gentlemen, with great pleasure, I would like to introduce you to… Sensation," Mayor James announced.

The banquet doors opened, revealing Sensation in the doorway. She wore a long black dress that had high splits along her legs up to her waist. The top of it was sleeveless and held together by a thin strap around her neck. The dress was backless and the straps widened to drape loosely over her breasts. Her stomach was left in view as the dress thinly came together around her waist. Her neck was laced with a diamond necklace and platinum bracelets were strapped around her wrists. Diamond earrings dangled from her ears. Her eyes were highlighted with purple eyeshadow, and her lips were accented with purple lipstick. Her fingernails were black with diamond studs. Sensation slowly approached the stage. She was closely followed by Sidious Craig and Coldred Black, both wearing the same long brown overcoats. The crowd gasped at her beauty. They were mesmerized by her elegance.

While everyone was stunned, Travis' Divine Eyes reactivated. The electricity momentarily paralyzed him. The feeling was unlike anything he had felt. He shuddered as the charges almost blew the sunglasses off his face. He quickly covered his eyes again and reached down to pick them up. Out of everyone who triggered his Divine Eyes, none had done so like Sensation.

 T. V. HOLIDAY

"Good evening, everyone," Sensation opened. "Thank you, Mayor James, for such a warm introduction. I am so pleased to be working with you. I promise that your dream of making Carnage Coast the most powerful city in America will become a reality. Thank you for giving me this stage on your night. It won't be forgotten.

"Ladies and gentlemen, as our wonderful mayor stated, I am Sensation. I've lived in Carnage Coast for many years. During that time, I've learned the essence of the world. I've learned what makes us who we are. I have learned what it means to be human. I found truth and freedom in Carnage Coast. I want to share that with all of you.

"We live by rules and traditions. We have morals and customs that we're taught when we're kids. We're fed stories to train us to think and live a certain way. We're made to believe there are horrible consequences for choosing to live the way we want. We're discouraged from living out loud and being free. Many of these rules, traditions, morals, and customs are instilled in us by religious institutions. It doesn't matter what religion you are or what you were taught. We were all taught something. And because of those teachings, we feel guilty when we shouldn't. We experience pain and suffering because we believe it is the right thing to feel. We're imprisoned by taught feelings.

"These religions and teachings tell us what love is and isn't. Who's to say what love is and isn't? Who has the right to tell you that what you're doing is wrong? I believe we have the right and the ability to feel and love as we want, without any restrictions. I firmly believe that true human desire is to be free. And as human beings, we are not free.

"Imagine a world where we had true freedom. The freedom to live how we want sexually, be what we want to be, and choose who we want to be with. Imagine that freedom. It's the only true freedom we really need. Think of the truths that would be revealed to us about ourselves if we didn't live within the confines of the past. There would be no need to fight about marriage. There would be no affairs. There would only be true happiness.

"I believe in God. I believe he is vengeful. He is hateful. He doesn't care about us. If he loves us like we're supposed to believe, why do we suffer? There was once a world where there was nothing but pleasure. Adam and Eve didn't know anything except his goodness. But once they had a desire for knowledge, God abandoned us. He allowed us to live lives of suffering that have never stopped. He curses us with bombings, mass shootings, and division. What is God's love if he can allow all of this? Why are we punished because we are smarter and knowledgeable about who we are? All he wants to do is control us. We're his creation and nothing more than pets. Pets of the highest order. But pets nonetheless.

"That's why I don't believe in religion of any kind. It's garbage that is used to control us. It's a sign of God's chaos. Why are there so many religions in the world? Religion is a prime example of God keeping us divided instead of bringing us together. If he is all there is, there shouldn't be the division we see now. Every religion consists of language to keep us in fear of hell. I believe the world we live in now is the hell we should truly fear.

"I believe love is all there is. I know we can experience true, free love if our desire is strong enough. Free love that allows us to be truly happy. We don't need God or any of the religions. All we need is the love we know to be true. That love will lead to the light we're desperately in search of.

"Tonight, I am launching my Free Love Initiative. My company will release information and produce different types of media about Free Love. The Free Love Initiative promotes only love, the abolishment of all religions, marriage for all, legalized prostitution, and drugs for everyone. It will also lead to the end of racism, legalized abortion, open carry laws for firearms, and free government housing for the homeless. Free Love will allow children to choose who they want to be. We can create a world of love where everyone is happy and feels at home.

Through our sheer will alone, we can make this happen. Through Free Love, people can be truly happy.

"Free Love will not be for everyone, though. For those who choose to embrace the Free Love lifestyle, registration will be required. Free Lovers will be allowed to enjoy all the benefits of a free-love society. Free Lovers will not be subject to jail or prison. If a Free Lover violates the initiative, then they will suffer imprisonment or, potentially, death. Those who do not sign up will be shackled to the chains of our loveless society.

"We don't need God to experience this. This is a concept that will change the world. I am talking about the end of division and the unification of the world. We can be the first people in the world to destroy hate. We can do what God has chosen not to do. As the first city to adopt the Free Love Initiative, we will show the world a new way to live. Carnage Coast will lead the way in a human revolution unlike anything humanity has ever experienced. Allow our city to start the very first world law in human history. We're not embracing chaos. We are shedding the chains and embracing lives of profound truth," explained Sensation.

No one was sure how to respond. Uneasiness lingered once Sensation finished. Some women were disgusted. Many in the crowd were shocked.

"How can you say such things? How can you even think to speak of a world with no God? You truly want us to embrace drugs and sex as if that is a better way of life? Are you crazy?" an older woman who stood next to Chief Olson asked. It was his wife, Elsie Olson, and she appeared disturbed.

Sensation grinned as she sauntered toward her. "No, I'm not. I'm not crazy at all. I can speak of everything I said because I believe in it. I live it. Let me ask you something: when was the last time you felt free?"

Mrs. Olson balked at Sensation's question but couldn't find an answer as seconds passed.

"Your inability to have a remote answer tells me everything," said Sensation. "You're trying to find a time, but you can't. I'm sure there is sadness in your life. Sadness you've been dying to escape but can't."

"Young lady, I assure you that I am free," Mrs. Olson reassured.

Sensation stepped down and approached Mrs. Olson confidently. "I am certain you're not free. Simply looking at you, I can tell that you've been longing for happiness. I see you're married, and I'm sure you know it's dead. You two probably don't touch one another anymore."

Mrs. Olson became uncomfortable and adjusted herself in her seat. Everyone's eyes became focused on her. They impatiently awaited her response.

"Young lady… I …we… that is none of your business," Mrs. Olson stammered.

Sensation stopped in front of her and Chief Olson. She moved her eyes toward him and gently placed her hand on his shoulder. She traced her hand to his neck and gently fixed his tie. Sensation moved closer while Chief Olson cracked a slight grin.

"Young lady, excuse you!!!!" Mrs. Olson yelled.

Sensation turned toward Mrs. Olson and gazed into her eyes. "Does this make you jealous? Chief Olson and I are good friends. I've met him recently and grown quite fond of him. How would you feel if I told you Chief Olson has been a practitioner of the Free Love Initiative even before tonight…."

Chief Olson instantly shook his head and motioned for Sensation to stop. His fear amused her.

"Don't worry, Chief, this won't hurt a bit. You see, Mrs. Olson, your husband has been sleeping with another woman for years now," Sensation revealed as she ignored his requests.

Mrs. Olson's eyes widened with shock and became tearful. Embarrassment and grief struck her heart like a wrecking ball. The news weakened her knees. She wanted to sink into her chair. She looked at Chief Olson, who stared away. He did not say anything while whispers could be heard in the crowd. He had felt disdain for his wife, but couldn't peek at her woeful face.

"Now, Mrs. Olson, I have a feeling you already knew that. I'm sure that you're so used to your lifestyle that you put up with it," Sensation continued. Mrs. Olson remained silent as tears rolled down her face. "I'm sure the Chief here was a happier person to be around… when he was around."

Sensation turned away from them and went back to address the crowd. "See what we put up with just to be happy. Mrs. Olson knew her husband was having an affair. And the Chief was a happier person. I'm sure he felt guilty initially. But it went away with every rendezvous. Imagine if my Free Love Initiative was in place. Both of them could be happy. They could continue enjoying the lifestyle they've grown accustomed to. Imagine if Mrs. Olson had someone to please her, too. Maybe their relationship would be better. They wouldn't feel the pain they're feeling now. If they didn't believe in God, there wouldn't be any pain, guilt, or shame."

People continued to talk amongst themselves until another voice sounded. "How do you expect this to take effect? How are we supposed to profit from a 'Free Love lifestyle?'" a man asked.

"There is nothing but profit to be gained. The Free Love Initiative will raise funds through my company's entertainment outlets. We will promote our ideals and tell people what the Free Love lifestyle means. I will donate fifty percent of my company's profits to the city. Carnage Coast will be the testament to the fact that a Free Love lifestyle can exist. This will put Carnage Coast on the map. We have to show that our love and happiness are greater than God's. We can produce crime statistics in the coming months to show how it will lower the crime rate. Our city's profits would increase by taxing prostitution and the legalization of all drugs. We'll have a universal healthcare system that'll allow us to take care of everyone. Other cities and countries will want what we have. For cities that want to adopt the Free Love Initiative, we'll tax them for adopting it. Freedom isn't free, and neither will Free Love," explained Sensation.

"But how do you expect this to go into effect?" the man asked again.

"There will be an election in three months. At that time, we can choose to vote it into law. It's as simple as that. Give me time to show you more, and I'll give you the world. Take the initiative and embrace free love... embrace truth," answered Sensation.

Silence settled over the crowd. They looked at each other and considered her proposal. Sensation sensed their curiosity. It appeared the majority were getting on board. She had planted the seed and watched it grow. Light sounds of applause could be heard. The applause slowly grew as more people clapped. Travis watched in awe as people showed their approval.

"How does... how does someone accept this Free Love Lifestyle?" Mrs. Olson tearfully asked. Her question surprised the crowd.

Words appeared on the TV monitors. Sensation gave them a moment to read the screen.

"On the screen is the Free Love Vow. Anyone who wants to accept the Free Love Initiative must take this vow. This is the only way we can achieve the dream. Those who chase their dreams are the ones who catch them. Chase this dream with me. You don't have to wait. We can take the vow now. It is your choice. Place both hands over your heart and repeat after me," explained Sensation.

Once again, the crowd looked amongst themselves. Doubt and skepticism remained. Mrs. Olson stood up and wiped the tears from her cheeks. She placed both hands over her heart and weakly gazed at Sensation. Her opposition had crumbled. Chief Olson stood next to her and placed his hands over his heart. They looked at each other and mouthed the words "I'm sorry." Another member of the crowd stood, followed by another, and another. Soon, the majority of the room stood with their hands over their hearts. Only a few people remained seated without doing so. A sinister smile spread across Sensation's face before she led them in the vow.

"I vow my life to be a free lover. I choose to accept and love everyone. I am an advocate for everyone to marry whomever they choose, no matter the gender, race, or age. I will not judge others. I will not discriminate or be racist to anyone. I will contribute to universal healthcare. I am an advocate for the right of women to have an abortion. I believe all drugs have a beneficial purpose. I will use the drugs I choose responsibly. I will ensure people have a safe place to use drugs. I will carry guns responsibly to ensure the safety of my fellow free lovers. I will reject God and all forms of formalized religion. I will accept free love as the only way of life. I will commit my heart and soul to the free way of life. I will give my life to the Free Love Lifestyle," vowed everyone.

Sensation felt a greater injection of ecstasy that took her breath away. Her blood pumped faster. Her hair grew longer. Her eyes became more vibrant. Sensation's skin became even more perfect. The commitment of new souls made her stronger.

Travis couldn't believe her speech or the crowd. He finally saw his purpose in The Seventh City. His mission as The Iron Warrior became clear. Sensation embodied everything he came to Carnage Coast to fight. She stood in front of everyone and outright denounced God. She was in a great position to spread her words and views. Sensation's plan was larger than he imagined. She was creating a movement. He repeatedly heard Mark's words in his head. He kept replaying Mark's statement of how important Carnage Coast was to the war between God and Lucifer. He felt crushed.

Sensation met with Mayor James, who introduced her to people. Travis fixed his sunglasses to make sure no one saw the electricity in his eyes. He had to leave. His eyes were going to give him away.

"Cheryl, I've gotta go," Travis abruptly told her.

She was caught off guard by Travis' sudden need to leave. "What's going on? Why?" Cheryl surprisingly asked.

"I can't explain right now. But do me a favor, don't do anything with Sensation. Don't set up any meetings or make any plans whatsoever. Okay?" he desperately asked.

Cheryl squinted her eyes and tried to read his face. It was obvious something was wrong. She heard his desperation. "Why… why don't you want me to do anything?"

He couldn't tell Cheryl that Sensation was evil. He needed a reason to give her, but didn't have one. It was evident she wanted to understand.

"I'll try to explain later. Right now isn't the best time. Trust me," said Travis.

Cheryl begrudgingly agreed and Travis walked away. He was close to the door and almost out of the room until he heard…

"Travis, wait!!!" a voice sounded. Travis recognized the voice; it was Mayor James.

Travis tried to smile and thought of ways to end the conversation before it began. He turned around and his face dropped when he saw who was with Mayor James. The electricity intensified, forcing him to close his eyes. He slowly opened them as Mayor James and his companion got closer.

"Travis, I want you to meet our special guest. This is Sensation… the woman who will put Carnage Coast on the map!" Mayor James exclaimed.

Sensation gazed at Travis with a delighted smile. She took slow, deep breaths as they got closer. Sidious and Coldred, who were behind Sensation and Mayor James, quickly surrounded Travis to prevent him from leaving. While Travis' body was charged with unbridled electricity, the ecstasy surged through hers. She hadn't felt anything like it after giving her soul to Lucifer. Her eyes blackened and turned fiery red.

The tension was thick enough to cut with a knife. They did their best to hide it from Mayor James.

"Nice to meet you," Travis hesitantly said. His voice cracked from the electricity flowing through him. He gritted his teeth and fought to control himself.

Her chest rose and lowered with every breath. She was a sight to behold. "Likewise. I understand you're new to Carnage Coast," she panted. Her voice became breathless after the pledge. The increase of souls made every word a seductive song.

"Yeah… I am. Everybody keeps telling me I need to get together with them," Travis told her as he flashed a sarcastic glance toward Mayor James. He realized why his Divine Eyes had activated earlier. Mayor James was in cahoots with Sensation.

She looked him up and down. There was something about him that was unlike anyone else she had met. "It's true. As the owner of the only sports game in town, you need to know everyone, especially me," she stated.

"Based on your speech, it sounds like I got to know quite a bit already. I have to admit I'm impressed with your Free Love Initiative. It sounds like a dream," he softly smiled.

Sensation smiled and giggled. She was flattered. "Thank you! Why know the truth and keep it from others? Everyone deserves to be happy and free. Did you take the vow?" she excitedly asked.

"No. And I wouldn't call that truth either," he firmly responded.

His staunch answer erased her smile. She had won over almost everyone in the room. His challenging demeanor surprised her. "What would you call it?" she asked.

Travis took a moment before he responded. He didn't care that Mayor James was with them. Sensation gave him an opportunity to address her directly and he didn't want to let it pass. He knew their paths would cross again. He wanted to send her a message. Travis stepped closer and peered into her eyes. Sidious and Coldred followed him to make sure she was safe.

"Honestly, I think this was smart. Very smart, actually. Everything you proposed is ideal. It's everything a person could ask for. Yet I listened to your vow. There was one key aspect that I don't think anyone noticed. You snuck in the rejection of God and pledging one's soul. Some may not think it's a big deal, but I do. We're not bigger than God. Every time we think that we are, he reminds us of how small we truly are. We can only hope that our will aligns with his. And let's not forget a person's soul. I see the value in it. I know what it's worth. Especially here in Carnage Coast. I'm not giving you my soul… or this city's," Travis calmly told Sensation.

She didn't know Travis. His words felt like a direct shot at her true purpose. She wondered how he could say such things. His message was clear, which spiked her curiosity. His attention to detail made her smile. She wanted to know more about him.

"Wow! That was definitely something. I appreciate how attentive you are. It's a shame to see a handsome man be so misguided. Once I ditched your sky daddy, I discovered the greatest happiness I've ever known. If you opened your eyes, you could know it too. But don't worry, in three months you'll know the Free Love I'm talking about. I promise," Sensation retorted.

She extended her hand and traced the lining of his suit. Travis grabbed her hand but was quickly restrained by Sidious and Coldred. He defiantly glared at them and returned his attention to Sensation, who had a devilish grin. She nodded, and they released him. He released hers as well.

"It's okay. Travis wasn't going to hurt me. He just needs a little time to get used to the idea," Sensation boasted.

"We'll see," Travis rebelliously responded.

     T. V. HOLIDAY

He left The Pavilion searching for answers. He had a mountainous challenge ahead of him. Everything Mark and Mike warned him about came to fruition. Sensation was trying to rid Carnage Coast of God's presence. He had to figure out a way to counter The Free Love Initiative. The fate of the world depended on it.

T.V. HOLIDAY

Sensation, Sidious, and Coldred returned to The Pit. She was confident others would buy into The Free Love Initiative. Her interaction with Travis enticed her. The heightened ecstasy signaled he was one to watch out for. As the elevator doors opened to her office, they saw a man sitting at her desk. Sensation noticed it was Luc who had a devilish grin. She hadn't seen him for weeks and was ecstatic. She. Luc didn't show up often, but when he did, he always had a gift.

She ran over and hugged him. "Luc!" Sensation shouted.

He held her softly and gently kissed her forehead. "Hello, my dear," he replied.

"What are you doing here?"

"I've come to tell you what a great job you've been doing. I'm so proud of you. You've started to become the woman I envisioned you to be. Your Free Love Initiative is priceless."

"You really like it?" she surprisingly asked.

"I love it! It's everything needed to drive God out of Carnage Coast. You're giving everyone what they want. You've become the most powerful woman in this city. Soon… the world will be ours. Once again, the fall of man will come from the hands of a woman. I couldn't have planned it better myself," Luc encouragingly said.

Sensation felt giddy and blushed. It was a feeling Sensation forgot. It had been years since anyone approved of anything she did. Now, she finally had someone who cared.

"Stop it! You know you could've done ten times better. I'm only here because of you," she stated.

Luc stepped aside and guided Sensation to her desk. Sidious and Coldred moved their feet together and bowed as Luc walked by. He complimented them for how they protected Sensation. He sat on the corner of Sensation's desk and calmly motioned for everyone to sit down. He asked her how the evening went.

"It was great. I got the mayor to give me a platform to speak about the Free Love Initiative. I proposed it and there will be a vote in three months to make it a law. I had a few non-believers at first, but I was able to change their minds. Before it was over, most of the room said the vow," Sensation explained.

"Good! Now tell me about the man you encountered. Tell me about Travis Holiday," Lucifer instructed.

Sensation was caught off guard by his request. Luc wasn't there but knew about their crossing. His question reminded her of his far-reaching presence. It was another sign of Travis' significance.

"Travis Holiday owns The Pavilion and runs the CCWA. For some reason, I had this strong feeling when I spoke to him. It was like I was speaking to you. It was weird," said Sensation.

"It wasn't weird. That is a man you're going to get to know a lot more," Luc told her.

"Why?" she asked, confused.

"Allow me to explain, lovely. To gain control of the world, Travis Holiday is the only one who can pose a problem for us. He is the only thing standing in my… I mean… our way from getting to where we need to be. Travis Holiday needs to be eliminated," Luc explained.

His explanation was logical. No other man, aside from Luc, made her ecstasy surge. Her confusion dissipated, replaced by a cool confidence. Her thoughts became clear. She was beginning to exert her power over the city. She wasn't going to let anyone stand in her way.

"Then we'll have him eliminated. No problem," said Sensation nonchalantly.

"No, dear. It will be. Travis has been chosen to stand against us. He is one of God's champions. Trying to kill him won't work. He's more complex than that," explained Luc. He remained gentle, but his tone deepened. Sensation sensed his urgency and was attentive.

"There is another reason why I came to you, Lynda. There is something you have. Just as God chooses his champions, I choose mine. I knew of this impending circumstance. I needed someone with

     T.V. HOLIDAY

the strength and willingness to carry out my will. Lynda, I chose you for Travis.

"Lynda, I was never meant for you. I wanted to bless you with happiness because you deserve it. You have a heart that yearns to be loved, and Travis is the man who can give it to you. He doesn't realize he's on the wrong side. I need you to open his eyes to the love you have for him. Make him understand he is fighting for a false hope. Travis is a decent man, but as you pointed out before, sex has been man's downfall.

"In order to defeat him, you have to get Travis to denounce God. Once he does, he becomes powerless. Make him lose his faith. Then he'll never be able to stop us. Once he becomes faithless, his fate is up to you. You can keep him for yourself if you want. If he refuses to stand by your side… kill him. Until you get him to denounce God and lose his faith, he is our greatest threat. Wear him down. Get him to lower his guard and he'll eventually crumble. The process has already started… now finish him," revealed Luc.

Luc's revelation took sensation aback. She was heartbroken to learn that her place was not by his side. He had given her more than any man ever did. He healed her wounds. She rediscovered her confidence because of him. Her life changed from one of despair to fully realized joy. She was gaining meaning and importance. She credited everything to him.

She was flattered and humbled that Luc chose her. His reference to God hinted at a greater purpose. Luc hadn't mentioned anything more than his desire for souls. To hear of God's champions made her realize she was part of something bigger than herself. None of that mattered to her. Sensation desperately wanted a man to covet her. She wanted someone to share her life with. She was perplexed by Luc's revelation about Travis. She only saw Travis as a challenger to her Free Love Initiative. Aside from the ecstasy she felt, his defiance was remarkable. She believed she could do everything Luc asked her to do. There was no way Travis could resist her.

She scanned Luc, searching for any sign that he might've been wrong. His demeanor remained the same. He confidently waited for her answer. Any hope she had of potentially being his woman waned. Her dreams of being with him were dashed. But as always, Luc gave her something new with his visit.

"I have a lot of things going through my head about this. But I'm going to do it because I trust you. You've been there for me more than anyone. Everything I have is because of you. If you say I need to get close to Travis… I'll do it," Sensation responded.

Luc smiled. He had a woman who was willing to do his bidding without question. Sensation couldn't do more to please him than destroy Travis.

"That is wonderful, my dear Lynda! Let me give you some things to prepare you for when it is time to make your move," said Luc.

Two weeks passed and The Free Love Initiative materialized. Commercials showcased people of different races and genders expressing their love to one another, walking in public with slung rifles, and smoking and snorting drugs. Free Love ads were played after every other song on the radio. It was on the front page of every newspaper. Free Love pop-ups cluttered computer screens. Free Love advocates posted videos on every social media platform, making them unavoidable. The Initiative's website had information along with pornographic videos and testimonies from Free Love converts. Headlines and taglines read, "Who needs a God when all we need is love? True love is free, so experience it with me. Love has no rules, so why choose a God who does? The Love Revolution is here; make history now." Free Love posters were plastered in elementary and high schools. Every piece of marketing included The Free Love Vow. Sensation appeared at the end of every commercial to remind people of the election. She wore a skimpy bathing suit to mimic Uncle Sam in every visible medium. Her movement was in full swing.

T.V. HOLIDAY

Travis watched as the Free Love Initiative swept across Carnage Coast. He had to find a way to reach people. He was brought to Carnage Coast to save the world from descending into hell. Stopping people on the street wasn't a solution anymore. He needed to showcase the ill effects of the Free Love lifestyle. People had to know that Free Love was not everything Sensation made it out to be.

To get the people in Carnage Coast to listen, they needed to know him as The Iron Warrior. Sensation made herself visible and told everyone what she was about. The only way for Travis to counter that was to do what The Warrior did. Using The Iron Warrior to truly represent the light in the darkness gave Travis an idea. It allowed him to develop a plan to create a movement of his own to stop the Free Love Initiative from taking effect. He planned to post footage of himself fighting Sensation's Double Ds. It was the only thing he could come up with to combat The Free Love Initiative. The Warrior hoped he could find something significant enough to post. Travis jumped into The White Ghost and rode into town. It was time to formally introduce Carnage Coast to The Iron Warrior.

Travis drove into a dark-lit alley and parked alongside a building. He transformed into the man he was meant to be. "I am the light in the dark. God's fist in the war, the man powered by faith, make me The Iron Warrior once more!" declared Travis. His eyes turned white as electricity pulsed through him. The silver and white metal covered his body. He became The Iron Warrior.

He walked through the alleys, but nothing triggered his Divine Eyes. Without having a starting point, it was as if he were trying to find a needle in a haystack. The Warrior wasn't sure what he was going to do. He only knew he needed to do something.

He headed back to The Ghost but a car pulling into an alley triggered his Divine Eyes. It stopped and the lights went out. The Warrior backed against a wall and watched from a distance. He stood back and observed until he realized what was going on. Women's voices could be heard, and after a while, the car rocked from side to side.

Meanwhile, inside the vehicle, Cassidy and Lovelyn spoke with a young white 21-year-old college student named Brittany. Cassidy and Lovelyn were Diabolical Donnas. They stayed on the streets to recruit new women. It was their job to find new girls and turn them into Donnas. Cassidy was a 35-year-old black woman who had worked the streets since she was a teenager. She loved the street life and led the Donnas' street team with Lovelyn. Lovelyn was a 28-year-old Filipino woman who was an expert Brazilian Jiu-Jitsu grappler. She was Cassidy's enforcer. She wanted nothing more in life and loved breaking in new women.

"Alright, B, you ready to become a Donna?" asked Cassidy.

Brittany was unsure if she was ready to embrace what she knew little about. She was enamored with the Free Love Initiative. She desired to live a life of pure happiness and freedom. She regularly passed by The Donnas and fantasized about their lifestyle. She knew the nature of their business. Cassidy and Lovelyn revealed they were part of The Double Ds and enticed her to become one. All she had to do was go for a ride. Brittany rode with them in search of true freedom. Now, in a dark alley, her quest for Free Love was awaiting an answer.

"Um… yeah," she apprehensively answered.

Cassidy climbed into the backseat of their luxurious BMW 745IL while Lovelyn locked the doors. Cassidy wore a blue jean skirt with a white, laced, see-through tank top. She sat back and looked out the window. Lovelyn unrolled a small sheet of aluminum foil and pulled out a small glass pipe. She placed a pill on the sheet and lit the bottom of the foil. She chased the dragon and passed it to Cassidy with another pill. Cassidy chased the dragon as Brittany watched.

"Listen, Brit. In order to be like us, you gotta' do exactly what we tell you. You cool with that?" Lovelyn asked.

Brittany had never been around drugs. She knew people who smoked marijuana, but they never did it around her. She knew the dangers of hard drugs and consciously stayed away. She questioned whether it was a good idea to be with them. Being a Donna was the pathway to the release she desired. She opened her mind to new possibilities, even if it included drugs. She sheepishly nodded and answered, "Yeah."

"Good… because to be a Donna, there is a process you gotta' go through. Somethin' we all do," Cassidy added.

Lovelyn gave Cassidy another pill. Cassidy placed it on the foil and chased the dragon again. She set the foil down and pulled Brittany closer. She kissed Brittany and exhaled the smoke into Brittany's mouth. Brittany pulled away and coughed.

"What was that?" coughed Brittany.

Cassidy slapped her and yanked Brittany by her hair. "You shut up and do what we say. You don't ask questions. You take it. You got that?" Cassidy snapped.

"But I thought you were going to show me Free…" Brittany started, but was slapped by Lovelyn.

"She said shut up! You don't know Free Love yet. You told us you wanted to be a Donna. Now take it!" Lovelyn yelled.

Brittany was overcome with fear. She suddenly realized she was in a dire situation. Everything she imagined about Free Love was no longer true. Her eyes watered and a cold chill trickled down her spine. Her body trembled. Something bad was about to happen. There was nothing she could do to avoid it. She tried to unlock the door, but Cassidy smacked her face against the window. The impact dazed Brittany. Her head throbbed while Cassidy and Lovelyn wildly laughed.

"I love it when they fight," Lovelyn commented.

"You want more? Or are you gonna' be a good bitch?" Cassidy callously asked.

Tears slowly fell down Brittany's face. Thoughts of the imminent future filled her mind. "You can beat me, but I'm not giving in to this. It's not like you can just kill me."

"Damn girl, you just don't know," said Lovelyn. She pulled out a switchblade and pointed it at Brittany. "We can. And if you don't go nicely… we will!"

"HELP!!!!" Brittany cried out.

Cassidy slapped Brittany again and Lovelyn sliced her shoulder. Cassidy forced herself onto Brittany while Lovelyn cut off Brittany's clothes.

Meanwhile, down the alley, The Warrior had seen enough. Although it could've been posted to social media, he thought against it. He couldn't let a situation like that get out for people to see. He was determined to find a way to sway people from The Free Love Initiative. That would come later. The girl in the car needed his help.

He ran to the BMW and punched through the rear window. Cassidy and Lovelyn stopped in awe of him. He ignored them and opened the door. He pulled Brittany out, who was in tears. She immediately grabbed onto him without looking.

"Help me, please, please help me," she cried horribly.

"Okay, okay… it'll be alright," The Warrior calmly responded.

Brittany slowly looked up and saw his face. She screamed at the sight of him. She squirmed and tried to get out of his arms. She pushed away and jerked while he firmly held her. He stood still and absorbed all her panic-filled strikes. He imagined her fright and didn't want to do anything to heighten it.

"Hey, relax! I'm here to help you," The Warrior calmly insisted.

Cassidy slid toward them and glared at him. Her awe was replaced by disrespect. "Who do you think you are!? She belongs to us, you fucking wacko! Look at what you did to our car! Give her back!!!" Cassidy snapped.

The Warrior nonchalantly glanced at her and kicked the door shut. "Shut up!" he responded and turned his attention back to Brittany. She settled down after he watched him close the door on Cassidy. His actions helped calm her. "Let's get you outta' here. What's your name?"

"Brittany," she responded.

"Okay, Brittany, I'll take you wherever you want to go. You name it, and we'll go," he stated. Brittany nodded her head. She was willing to let him take her anywhere as long as it was away from Cassidy and Lovelyn.

Inside the car, Cassidy was in disbelief. "No, this motherfucker didn't! Go get her back. I'm going to send a text real quick. I'ma let them know we gotta' problem," said Cassidy.

Lovelyn nodded and stepped out of the car. She shouted, "Hey pussy blocker! You're walking off with my girl. I didn't get a chance to hit that yet. I'll give you a chance to leave with your life, though. Keep walking and give her back."

The Warrior turned around and cracked a slight smile. "Pussy blocker, huh! That's not the first time I've heard that one. Look, sweetheart… I'll put it to you this way. We're leaving. If you get too lonely, wait here, and I'll come back for you."

She stood with her mouth open. Lovelyn couldn't believe his response. "Wow! Crazy and you got balls. Shit, you can join us! But she is coming back, though."

He turned around and walked away with Brittany, who watched timidly. "Goodnight," said The Warrior.

Lovelyn laughed while he left. She liked a man who was willing to stand up to her. She ran toward them with her blade out and tried to leap on his back, but The Warrior ducked. He back-dropped her to the ground. The fall made her release the blade. Lovelyn held her back and groaned. He grabbed the switchblade and threw it into a nearby dumpster.

"Go home," The Warrior mockingly said.

He grabbed Brittany and helped her toward his truck. She stumbled over her feet. She felt lethargic. Her pupils got smaller. Her body quivered. She held her stomach in pain.

"Hey, what's wrong?" The Warrior asked. He recognized that she was in bad shape. He wondered if she would have to go to a hospital.

"I don't know. I feel sick," Brittany replied.

While he tended to Brittany, five large men wearing biker vests exited one of the nearby buildings. They met with Cassidy in front of the BMW. One of them held a phone that was set to record.

"Hey wacko!!" yelled Cassidy. "Now you're gonna' get your ass stomped for stickin' your nose in shit that don't concern you. GET HIM!!!"

The Warrior quickly thought about how to fight off the group and keep Brittany safe. She was getting worse and couldn't care for herself. He figured his best bet was to keep her by him. He heard Lovelyn snicker as the group charged at him.

"See… you're not just a pussy blocker, you're cock blocker too. They had next after us. You shoulda' listened. I was gonna' let you get some of her and me. Dumbass!" stated Lovelyn.

Lovelyn snatched Brittany and yanked her back to Cassidy. The Warrior reached for Brittany but was intercepted by a biker who tackled him to the ground. Three more surrounded The Warrior while the fifth recorded the beatdown. They kicked him all over. One of the bikers headlocked The Warrior to hold him down while another pulled out a chain. The biker whipped his back while the other clamped down on the headlock.

Meanwhile, Cassidy and Lovelyn threw Brittany in the backseat of the BMW. They picked up where they left off. Cassidy slapped Brittany around as Lovelyn ripped her clothes. The drugs took full effect and zapped Brittany's resistance. She was at their mercy and they had none to give.

Back in the alley, The Warrior had his hands full with the bikers. They continued to whip and beat him while the fifth biker filmed

     T. V. H O L I D A Y

everything. The Warrior caught a glimpse of the car and Brittany's screams suddenly stopped. All he could see was Cassidy sitting upright in the backseat. A pair of legs was spaced apart underneath the open backseat door with Lovelyn stooped behind it. Something bad was happening. The Warrior had to get to her.

His body surged with electricity and he became impervious to their strikes and whips. He stood and hoisted the biker, who had him in a headlock, onto his shoulders. The other bikers stepped back in amazement. The Warrior tossed the biker into the other three while the fifth watched with his camera. The chain fell to the ground as the group scrambled to their feet. He grabbed the chain and eyed it. Thoughts of a fair fight entered his mind, but vanished when he glanced at the car again. They were in an alley. Fairness had no home there.

He whipped one of them in the leg. The biker wailed and buckled to his knees. The Warrior kicked his face like it was for a field goal. The biker spun to his back and unconsciously flattened out. Another biker pulled out a knife, but The Warrior whipped his face with the chain. The impact broke his jaw and knocked out his teeth. He fell face-first to the ground and lay next to the other unconscious biker.

Two bikers were left. They stood between The Warrior and the car while the fifth kept recording. They charged toward The Warrior and he responded with a double clothesline. He wrapped the chain around his fist and punched one of them. The blow broke the biker's face as well, while the fourth biker crawled away in search of a weapon. He realized that he was outmatched and needed something. The biker found a cinderblock under a stack of trash bags. The Warrior reached for him, but the biker smashed his face with the cinderblock. The cement crumbled on his face as he stood still. He amusingly wiped off the dust while the biker peed his pants. He couldn't believe The Warrior withstood a cinderblock to his face and stood unfazed. He eyeballed the biker and growled under his breath.

"Run!" The Warrior growled.

The biker ran away in utter terror. The Warrior turned his attention to the last biker who recorded the fight. The biker violently shook as The Warrior got closer. He turned the phone around and showed that the recording was for a social media site. He placed his finger over a portion that The Warrior couldn't make out.

"Come closer, and I'll press this button," the biker fearfully threatened.

"If I make it to you, I'm puttin' you to sleep like your friends over there. And that's not a threat. I'm simply telling you what's going to happen," said The Warrior.

He dashed toward the biker and squeezed his hand over the phone. The biker wailed in agony as The Warrior crushed the phone in his hand. A clicking noise came from the phone that caught his attention. He grabbed the phone and saw a message that read, "VIDEO POSTED." The Warrior's heart skipped a beat in trepidation. He hoped the message didn't mean what it could've meant. He hoped the video wasn't posted on a site.

"Video posted? Please tell me that video wasn't for a site?" The Warrior angrily asked.

The biker held his hand and whimpered. "That video just went out on the largest social media platform there is. Now everyone is gonna' know who you are. They're gonna' see how you attacked us and let that little cunt get-"

The Warrior aggressively kicked him in the chest. The force flung him against a building. His ribs broke and his head smacked the concrete. The biker slid down the wall and unconsciously slumped over. The Warrior was frustrated at the thought that others would see the video. He imagined what people would say. He shook the thoughts and tried to stay in the moment. Brittany still needed his help.

Inside the car, Cassidy was horrified when she noticed The Warrior coming.

"Lovelyn, get up!" Cassidy anxiously shouted.

Lovelyn raised her head from between Brittany's legs. "Are the boys comin'?" she asked.

"No! It's that silver motherfucker. I don't know what the hell happened, but he's comin' back!" Cassidy nervously said.

"No way!" Lovelyn surprisingly responded. She saw The Warrior getting closer and grinned. "I'm really going to have some fun tonight," she mumbled.

"Don't worry, Cass, I got him. Take her in and keep working on her. I won't be too long," Lovelyn urged.

Cassidy watched as Lovelyn wiped a trace of blood from her face and grabbed her gun. Cassidy dragged Brittany, who was partially unconscious, out of the car and down another alley corridor. The drugs incapacitated Brittany.

The Warrior walked toward Cassidy and Brittany, but was cut off by Lovelyn.

"Oh no, no, no, no, no!" she said. "Me first!"

"You sure about that?" asked The Warrior. "I've always prided myself on not hitting a woman. But you're making it really hard for me tonight."

Lovelyn aimed her gun at him to allow Cassidy to get away. "Ooooh! Sounds like I'm doing somethin' right. Y'know, I'm not too big on men, especially freaks. They've never been tough enough for me. But you... you're different. I could love you. And I mean like really love you."

"Don't I feel like the special one?" The Warrior sarcastically responded.

Lovelyn laughed. "God, I love it! I finally found a guy with some balls. Come on, baby, let's take this fight to the bedroom. You're too fun to kill."

"Either blow me, and I'm not talking about the one that you're good at. Or... well, you probably suck at that too. Just get the hell outta' my way," he snapped.

"Agghhh! So be it. Too bad, though," said Lovelyn.

She shot him, but he didn't move. Lovelyn was stunned. She fired eleven more rounds and he still didn't move. The bullets bounced off him. Dented casings fell to the ground. He cracked a slight smile as Lovelyn pulled the trigger on an empty gun.

"You still havin' fun?" The Warrior cynically asked.

Lovelyn dropped her gun and walked toward him. She hit him with a roundhouse kick to the face, but it barely fazed him. She slapped him, kicked his groin, and spun around with a backhand to his face. But nothing affected him.

"You done yet?" he facetiously asked.

"No. I'm in love with you. I've never seen a guy take all of that and look at me the way you do. Oh, baby, I'll do whatever you want. Forget that broad, fuck with me," said Lovelyn.

She moved in to hug him, but quickly pulled out a knife. Lovelyn tried to stab his face, but The Warrior caught her arm. He clenched his fist and instinctively reached back to punch her.

"Come on, baby. You're one of the good guys. You're not going to hit me. That wouldn't be fighting fair," she slyly told him.

The Warrior squeezed the knife out of her hand and walked her back toward the car. "I stopped fighting fair." He grabbed her head and rammed it through the car window. He looked at her and immediately regretted his actions. He wondered if that was necessary. She could've been seriously injured or possibly worse. He tried to put that aside. He needed to get to Brittany. His night wasn't over yet.

Meanwhile, inside the building where the bikers exited, Cassidy took Brittany to the basement. The building was known as The Gutter. The front of it was a bar that served as a cover. The bartender worked as a scout for new "recruits." It was also where the local gangs waited for their turn to break in recruits. Cassidy strapped Brittany to a table. She turned on the lights that revealed a torture room. Objects hung on the wall and ceiling. It was a room meant to break spirits and crush souls. The walls echoed with screams. The floor was covered with dried tears from past recruits.

"We had a minor setback, but I promised you Free Love," said Cassidy. "You may think this is hell now, but you're gonna' be stronger from it. You'll know the true meaning of Free Love. You'll be a Diabolical Donna. But first you need to know real pain."

The basement door opened and the light from upstairs silhouetted a figure at the top.

"That you, Love? That silver bastard took you longer than I expected. How was he at the end?" Cassidy asked.

Footsteps echoed down the stairs throughout the room. A light followed along the footsteps. Cassidy looked up and saw The Warrior. His eyes were filled with utter contempt.

"I guess you could say I'm pissed because my night ain't over yet. You still have something I want," said The Warrior.

"Who are you?" asked Cassidy. She slowly backed away from Brittany and grabbed a whip from the wall. She walked backwards until the wall stopped her. Her heart pounded like it was going to burst.

The Warrior unstrapped Brittany from the table. Her eyes fluttered and rolled back into her head. He checked her pulse and was relieved to learn she was still alive. She had passed out.

"I want you to pass a message for me," he said while looking down at Brittany. "Tell Sensation, I am the light in the dark, God's fist in the war, the man powered by faith. I am The Iron Warrior, and I'm here to stay."

The Warrior picked up Brittany and carried her up the stairs. He paused and looked back at Cassidy, who was terrified.

"I trust you can pass that along," he told her.

Cassidy was frozen as she watched them leave. She didn't know what to make of him. She worried about what to tell Sensation and the Donnas. They had a big problem on their hands.

The Iron Warrior took Brittany to Last Hope. He believed Mike was the best bet to take her to the hospital. He couldn't make himself a suspect by walking into the hospital with her as Travis Holiday or The Iron Warrior. He believed Mike could pass as someone who wanted to help a battered young woman. He hoped Mike was awake. It was two o'clock in the morning.

He parked The White Ghost behind the church and carried Brittany inside. He rampantly searched and shouted for him. There was no sign that Mike was there. His hope diminished. He didn't know where Mike lived. The Warrior began to consider taking her himself. She needed medical attention, and he couldn't waste more time. He walked back in and knelt next to Brittany. Her eyes swelled. Her bottom lip was busted. Parts of her hair were pulled out. Her clothes were ravaged, and she had scratches and lacerations all over her body. He felt guilty. He was there from the beginning. An innocent person was in pain. She suffered because he didn't act soon enough. He was filled with remorse.

"I'm sorry I didn't act sooner," The Warrior quietly told her.

He heard a noise near the sanctuary entrance. The Warrior was relieved when he saw Mike walk through the doors. The Warrior sprang to his feet and motioned for Mike to come over. Mike was relieved to see him, but stopped when he saw Brittany. Her vulnerable state saddened him. He immediately wanted to help her. "Oh, dear Lord, what happened?"

"She was assaulted. Can you take her to the hospital? I'm asking because…" pleaded The Warrior.

Mike motioned for The Warrior to stop. "I don't need an explanation. Without question, I'll take her. Did you at least catch the people responsible?"

"Yeah," The Warrior heavily sighed.

The Warrior's dejected demeanor confused him. His reply sounded as if nothing went well. "What happened?" asked Mike.

"I don't know. I may have gone too far tonight. I did everything I believed was necessary to help her. I'm not sure if I should've gone as far as I did," explained The Warrior.

Mike was perplexed with him. He wondered what The Warrior could've meant. There was more to the situation than he let on. Mike wanted to ask more questions, but taking Brittany to the hospital took precedence.

"It sounds like you need to talk. I'll be here if you need me. You are in church. If it's as bad as you make it sound, there's no better place to be than here. Do me a favor and lock up before you leave," Mike suggested.

He carried Brittany to his car and left for the hospital. The Warrior looked around the sanctuary, noticed a cross on the stage, and prayed. He asked God to give him the strength to continue. The Warrior knew he wasn't strong enough to walk his path alone.

T.V. HOLIDAY

Later that day, Carnage Coast Police Detective James Hicks entered the emergency room at Seventh City Memorial Hospital. He was an 18-year veteran assigned to investigate Brittany's assault. News of it spread like wildfire through social media. The Carnage Coast Police Department needed to show they were handling the matter. The Police Chief declared The Iron Warrior was a vigilante and called for his arrest. Hicks watched the video to educate himself before he met Brittany. After watching it, he knew it would be a delicate situation to handle.

A nurse walked him to her station. He learned her full name was Brittany Candace Lexington. The nurse told him that Brittany suffered a concussion and had multiple bruises and scratches. The hospital staff were distraught after they saw what happened to her. She encouraged him to arrest the people who harmed Brittany.

They arrived at Brittany's room, where she lay with bandages wrapped around her wrists. Her upper lip was swollen and her left eye was blackened. She attempted to sit up as they entered. Her injuries took him aback. He had seen people gruesomely hurt throughout his career. No incident was ever the same. Seeing Brittany's condition angered him. She reminded him of his younger sister. His heart went out to her.

"Hey, sweetie! I have a police officer here who wants to speak with you," said the nurse as she helped Brittany sit up. She fluffed her pillows and made herself comfortable. "I'm going to give you two some privacy. Let me know if you need anything," said the nurse before she walked out and closed the door.

Hicks sat at her bedside while she tried to focus on him. His face was worn and gruff. He was in his early 40s, but the stress of the job aged him. He appeared to be closer to 50 instead. His brown overcoat was dirty with coffee stains. His mustache protruded over his mouth. Hicks was supposed to be clean-shaven, but had a five o'clock shadow mere hours after his shift began.

"Hello, young lady. I'm Detective Hicks. I need to talk to you about what happened," he opened.

Brittany's eyes watered at the mere mention of the event. The night replayed in her mind constantly. The only respite was when she was asleep. She hoped it was a nightmare. She tried to convince herself that she was in the hospital for a different reason. Hicks's presence was confirmation that everything was real, much to her dismay.

"Now Ms. Lexington…um, is it okay if I call you Brittany?"

Brittany nodded without saying a word. He knew speaking to her shortly after it happened was the best time. Her statement would be raw. Her account would be fresh, without the chance to second-guess what occurred. Her silence made him wonder if she would be able to speak.

"I'm sorry to meet with you under these circumstances. I have to ask specific questions that are going to make you re-live last night. As tough as it is, it's necessary to ensure I get an accurate account of what happened. You can tell me whenever you're ready?" Hicks opened.

Brittany nodded again and sat, staring blankly. Tears fell as she recalled the night.

"I never… I never thought I would be in a situation like this," she started. "Growing up… you hear about women getting assaulted, and you hope it doesn't happen to you. How am I going to tell anyone about this? I can barely think about it."

Her pain moved him. He was hesitant to answer. Although he was there to do his job, he empathized with her. Hicks knew how tough the road ahead for her would be. He had seen victims of sexual assault. Some of them were able to live with the incident. He worried whether she would be able to do so.

"Y'know, Brittany, you don't need to have the answer right now," Hicks responded.

She sobbed and cupped her face in her hands. She was embarrassed and ashamed. Despite his appearance, Hicks put her at ease. She wanted to talk to him. "Thank you," she whimpered.

"You don't have to thank me, Brittany. I haven't done anything. Are you ready to try and tell me what happened?" Hicks empathetically asked.

His question helped her fight through the tears to give a statement. She wanted to get it over with. "Yeah… I've been or… was intrigued by this whole Free Love thing. You know that whole Free Love Initiative, where everything is supposed to be peace and love. It's all over the TV, on every wall, in every magazine, it's everywhere. I love what it means. Everyone is accepted. There is no more division through religion. Free love and free choice are what a person lives by. I love that concept. I mean, who wouldn't want that right?" stated Brittany.

"I'm pretty sure there are a few out there who would disagree," shrugged Hicks.

"Maybe they're the smart ones. Well, I always saw these two girls named Cassidy and Lovelyn. They're Donnas. Every time I passed them, they spoke to me. They were always so nice. It was like knowing the bad girls on the block. They always had people coming to them for everything. I felt stupid being a college student and working hard. It was like, why am I doing all of this just to try to be like them eventually? They seemed so strong and in control of their lives. That's what caught my attention about them. I wanted to become a Donna.

Then all of this Free Love stuff started. I told them how much I loved the whole concept. They told me The Donnas were part of the Initiative. That's how they got me. They kept telling me I was pretty and could be a Donna. It really hit home for me. I told them no. I was going to stick to school. But every day I thought more about what they said. It all made sense and they looked so happy, y'know. When they asked if I wanted to join… I gave in," explained Brittany.

"That's why you were with them?" Hicks asked.

"Yeah. And it was nothing until they drove into the alley. I thought it was strange but didn't think too much about it at first."

"Did they tell you anything?"

Brittany shook her head to say yes, her eyes watering again.

"Take your time. Take all the time you need," Hicks reassured while she sobbed. He waited patiently. He felt it was necessary to let her cry it out. He knew she was going to shed more tears before she could ever get over what happened.

"They didn't really say much. All I remember is Cassidy getting high and them saying, 'You ready to get the real free love?' Then Cassidy forced herself on me and blew some smoke in my mouth. I hated it. I didn't know what was going on. I couldn't understand why it was happening. I pushed her off, but they started hitting me. I was so scared," she continued.

"What happened next, Brittany?" Hicks asked.

"I told them I didn't want their lifestyle. I told them I didn't want anything to do with them. I knew what they were going to do. I was so afraid. I hoped God would help me. I kept hoping I'd pass out and wake up after it was over. It was such a mistake. I kept wishing that something, God, or someone would make them stop. That's when *HE* showed up....

"He was like this bright light. He scared me. He took me out of the car and tried to take me away. But whatever it was Cassidy blew in my mouth made me sick. I got really weak and could barely stand. Cassidy and Lovelyn tried to take me back, but he stopped them. I can't remember much else. Everything is really fuzzy after that," concluded Brittany.

Hicks took notes during her statement. Her story was what he expected to hear after seeing the video. He wanted to ask more questions, but didn't think she'd be able to add anything else. "Thank you for telling me what happened, Brittany. I know it took a lot for you to tell me that."

"Don't thank me. I don't want to ever tell that story again. I feel so dirty. I want to wash myself over and over again to get rid of it, but I can't. I feel so worthless. What man will ever be with me now? I wish I could block out that night for the rest of my life," she cried.

     T. V. HOLIDAY

Hicks didn't want to leave her down and broken. He never offered advice to people. He had been burned in the past. People turned his good intentions against him. He felt compelled to help Brittany. He didn't care if it would come back to bite him. She needed to hear something uplifting.

"Hopefully, Brittany, a time will come when you can use this experience to help someone. All you can do right now is let time take its course. Try to use some of the resources the initial officers left you. Don't let this be the end of you. There is a reason you're here today. I think God has a lot more in store for you," said Hicks.

Brittany again wiped her tears as she took in Hicks' comment. She sensed his sincerity. She never interacted with police officers. All she knew was what she saw on TV. Hicks seemed like a genuine human being. She believed he was there to help.

"You believe in God?" she asked.

He hesitated to answer. It was a personal question. He reminded himself that she was completely vulnerable and opened up with him. He wanted to respect that. Hicks believed his vulnerability was appropriate considering the circumstances.

"I do. In my line of work, I need a foundation to handle what I encounter daily. God is my foundation. I couldn't do this without him!" Hicks exclaimed.

"I always believed God existed, but never really put much into it. I always thought it was a religious thing. Even after all of this, I'm still not sure what to think. Who's to say the guy who helped me wasn't a mere coincidence? I'm glad he helped, but it seems too coincidental. God doesn't answer people that quickly. It's always supposed to be a long wait," said Brittany.

Hicks gently smiled, "Sometimes God answers us in ways that'll open our eyes. Maybe God answered quickly for you to realize he's real. People always say there's no real evidence he exists. I think the proof is in our experiences. If not before, I believe you have proof now."

Brittany contemplated Hicks' words. She felt there was wisdom in what he spoke. The man showed up when she needed someone. She couldn't think of a way anyone else would've found her. Nobody knew where she was. There was no logical explanation for his intervention. She wondered if Hicks was right.

"Maybe… I heard he can be a hard teacher. Hopefully, there won't be any other lessons as hard as this one."

Hicks suddenly became melancholic. He remembered to tell her about the video. He knew it would hurt her. He didn't want her to find out from someone else. He felt it was his responsibility to break the news to her.

"Brittany, there is something else I have to tell you. There is a video of what happened to you," Hicks reluctantly told her.

Brittany's heart dropped. She couldn't breathe. She didn't want to believe it occurred. Talking about it with Hicks made her relive it. Knowing it was visible to the world devastated her. "How? Where did it come from?"

"We spoke to the biker who recorded everything. He said the guy who saved you posted it."

"Posted?" she yelled. "You mean there is video of me getting raped on the Internet!?"

Hicks hung his head and closed his eyes. He felt her anguish and didn't want to look at her. He could hear her quietly utter the words "No, no, oh God, please no, why?" Hicks' eyes teared up as well.

"Yes, Brittany. The video is viral. We don't know who the man is. But we're trying-"

"TRYING!!! I don't care what you're trying. I feel like dirt. I was beaten and shamed, and now the whole world can see. I don't want to hear what you're trying. Just leave me alone!" snapped Brittany.

She covered her face with a pillow and wailed. The news shook Brittany to her core. She felt like she could never show her face again. Hicks left but paused at the door. Her cries echoed in his ears. Her pain rattled his bones. He couldn't help but feel that she was destroyed. He looked over his shoulder and saw that the pillow was still over her face.

Before leaving, he muttered, "I'm sorry, kid."

Hicks returned to the ER station and asked about who brought Brittany to the hospital. He knew who his prime suspects were. Their arrests felt secondary. He wanted to find the man in the video. He felt Brittany deserved an explanation as to why it was posted. The only one who could answer it was him. Hicks made it his personal mission to track him down.

T.V. HOLIDAY

During the days that passed, the video was the biggest topic in Carnage Coast. News stations and talk shows condemned its violent nature. Talk of who posted it sparked great discussion. Everyone speculated on who it could've been. The identity of the man who saved Brittany was on the tip of everyone's tongue. Although he saved Brittany, his methods were attacked. The police department and the news media vilified him for his savagery.

Sensation capitalized on the news and used it to push The Free Love Initiative. She used her newfound political pull to keep the focus off Cassidy and Lovelyn. She had Cassidy and Lovelyn turn themselves in for the assault. Thanks to her influence within the police department, the vital evidence that would have convicted them disappeared, and they were released. She claimed the Free Love Initiative would prevent assaults from ever occurring. She had therapists give seminars on repressed sexual urges for why the assault happened. She paid for Brittany's medical bills and any future assistance she would need. Sensation used every possible angle to heighten it.

Outside of the public eye, she gathered her head Donnas, including Cassidy, Lovelyn, Domino, and Vivian. Cassidy relayed The Iron Warrior's message to Sensation. She directed The Double Ds to hammer him anytime they could. She took the time to carefully plot a way to weaken his faith. Sensation planned to tear him down on all fronts.

Meanwhile, Travis tried to find a way to counter Sensation's Free Love Initiative. He was now a wanted vigilante, which limited his ability to fight as The Iron Warrior. His violent ways came back to do more harm than good. He was viewed as the criminal while the true evil in Carnage Coast was praised. He tried to compartmentalize his family. He believed it would help him cope with his new life. But there was no way of forgetting them. He loved them too much. It only dulled the pain. It didn't erase it. There was nowhere he could turn without feeling down. He was losing himself. Travis allowed Cheryl to set up a dinner meeting with Sensation. He needed another opportunity to speak with her. He hoped it would give him an opening to stop her.

He arrived at Habanero's, which was a classy, upscale restaurant. It was surrounded by glass and sat along the bayside with an ocean view. Valets carefully parked customers' high-end vehicles. As he walked inside, the live jazz band filled the darkened room with its music. The moonlight's reflection bounced off the ocean, imbuing the restaurant with a stirring ambiance. The aroma of exquisite cuisine permeated throughout the room. Travis's black suit jacket and dark blue shirt helped him look like he belonged. His mirrored glasses allowed him to hide his Divine Eyes when they got triggered. He was counting on it happening again.

"Hey, good evening. I have a reservation here for Travis Hol…" Travis started.

"Ahh, yes!" the attendant exclaimed. "Mr. Holiday. What a lucky man you are! Ms. Sensation is already here. We have a special table set aside for you two right by the window. Follow me."

Travis' Divine Eyes activated when he saw Sensation and didn't stop. The rousing aura he felt when they met returned. She wore a dark violet Versace evening dress. Her jet-black hair was curled. Black and purple eye shadow accentuated her eyes. Her crossed legs exposed her dress's split and diamond open-toe high heels. The low table light spotlighted her like a 1940s screen siren. She was ravishing.

"Ms. Sensation… here is Mr. Travis Holiday," said the attendant who motioned for him to sit.

Sensation breathed heavily upon seeing him. The ecstasy rippled throughout her body. She traced her tongue along her cherry-red lips. She leaned forward and showcased her voluptuous breasts. She wanted him to take in her beauty. She closed her eyes and savored the rush.

"Thank you, Jeremy. Can you please bring us the Chardonnay? We'll be ready to order afterwards," Sensation smiled.

Jeremy nodded and left while Travis adjusted himself at the table.

"Can you feel that?" she asked. Her breathy tone was provocative and sounded like sex. It was effortless.

He knew what she referred to, but didn't want to get lost in her extravagance. He wanted to play it cool. "Feel what?" he coyly responded.

She didn't buy his response. His distance excited her. "Oh, come on. You know what I'm talking about. That feeling running through your body right now. You felt it last time. And you're feeling it again."

"What makes you think I feel anything for you?" Travis asked.

"Because I feel something for you. I felt it when I met you. I feel it whenever your name is mentioned. And… I felt it when you pulled up to the door. Besides, I can see through those glasses. Your eyes are telling me what you won't," she explained.

Travis smiled and let out a soft laugh. She saw right through him. His approach wasn't going to work. He had never been good at pretending to be someone he wasn't. There was no point trying to fool her.

"I guess you're right. I needed something for my eyes. At least yours don't spark whenever I come around. Sunglasses at night aren't as cool as the song," Travis responded.

His cynical response made her smile. "I get why you're wearing them. It's nice to know I can get a reaction out of you. Your eyes spark, but I get buzzed in all the right places. Which one would you rather have?"

Her flirtatiousness made him blush. Travis couldn't remember the last time he felt that way. He tried to snap back to his senses. He had to remember why he agreed to meet with her in the first place.

"Why did you want to meet? I mean, this is a little strange. Shouldn't we be fighting or something? Not meeting in a place like this?" asked Travis.

"We know who each other really is. I wanted to speak with you. Get to know you."

"Before you try to kill me?" Travis jokingly interrupted.

Sensation sighed and ignored his comment. Her intentions were earnest. She wanted him to see that.

"I'm hoping it doesn't come to that. I wanted to give you a chance to join me without ever lifting a finger against one another. I'm not much of a fighter anyway. You and I are unlike anyone else. We're different. We both know what's looming over this city. I wanted to know where you stood," she answered.

Travis was intrigued by her question. He didn't know what to expect heading into the dinner. Her curiosity about his position was unimaginable to him. If their dinner was chess, she was already two moves ahead.

"How do I respond to that? I thought it was clear that I stand against you. I mean… you represent evil. You're everything I was brought here to stop. It doesn't seem like it's a matter of question," Travis said.

His answer upset her. Before she could respond, Jeremy returned with the bottle of Chardonnay. He poured them a glass, but Travis stopped him.

"Hey, my man, don't worry about me. I won't be drinking tonight," said Travis. Jeremy graciously obliged and took their order before leaving again.

"I want to respond to your last comment, but first I have to ask… Why didn't you let him pour you a glass? Are you really going to let me drink alone?" asked Sensation.

"I don't drink alcohol or smoke," Travis explained.

Sensation felt awkward upon hearing his refusal. She had never been with someone who didn't drink. She felt slightly self-conscious about drinking in front of him. She pictured him as a self-righteous Christian. Something she wasn't fond of.

"Are those supposed to be evil, too?" she smirked. She waited for the typical holier-than-thou answer she was accustomed to hearing.

     T.V. HOLIDAY

Travis sensed her judgment through her body language and tone. "No. I don't have anything against people who smoke or drink. It's just a personal preference. I never really had the desire to do either. I've known alcoholics. I don't think I'd become one by having a drink. But I've seen what happens when it's uncontrolled. I've also met people who were hit by drunk drivers. There's so much that can come with both. I guess it's something I've stayed away from. Now I don't even think about it," he clarified.

His explanation relieved her. She understood his reasoning. He wasn't as judgmental as she thought. "You are different. I never met anyone who didn't at least drink occasionally," said Sensation.

"You can check that off your list of firsts," Travis remarked.

Sensation leaned forward and glared through his glasses. She wanted him to have a clear view of her eyes when she asked her next question. "You said something a minute ago that bothered me. Do you really think I'm evil?"

Travis paused. He didn't mean to offend her. It didn't matter if she was evil; he didn't want to tear her down purposely. To be rude and offensive wasn't reflective of the man he chose to be.

"Help me out then. What am I supposed to think? I mean… from how it seems, you run this city. My eyes light up, and not in a good way, when it comes to you. They only light up when someone is connected to evil. You're pushing this Initiative that's calling for people to reject God and give up their souls. If you're not evil, you're not doing a great job of showing it. I don't know what I'm supposed to do with you. That's why I'm here. I've never killed anyone, nor do I want to. I was hoping, like you, to find a way to stop this without fighting," he answered.

She felt the word 'evil' painted her with a broad brushstroke. Once again, Sensation understood his reasoning. Although it was from a different perspective, he seemed willing to discuss it. Knowing that he didn't want to fight either gave her the confidence to sway him. It was an opportunity she didn't want to pass up.

"I'm not evil, Travis. You don't have to kill me. I simply don't have any skin in this game. I've been spat on, kicked and beaten to the point where I don't care what happens anymore. This world is ugly. Who can say we aren't in hell already? Look at how we treat each other. It's disgusting. No one cares about anyone but themselves. People lie, cheat and steal to get what they want. You can't tell me this world is worth fighting for after all the brutality I've witnessed," Sensation achingly explained.

Travis felt sorry for her. He could tell she had experiences that led her to believe what she said. He didn't think he would change her outlook with one conversation.

"Some of that is hard to argue. This world can be very ugly. But I know it can also be very beautiful. I've had my share of storms. But I've been blessed to bask in the sunlight that comes after. If all you see is darkness, you'll miss the light that's right around the corner. Everyone deserves to feel that light—that warmth. Your Initiative is the gateway to hell. If that passes, no one will ever know that light. They'll never experience that warmth. They'll never get the opportunity to feel loved, which is the most beautiful feeling anyone can ever experience. What about them?" Travis pleaded.

"I don't care," said Sensation callously.

Her response sank his heart. He had hoped there was a semblance of humanity still in her soul. He hated the damage that was done to her heart. He wished there was something he could do to heal it.

"What about you? What do you get out of all of it?" asked Travis.

"I only want to be happy. I've suffered too long. This world can go to hell in a handbasket. It's already going that route anyway. I might as well be on the winning team when it's all said and done," she declared.

"You really think you've made the right choice, huh?" Travis skeptically asked.

Sensation sat back and looked out the window into the ocean. "Imagine going all the way out there hoping to see God. You sail, and sail, and sail away. Merely hoping for the chance to see him. You and God alone. And imagine that you keep sailing and eventually run out of food. You try to keep going because you have faith that God will pull you out of it. But instead of pulling you out, a storm comes. You're about to drown and you ask God to save you. And you know what … God saves you. He saves you just enough to make it to the next day and the day after, while leaving you in immense pain. All of that pain because you wanted to see him.

"Then you realize you did see God. You saw his true nature and learned how small you are. You can float and suffer for all he cares. Carnage Coast has been my sea, Travis. I drowned in it for years. It wasn't until a while ago that someone, not God, came to my rescue. He lifted me from my life. The captain of my team changed it for the better.

"I don't have pain and suffering like I did as a woman of God. I'm free now. I don't have rules as you do. I live however I choose, and no one is going to punish me. I feel like I finally have the strength to be who I always wanted to be and it's not because of God. I'm listening to my emotions and instincts. There's nothing wrong with that. With all of that, there isn't a doubt in my mind that I'm on the right side. I bet you can't say the same?" Sensation said.

Travis looked at the wedding ring on his finger as a reminder of what he no longer had. He had been suffering since he arrived in Carnage Coast. He could relate to what Sensation said. Travis had been at the end of his rope. He desperately needed help to hold on to his faith. But he became weaker every day.

"See, Travis, I know a lot about you. I know how you got here. I know you had a family and how much you loved them. I also know how unhappy you've been," Sensation continued.

He was floored by what she divulged. There was no way for her to know about his family. No way for her to know anything she spoke of. Travis scrambled to keep his composure.

"How did yo…" Travis started.

Sensation turned back to Travis and smiled. "My guy hasn't left me since I turned to him. I see him regularly. He's there for me whenever I need him. Unlike me, you're here alone. You did everything right and still ended up alone. Everything you loved was taken from you for nothing. Tell me why? What possible explanation were you given?"

He felt like a caged dog. She poked and waited for him to snap. His heart raced as his frustration amplified. He wanted to respond, but couldn't find the appropriate words. He was angry. She tapped into the misery he bottled up inside. Travis' face reflected his internal struggle.

"I… don't… I don't have… Look… I'm on the right si…" Travis stammered.

"Side? You can't even finish it. You're broken like I was. The difference is that you're still living in denial. You're holding on to a faith that will lead you to despair. God will let you suffer. I won't. There's nothing for you to stop. I don't want to fight you. I'd rather give you the same happiness that was afforded to me. I can tell you aren't happy. Come with me. I'll make you hotter than you've ever felt. Let me make you happy," offered Sensation.

Travis was visibly shaken. He felt like she gut-punched him. He wasn't sure if she was right. He didn't want to believe her. He tried to tell himself it was a mental game, but her words were genuine. Travis felt like he was losing again.

"I need to get back to my family. The only way that is going to happen is if I stop you. I love my family too much, and I miss them," Travis declared.

Sensation sighed and shook her head. His struggle was evident and she pitied him. "Poor Travis, they keep feeding you lies. You're never going to see your family again and you know it. You can't even find your way out of this city. You don't even know how you got here. Face it …you're stuck. I'm the only one who is here for you."

"I'm not stuck here. I will see my family again," Travis defiantly exclaimed.

     T. V. HOLIDAY

"You keep that hope alive, handsome! But when you wake up, and you will wake up, I'll be the one here for you. Not God, not your family, and not anyone else. My door will always be open, too," said Sensation.

Sensation felt he had heard enough. She saw the effect their conversation had on him. She was satisfied. She went over and whispered in his ear while he closed his eyes and turned away, "There is one thing I want, and it's very important to me. I want your love. The love you have for your wife is something I've never known. I want you to love me that way. I'll be here whenever you need me. Let me love you and hopefully… our love can save us both."

Travis fumed in his seat as he watched Sensation sashay out of the restaurant.

T.V. HOLIDAY

Travis left the restaurant and walked along the boardwalk, which was eerily empty. He looked out into the vast ocean and thought about Sensation. He was angry. She desired his love. Hearing those words from her was heart-wrenching. It served as another reminder of what he no longer had. Travis had reached his end and couldn't contain his frustration anymore.

"I'm trying to play by the rules, God. I'm getting tired of doing things the right way. I quit. I sat right in front of this woman who is supposed to be my enemy and she picked me apart. Why did you pick me to fight for this world? I'm trying to walk the line, but it doesn't seem like it's worth it anymore," Travis prayed aloud.

He walked back to the restaurant but heard scuffling. The noise came from a nearby walkway between two buildings. It sounded like someone was fighting. Travis paused and pondered whether to follow the noise. It was what he was chosen for, but he felt conflicted. He wanted to go home; however, he didn't want to walk away from his calling. To walk away would go against being the man he chose to be. Going in was the only option.

Travis entered without hesitation and ended up in another alley. He saw two women leaning against a wall. They were dressed in scantily clad clothing. The dim alley light revealed a smirk on one of their faces. She stepped away from the wall and drew near.

"Don't play with him! Just do it," the other woman shouted.

Travis recognized the woman's voice. He also recognized the woman approaching him. It was Cassidy and Lovelyn. Cassidy's comment caught him off guard. He never changed in front of them. He wasn't sure whether to respond as if he knew them or act like a stranger.

"No! I want to see it happen," Lovelyn shouted.

"Um…." Travis started.

Lovelyn raised a 9mm handgun to his chest and racked the chamber. "Cut the bullshit! You know us and we know you. I've been dying to get another taste. Change! Change now before I stop your heart," exclaimed Lovelyn.

Lovelyn's frankness cut through his defenses. She called him out. She opened an emotional door he was tired of keeping closed.

"Cut the bullshit, huh? Fuck it! Do it. I'm so sick of this. I don't want this anymore. Put me to sleep! Come on, you crazy bitch! I got nothing left to lose. Kill me," Travis snapped.

Lovelyn excitedly jumped up and down. "No way! This is why I've been dying to see you again. I don't have to do this. Come back with me! Let me fuck your brains out!"

"I thought you were heartless. You can snatch up a female and have your way with her, but you can't put a bullet in me when I tell you to. What makes you think I want an incompetent broad like you?" goaded Travis.

Cassidy frustratingly watched from a distance. She was used to Lovelyn's antics, but her patience wore thin. She didn't want to see him change. He was too dangerous. "Dammit, Love! Do it now!!!" shouted Cassidy.

Lovelyn shot him in the chest. The blast knocked Travis onto the ground. Pain jolted through him like a lightning bolt. His clothes became increasingly warm as the blood rushed out. He clutched his chest and doubled over in agony. Cassidy shouted for Lovelyn to shoot him again but was ignored. Lovelyn laughingly walked around Travis as he clutched the gunshot wound. She kicked him in his lower back with her boots. Travis yelled in misery to her delight. She begged him to get up and change. She shot him twice more in his abdomen and chest as she shouted, "CHANGE!!!!" Travis bellowed as she knelt and clenched his face.

"I was expecting so much more out of you. I'm kind of glad it works out this way. Sensation isn't going to want you now. You're nothing like what she said. After what I saw last time, I didn't think it'd

 T. V. HOLIDAY

be this easy. But since you're counting your last breaths, I'm going to get my taste before you go," said Lovelyn.

She jammed her fingers into his abdomen wound that made him wail. Lovelyn cupped his head and kissed him. The pain was excruciating as Lovelyn forced her tongue into Travis' mouth.

Lovelyn pulled away and smiled. She aimed her gun at his face and blew him a kiss. "Bye-bye baby, you were so sweet. Anything you want to leave me with?"

Travis' anger turned to rage. His body cooled while he bled out. His pride swelled. He had been through too much. It was time to die. It was time to come alive. He dug deep to give himself a chance to survive.

"I am…" Travis started, but was stopped as he began coughing up blood. "I am… the…light…"

Lovelyn straddled Travis and leaned over him. She leaned toward his ear and softly whispered, "What was that, lover? I couldn't hear you."

"I am the light in the dark. God's fist in the war. The man powered by faith, make me the Iron Warrior once more!" Travis spoke into her ear.

Travis' body illuminated. His Divine Eyes sparked as he flung Lovelyn off him. Metal appeared as he transformed into The Iron Warrior. Travis' wounds were no longer present. He slowly rose to his feet and spotted Lovelyn, who looked at him in astonishment.

"Is it everything you hoped for?" The Warrior asked.

Lovelyn giddily kicked her feet and shouted with joy. "Hell yes!!! Now let's see what else you got."

The rumbling of feet running across the nearby buildings drowned out the noise in the alley. The Warrior looked up and saw shadowy figures outline the surrounding rooftops. Every shadow had a weapon pointed at him. Almost twenty Donnas had guns, ranging from shotguns and machine guns to rifles, magnums, and basic 9 millimeters.

The Warrior turned his attention to Lovelyn. She perversely smiled and backed away. He looked back to find a fearful Cassidy disappear into a building. It was an ambush. There was no place for him to run or hide.

The Iron Warrior raised his arms and looked up. "Bring it!!!" he shouted.

The Donnas fired at him. The gunfire reverberated throughout the streets. The alley was like a fireworks display. Casings rained down as The Iron Warrior took the gunfire. Passing citizens screamed as they watched them gun down The Warrior. The gunfire ceased and smoke clouded the alley while police sirens blared. Apartment lights came on. People went to their windows and peeked outside to witness the aftermath.

In the alley, Lovelyn slowly approached The Warrior who stood with his arms raised. His head was still tilted back with his eyes closed. The casings clicked and clacked as Lovelyn got closer while he remained frozen and quiet. She raised her gun to his face. Her giddiness was replaced with apprehension. He took hundreds of rounds and was still standing. He lowered his head and opened his eyes to see Lovelyn. The Warrior sensed her trepidation.

"Aww, what's the matter? Why so sad now? I thought this was what you wanted," growled The Warrior. His voice was raspy and broken. His wails and anger distorted his voice.

Lovelyn moved closer. Her finger loosely wrapped around the trigger. Her bottom lip quivered from a mix of fear and excitement. Something inside bubbled to the surface. It made her uneasy.

"Here, let me help you this time," said The Warrior. He grabbed Lovelyn's hand and aimed the gun at the side of his skull. The Warrior placed his finger over Lovelyn's trigger finger. "See, this is how. You squeeze slowly until…"

Another gunshot went off and The Warrior quickly stepped away. He held his head and jumped up and down, hollering. He suddenly stopped. His screams changed to eerie laughter. He glared at Lovelyn and removed his hand from his head. In the palm of his hand was the crushed bullet. He ran up to Lovelyn and showed her the bullet.

"Ya' see! You couldn't end me with me pulling the trigger. I'm not the guy I'm supposed to be. I can be something much, much... much worse. I'm an equal opportunist. I believe in equal rights. I'll put it to you this way. If you ever shoot me again, your life will cease to exist. I'm tired of playing by the rules. And you're going to be the first one I break them with," The Warrior told her.

Lovelyn cracked a fearful smile, "Promise?"

The Warrior headbutted Lovelyn and knocked her out. "Promise," he retorted.

Red and blue lights bounced off the alley walls. Cars screeched to a stop at every possible exit. The Donnas cleared from the rooftops. They left Lovelyn behind with a broken nose. Police spotlights revealed his presence to everyone. The Iron Warrior was surrounded.

"This is the Carnage Coast Police Department! We have you surrounded. Keep your arms out and lie down on the ground. If you do anything other than what we tell you, you will be shot," the P.A. blared.

The Warrior looked at the cars and people around him. His anger subsided as he wondered what the officers were thinking. He imagined the nerves, the excitement, and the adrenaline everyone might have felt. Those feelings snapped him back to reality. The Warrior slowly raised his arms as he was instructed. He surveyed the alley with hopes of finding a way out. He didn't want to hurt the cops. He wasn't going to put a cop's life in jeopardy.

"GET DOWN NOW!!!" another voice blared.

The Warrior ignored the instruction and walked toward the officers. He noticed a cracked door to his right. It was where Cassidy stood moments earlier. The Warrior glanced back toward the officers and sprinted toward the door. He burst through it and stumbled into a wall. He heard footsteps approaching the door. He knew they would create a perimeter around the building. The Warrior ran through the building, trying to find a way out.

He raced to the roof and heard a helicopter. He was sure it would be a police helicopter. Escaping would be impossible once it arrived. The Warrior looked down and spotted officers at the corners of the building. The only way off was to jump to the next roof. He backed up and sprinted toward the ledge. The Warrior leapt and crashed onto the next building. He rolled and swiftly got back to his feet. He ran in the same direction and jumped onto another building toward another nearby building. He didn't know where he was going. He only ran to get away as fast as he could. The Warrior looked over the ledge and saw the police cars nearly three buildings away. He created some distance between himself and the police. He had to find a way off the roof.

The Warrior found a door and kicked it open. He closed the door to cover his tracks and ran down the stairs until he found a door with an exit sign. It was locked. The Warrior tried to open it again but was stopped by the sound of a gun being racked.

"What the hell do we have here?" a raspy voice blared.

The Warrior did not move or say a word.

"Come on, bright light, I asked you a question," the voice blared again.

The Warrior quickly turned around and slapped the weapon out of his hand. He struck him with a forearm to the face. The impact knocked him unconscious. The Warrior caught him as he slumped to the ground. He took the man's body and threw it against the door to open it. The door opened into another alley that led toward the ocean seawall. He checked to make sure there weren't any signs of the police nearby. He transformed into Travis and hailed a cab back to Habanero's. Once there, he got in his car and drove home. There was a lot on his mind. He had to decide whether he had any hope of eliminating Sensation.

Chapter
18

As Travis approached his home, he noticed a newer model Mercedes-Benz parked in his driveway. His Divine Eyes sparked. Something was amiss. After the night he had, he simply wanted it to be over. No one should've been at his house. The lights were dimly lit and the front door was cracked open. He didn't have a weapon, but Travis didn't need one. He was the weapon. He walked inside with reckless abandon but was stopped by the sight of rose petals on the floor. Travis slowly walked toward the kitchen, frozen by what he saw.

Sensation sat at the table, dressed in a purple negligée and open-toed high heels. Her shoes displayed her painted toenails that matched her manicured fingernails. There were two plates of sliced cheesecake beside her. She held a glass of water near her red lipstick that highlighted a conniving smile.

"Surprise, baby," she said.

Travis' heart pounded. She dragged him through the mud at Habanero's. He was positive she had to be behind his ambush. He couldn't believe she dared to show up at his house. He looked around to make sure she was alone. Sensation was by herself.

"Why are you here?" Travis angrily responded.

Sensation was undeterred by his anger. She expected it. "Oh, don't waste your time being angry. I told you what I wanted. How else is this night supposed to end?"

Her arrogance only agitated him more. He approached her while she unflinchingly uncrossed her legs and leaned forward. Her movement made him pause. He recognized it as a tactic to break him down. It wasn't enough to dull his anger. "You just tried to have me killed?" Travis furiously snapped.

"Naturally," she shrugged.

Travis raised his eyebrow and shook his head, "Naturally?"

Sensation sighed, "I told you I didn't want it to come to that. I don't care about this war. I only want to be happy. The happiness I want can only be had with you. My guy told me you're the one for me. I believe him. You clearly haven't been happy. Why are you fighting this?"

Her words broke through his irritation. He hated that he could understand how she felt. He was unhappy. No matter how much he tried to hide it, she wouldn't let up. She said all of the right things that would make his heart sing. He did his best to remain strong.

"We cannot…."

Sensation stood and sauntered toward him. "What, because you're married? Let me ask you something, lover: how many times have you reached out to your wife and been rejected, huh? How many times did you try to prove your love to her, only for her to never trust you? How much therapy did you go to just to make yourself better for her?"

Travis was shocked. His eyes widened and his mouth dropped. Doubt cluttered his mind. "How the hell do you know all of this?" he asked.

"I know things about you, lover. Your pain. How much you've tried to be a better man for your family. How much they mean to you. How you've stuck it out even when others have called you crazy. I know how lonely you feel. I know how you feel like you're never good enough.

"You're not the monster she makes you out to be. You're a gentle soul who shows it in every way. You make sacrifices when you don't want to. She's wanted to leave you multiple times. She's accused you of cheating, but you've always been faithful. You're a good man. Why wouldn't I want a man like you?"

Sensation looked into his eyes while she gently caressed his face. His anger gave way to pain from his past. All of the rejection and abandonment he felt during his marriage flooded his heart. He knew life would be filled with suffering. There were times he wanted to turn away. Times when the pain was overwhelming, but he fought through and stayed.

"I know you've been alone in your life. You had to take care of yourself. I don't want to abandon you. I can appreciate a man like you.

A man who will tirelessly fight for my love. One who'll reject other women because I'm his queen. Who'll sacrifice for me like no one else has. I want that love. We don't have to be enemies. We don't have to fight," she stated.

Sensation softly ran her hand over his gunshot wounds that healed on his way home. His shirt was stained with blood. She lay her head on his chest and wrapped her arms around his waist. She pressed her body against his. Travis' heart raced as he felt her warmth. It had been a long time since he felt the warmth and comfort of a woman. She was soft, and her fragrance was intoxicating. Sensation was everything he dreamed of. She didn't sound evil… or feel evil for that matter either.

"Physical touch is your love language, right?" she softly asked. Sensation grabbed his arms and wrapped them around her waist. "You can touch me."

Travis didn't fight her off. He couldn't. She felt too good. He tightened his grip around her and pressed his cheek against her head. He closed his eyes and stilled the feeling of his hands on her body. She felt like love in his arms. At that moment, his mission, the reason why he was in Carnage Coast, didn't matter anymore. He had what he wanted so badly. He had a beautiful woman in his arms who professed a desire to be with him.

Sensation felt his strength weakening. She listened to his heartbeat as they breathed in sync. It felt like she was where she belonged. "Are you still sure you're on the right side?" she asked.

"You know me, right?" His voice cracked.

Sensation exhaled and nodded her head, "Umm, hmmm."

Travis' eyes watered. "Then you know as badly as I want this, but I can't," he said as a tear rolled down his face.

Sensation stayed in his arms and gently squeezed him tighter. "You can. You don't have to take the high road. Let God go," she daringly responded. Sensation removed her arms from around his waist and gently placed her hands on his face. She focused his face on hers and wiped away his tears.

"Let God go and come with me. You don't have to sacrifice yourself anymore. Come with me and live for you. Live for us. I can love you better than he ever could. You can love me however you want. My love won't hurt you," she softly urged.

Travis opened his eyes, and Sensation's smile gave way to desperation. She sounded genuine and her words felt real. Her offer was a release from his misery. Travis wrestled with giving in. He remembered all the times God carried him through his suffering. He thought about how God blessed him with a son after losing their first baby. Whether as a Marine or a policeman, Travis lived a life greater than he ever imagined. He experienced that life by denying himself and turning to God instead. No matter how much pain he was in. No matter how long it lasted. God carried him through. This time had to be the same. He had to believe that. He had to believe it, no matter how much he wanted Sensation.

"This isn't fair. You know where I'm weak. To go with you is to go against everything I fought for in my life. You're everything I want and everything I can't have. I don't want to let you go. I'm supposed to stop you. Now I'm looking in your eyes, and all I want to do is kiss you. Why did you do this to me? It was hard enough being here on my own. Now you show up here begging us to love each other. You're too good to be true, which is why I can't have you," he sadly answered.

His response rocked Sensation. She felt like someone had punched her heart. She couldn't understand why he wouldn't give in. She saw his tears. She knew he wanted her from the way he held her. She didn't want to let go. She didn't want to leave him.

"You can have me. You simply have this misplaced sense of faith that says you can't. Look me in my eyes and listen to me when I say that you can have me. You have me right now."

"STOP!!! This can't happen. You need to either kill me or leave," he pleaded.

Travis's outburst took Sensation aback. She stepped back and was unsure whether to fight for him or respect his wishes. He was visibly shaken. She didn't want to make things worse. Between their dinner and The Donnas, Sensation knew he had been pushed. If she pushed too far, she worried that she'd never win his heart. She grabbed her jacket and walked toward the door. She paused and looked back. He couldn't hide the conflict, and deep down, she felt conflicted too. They were on a path to oppose each other, yet neither was prepared to take it.

"Bye, lover," she said softly as she left.

Sensation returned to The Pit. Her interaction with Travis weighed heavily on her mind. She learned about him, but did not have the chance to get to know him until tonight. His connection to his family was strong… maybe too strong for her to overcome. She had to find a way to get him to forget his family. Sensation ran a bath and soaked in the tub.

"His will is strong, isn't it?" a voice slyly crept into the bathroom.

Startled, Sensation sat up quickly as the door slowly opened. Sidious and Coldred were in the apartment, but somehow someone got inside. Before she could wonder who it was, she recognized a familiar face. It was Luc.

"Relax, my sweet, I felt you could use some company after tonight," he smiled as he sat atop the toilet seat and turned toward her.

She lay back in the tub and let out a sigh of relief. "You scared me, baby."

"I'm sorry, lovely. What's on your mind?"

"Travis… he…. This isn't going to be what I thought it would be. It seems like it's going to take a lot to break him," said Sensation.

"Did he hurt you?"

His question threw her off. She didn't want to admit that Travis hurt her. Sensation thought about Travis' wife. She found herself envious of her. The thought of being jealous angered her.

"He rejected me! Nobody has been able to resist me since you've come into my life. How can that be? Why would he say no? What is so special about his wife? Who the hell is she that he can't see her for months and still reject me? I don't get it," she explained.

Luc grasped her envy. He had the solution she needed. "Don't worry, she can be overcome. All you have to do is be you. Share your dreams with him. Share your desires. Share the moments in your life that are important to you. Be vulnerable. He won't be able to resist you then."

"Why would that make a difference?"

Luc kneeled along the bathtub and looked into her eyes. "Because no man can resist a woman when she opens her heart to him."

Sensation saw the confidence in Luc's eyes but still felt doubtful. "Do you really believe that?"

"Absolutely, my dear," Luc reassured. "That's one of the reasons I chose you. I see the love in you that has been dying to be set free. I've given you many gifts. This will be my greatest gift to you. Besides, I have something that will help sway his heart to you even more."

Chapter 19

T.V. HOLIDAY

Travis was still conflicted about the prior evening. During the ambush, he went to a dark place, and his anger spilled out again. Sensation's words replayed in his head. Her yearning for his love tugged at his heart. She attacked him in a way he wasn't ready for. He had been pushed over the edge. Something wasn't right within him. He felt something was off.

Travis sat up to get out of bed but felt a sharp pain in his right side. It was intense and drilled into his abdomen. He raised his shirt to examine it, but there was no visible injury. His skin darkened into a bruise. Soreness spread throughout his body. None of it made sense. He was supposed to be impervious to pain. There weren't supposed to be any bruises or broken bones. He couldn't understand why. He needed answers. Mike was the only one who could explain what was happening. He planned to find Mike after work.

Travis left for work. The aches remained and pain never ceased. He arrived at his office and looked over the city. He wondered how God could allow a place like Carnage Coast to exist. It was a battleground. There was a time when Travis volunteered to go to a warzone but was spared only to be thrust into the greatest battle in human history. A seemingly invisible battle. But nothing was invisible now. It was real.

A knock at the door disrupted his moment. Cheryl walked into the room with an apple pie. She greeted him with a hearty welcome as she set the pie on his desk. It was apparent to her that he was in deep thought.

"What's going on?" Cheryl asked as she sat across from him. She could tell he was contemplating something.

He hesitated to answer. Travis didn't know Cheryl. Their interactions always centered on work. He decided to take a chance and open up to her. "Does this city feel like home to you?"

Cheryl cracked a slight smile and was amused by his question. "Of course it does. I grew up here. I can't imagine living anywhere else."

"Really!? You really can't imagine living anywhere else?" Travis shockingly replied. He was surprised to hear she spent her life in

Carnage Coast. He wondered if she had any clue that she was in the midst of a warzone. He remembered Mark telling him that every person in the city served a purpose.

His confusion surprised her. It made her more curious about what was on his mind. "No. I don't feel like I'm missing out on anything elsewhere."

Travis read Cheryl's reaction. He tried to be mindful of his mannerisms. He reminded himself that no matter what he thought, Carnage Coast was her home. "I don't mean any disrespect. I've only been here for a short time. And maybe it's just me. But something doesn't seem right here. It feels like there's something lurking," said Travis.

Cheryl tried to interpret his feelings. She was uncertain about what he was hinting at. "Lurking? I don't know about that. Don't get me wrong, we have our fair share of crime. But the people here, for the most part, mean well. There are good people here, just like any other place."

Travis realized he was being too vague. They were in the battleground between heaven and hell. He believed she had to have seen something strange.

"Let me put it this way, I can't imagine another city that would entertain this Free Love Initiative. And when I say entertain, I mean look at how it's spreading. There are billboards, flyers, posters, local TV ads, and everything you can think of to promote it. It's like all of the businesses are behind it. And have you looked at the vow? It's unnerving. Even more worrisome is that it's getting so much support. I don't think this would ever fly anywhere else," he clarified.

His explanation gave her greater clarity. She felt his honesty. Being a woman, she was unsure about giving her true opinion. She was in a great position within a large company. He promoted her because of her work. She didn't want to lose it because of her opinion.

"To be honest …this Free Love Initiative bothers me too," she hesitantly answered.

Travis' eyes lit up with surprise. He leaned forward and asked, "Why?"

His reaction made her nervous. He seemed intrigued to know more. Cheryl wondered whether she would regret speaking up. It was too late to backtrack. "It's vowing to do things that should already be done, like, for instance, accepting people. I don't have to vow to accept people. If you really have love, then loving people doesn't need a pledge," Cheryl explained.

"True... so what about the rejection of God and religion?" Travis asked.

"I don't like that at all," Cheryl answered firmly.

Travis breathed a sigh of relief that caught her attention.

His sigh sent her into a tailspin. Cheryl pondered if she watched her career flush down the toilet. She did her best to hide it. "What's that for? Don't tell me you thought I was all for it?" she snapped.

"I had no idea. I'm so thankful you're not," said Travis as he leaned back into his chair. Her feelings gave him hope. They let him know some people wouldn't be easily swayed.

Cheryl was relieved as well. She felt her career was still intact. She also felt safe to be honest with him. That safety freed her to be more open.

"Of course not. How could I reject God? I can't even fathom that. There are things in that vow that'd be nice to see happen. No racism, universal healthcare, accepting people, and showing love to people... all of that is a dream. But it's not worth the cost of my soul. I would never sign anything that would require people to register for those things. Then what happens to those who don't sign? They're subject to whatever consequences Sensation or someone decides. No... absolutely not. I don't support it," Cheryl explained.

Travis smiled and nodded approvingly. He felt he could trust Cheryl more than he did before.

"Speaking of Sensation, two things. 1. How was your meeting with her last night? 2. She had this apple pie delivered with a note," asked Cheryl. She removed the note from her pocket and placed it next to the pie.

His smile slowly eroded at the mention of the last night. He looked away from Cheryl to find his answer to her question. "She gave me a lot to think about."

"Okaaayyyy… like what?"

"I'm still trying to figure that out myself," Travis solemnly answered.

Cheryl was slightly disappointed that he wouldn't go into more detail. She hoped he would feel comfortable sharing more. She didn't want to press him any further. She stood and went to leave. "Let me know when you figure it out. Enjoy that pie too. It's from a really good bakery."

Travis grabbed the note from Sensation and read it.

Dear Travis,

I'm sorry for the way I came on last night. I realize that may have been a bit too strong. Can we get a do-over? Please accept this pie as a gift and a gesture of good faith. I want a future with you. I want you to know that it is possible.

Sincerely,
Sensation

Travis didn't know what to think. It had only been one day of interacting with her and she was overwhelming. He looked at the package to see if it had been tampered with, but it wasn't. He contemplated whether it was smart to eat it. He had been shot and stabbed since being in Carnage Coast. He wondered how a pie would hurt him. No matter how their interaction ended, Sensation still had him attacked. He had to stay sharp.

Travis shrugged off the doubt and ate a slice. He sat back and thought about his next move. He needed to see Mike. His abdominal pain was still present, but didn't hurt as much as it had earlier. He still needed to understand why he felt anything from the night before. As he sat in the chair, he felt a wave of fatigue wash over him. His vision became hazy. It was the pie. He lost feeling in his legs. His eyes slowly closed while everything faded to black.

A dim light sparked. The room was dark. A spotlight shone on a set of red curtains. Travis looked around and realized he was in an empty room. The curtains retracted to reveal a movie screen. The images of a man and a woman appeared on the screen. It was Travis and his wife. They were in a room. She stood and he was on his knees. Her face showed the sadness in her heart. She softly told him, "I'm not good for you. You should leave me and find someone else." He disapprovingly shook his head. "I don't want anybody else. You're the woman I want. I want to spend my life with you," he desperately responded. It had only been months after he proposed. In less than a year, he was on his knees fighting for her.

The screen cut to Travis sitting in handcuffs at the bottom of a stairwell. She called the police to make him leave. She was afraid their arguing would cause the loss of another child. Her tears were ingrained in his memory. He wouldn't be able to handle another loss. The visual shifted to her moving into a house. She wanted space. He wanted to be there for his family.

The screen faded to black while her voice played throughout the theater. "I can't do this anymore with you. You have to change. I don't love you as I should. You've hurt me and I'm afraid I'm going to resent you. I wasn't sure about you when we got married. I chose you because the one I wanted didn't want me and you did." They were from different times throughout their marriage. Times he wished he could forget. He buried those moments, but they wouldn't go away. They regularly gnawed at him. Each one chipped away at his happiness.

Another image appeared that showed him walking into an office. He sat down and asked a woman how much the monthly rent would be. The visual glitched like a grindhouse film and her outfit changed colors. The film repeated the conversation, but they spoke about a different apartment. They were different occurrences. Times he prepared to move only for her to change her mind.

A montage played of them in different counseling sessions, sleeping in separate bedrooms, and him moving into different apartments. Journal entries from multiple dates with the same prayer visualized. "Help me, Jesus. I just want my family. Please don't let me lose my family. I'm tired of going through this, God," flooded the screen. He tried to get up, but straps were wrapped around his waist and wrists. He was locked in. There was no escape from reliving his suffering.

Behind the images, her words played again. "You should be with someone else who can love you better than I can. I'm not important to you. I feel like I don't matter. I'm afraid of you. I hate talking to you. I get treated badly …maybe I deserve it. I can't connect with you emotionally. You are harsh. I resent you. I want a divorce. I want a divorce. I want a divorce." Travis tried to rip himself free of the straps, but he couldn't move.

All the images were replaced with one of him standing in line at a courthouse, holding divorce papers again. It was a moment he had never experienced. His heart dropped to his stomach as he watched. On the screen, he had no shame that time. No sense of failure. Only acceptance. Acceptance that it was over. Acceptance that the woman he loved more than any woman in the world was leaving. It was for real that time. No more do-overs. No more second chances. No more hoping. No more living like roommates. No more tears. No more being blamed for her pain. No more family. No more Chantel Holiday. No more.

The curtains closed and the lights went out. It was quiet. He was left in the dark. Left with his pain. He was alone.

T.V. HOLIDAY

Detective Hicks went to the afternoon lineup before his shift. The officers were buzzing from the incident with the vigilante. Hicks wasn't at the shooting but heard about it. Sgt. Sampson walked in with a stack of papers as he chewed on his cigar. He passed around Be On the Look Out sheets to everyone in the room. The vigilante was the subject of the BOLO sheet.

"Listen up! This jerk needs to be found. He is wanted for battery against those girls in the alley and resisting arrest. He needs to be arrested. This is coming down from the Chief! Finding him is the top priority," Sgt. Sampson blared.

Hicks wanted to find him on his own. The vigilante needed to answer for the video of Brittany's assault. He made his way to Last Hope church. He had never been there before. The nurses told him a man named Mike Ocean dropped her off. Mike Ocean told the nurses that Brittany was brought there by the vigilante.

He entered and noticed the lobby was empty. He continued into the sanctuary, which was also empty. It was lit by the sunlight that shone through the stained-glass windows. The pews had a light layer of dust on them. It was apparent people hadn't been in the church for a while. Faint footsteps could be heard near the entrance. A bald white man with a welcoming smile appeared.

"Welcome! Can I help you with something?" he politely asked.

"Good afternoon. My name is Detective Hicks with the Carnage Coast Police Department. I'm looking for Mike Ocean. I was given this address for him," Hicks responded.

Mike was surprised by Hicks' visit. He knew the purpose of it was to talk about Brittany. He was positive Hicks would question him about The Iron Warrior, too. "Oh! Yes Detective. I'm Mike Ocean. I'm the pastor here. What can I do for you?" said Mike as he approached and shook Hicks' hand.

"Sir, I'm here regarding the young lady you took to the hospital a few days ago. I was told you were the one to take her in. I had a few questions if you don't mind," said Hicks.

"Absolutely. I wasn't sure if someone would eventually come by to ask more about it. Please let's have a seat and you can call me Mike. Sir is very formal," Mike responded. "Or we can go to my office if you want."

Hicks looked around the sanctuary. Their conversation needed to be private. There were no signs of life in there aside from them. Because nobody was there, Hicks didn't feel the need to move. "This should be fine. Who brought the girl here?"

"It was the guy who has been on the news," Mike answered.

"Why did he bring her here? What did he say to you?"

"He told me she had been assaulted and asked me to take her to the hospital," Mike told him calmly.

"How was she when he brought her in?"

Mike remembered how badly bruised Brittany was. He felt sorry for her. His sadness returned the more he remembered. "She was in bad shape. She was in and out of consciousness."

"Why did he bring her here, though? This is a little way away from where the incident occurred," Hicks inquired.

"Umm… I don't know. I'm just glad he did," Mike told him.

Hicks tried to read Mike. He believed there had to be a deeper explanation as to why Brittany was taken to the church. Mike didn't seem to be deceptive.

"Is there anything more you can remember?" Hicks asked.

Mike didn't want to reveal his connection to The Iron Warrior. He wanted to help Hicks catch the people who harmed Brittany.

"Unfortunately, that is all I have," said Mike.

Hicks was satisfied with Mike's statement. He tried to think like the vigilante. Hicks imagined how unusual it would've seemed for him to show up at a hospital with her. It would've raised eyebrows and drawn massive attention. He rationalized that a random church would be the best option to help. Hicks glanced at Mike and remembered his standing as a pastor. If anyone would've helped the vigilante, it would've been Mike. He couldn't imagine a pastor sending someone in need away.

"Thank you for cooperating. Have a good rest of your day," said Hicks as he stood to leave.

Mike's curiosity got the better of him. He wanted to have something to tell Travis when he saw him again. "Actually, Detective… what happens next?" Mike asked.

Hicks was contemplative. He lost his composure. His face displayed the deep thought process going on in his head. "I have to find the vigilante. Our entire Department is looking for him after what happened last night," said Hicks.

Mike picked up on his meditative demeanor. He could tell there was something more nagging at Hicks. Mike was well adept at reading body language, too. Hicks' tone and mannerisms said what his words wouldn't.

"It seems like you may have another reason for finding him," said Mike.

Hicks sighed, "No. I met that young girl in the hospital. She's traumatized by what happened. She was even more hurt to learn that it was posted all over social media. I can't unsee her sadness. I can still hear her crying. I have to know if he posted it. I don't think he knows the damage he caused to that young girl. If he contacts you, please let me know."

"Sure thing, detective," affirmed Mike.

T.V. HOLIDAY

It had been a few days since Brittany returned home from the hospital. Home was a tiny studio apartment on the lower southside of Carnage Coast. She was a college student majoring in sociology. She worked as a waitress and lived off campus. Her life was average until everything was turned upside down.

Brittany's attack rocked her to her core. Her beliefs were shattered that night. Her hope for Free Love was turned into a dark cloud. She put her trust in Lovelyn and Cassidy. They took advantage of her in ways she never dreamed could happen. She was violated by The Donnas she wanted to be like. Worse yet, they hinted at a future far darker than she could imagine.

The vigilante saved her but brought more harm in the process. Her assault was shared for everyone to see. He shared a moment that was never meant to happen. One where she was defenseless. Where she was treated like nothing. One where she never felt more inhuman. A moment of shame. Everyone in the hospital knew who she was. Her story was the hottest topic on the news. Brittany never desired to be famous. She wanted to advocate for people less fortunate than her. She felt it was taken away with the Free Love Initiative.

Brittany stood from her bed while the TV played in the background. She examined herself in the mirror and could still see faint images of her bruises. Reminders that her ordeal was more than a nightmare. It was real. None of it was worth her dignity. None of it was worth the shame that she couldn't shake.

Brittany felt a swell of disgust. She hated what she had opened herself up to. She felt guilty for allowing herself to be in that situation. It was her fault for getting into it and the vigilante's for shredding any dignity that could've been salvaged. She could no longer stand the sight of herself. Brittany felt like she could never be beautiful again.

"And a manhunt has been issued for the vigilante," said a news anchor on the TV.

The news caught Brittany's attention. She wanted them to catch him. She wanted him to answer for why he posted her assault. Brittany was enraged that Cassidy and Lovelyn had already been released and cleared. Her mind flashed to images of that night. It was overwhelming.

Brittany leaned back and rammed her head into the glass mirror. She let out a primal yell as the glass cracked. Shards fell into the sink. Blood ran down her face from the laceration on top of her head. Tears fell to compensate for the pain that raced through her head.

Brittany looked into the mirror pieces that were still in the frame. Her blood only intensified the disdain she now held for herself. Now she would have more scars to show of her pain. Scars that showed pain she didn't want. Pain that she didn't deserve. Brittany felt there was one solution to escape the nightmare she found herself in.

She picked up one of the jagged glass shards and held it to her wrist. Brittany paused and thought about her parents. She wondered what they would think. She thought about her friends. Brittany thought their pain would only last for a moment. There was no one to tell. There was no one to care. She slit her wrist with the glass shard.

There was a knock at the door. "Hello! Are you okay in there? I heard a scream," said a voice.

Brittany didn't know who it was. She walked toward the door as the blood rushed out of her wrist. The room began to spin, and she became lightheaded. The door was only a few feet away, but felt more distant with every. She felt weak. She reached for the door but missed the handle and fell against it. Her body made a loud thud upon impact.

"Hey, are you okay in there?" asked the voice outside. The person knocked and tried to open it, but the door didn't budge.

Brittany lay there as she faded. The end of her nightmare was approaching. She had found a solution. She wasn't going to have to live with the memory of that night anymore. It was only a matter of time.

T.V. HOLIDAY

Back at the Pavilion, Travis awakened from his slumber. As he regained his sight, the visions replayed in his head. Hours had gone by since he passed out. He didn't care what happened at work. He needed to get to Mike. He needed help. Travis left and went to Last Hope. He burst in looking for Mike and found him vacuuming the sanctuary floor.

"Mike, we gotta' talk," urged Travis.

Mike set aside the vacuum and motioned for him to sit. Travis' urgency alarmed him. "What's going on?" he asked.

Travis sat and was visibly shaken. He made a concentrated effort to control his breathing. He wanted Mike to understand him. "I just had the weirdest dream. It's like I was watching a movie, but I kept seeing visions of my wife. There were so many," explained Travis.

"What were the visions?" Mike inquired.

Travis looked down as he recollected. He didn't want to relive the visions. They were memories he did his best to bury. Memories that chipped away at him. "It was all the bad stuff. Moving into apartments, she said that she hated me… that she didn't love me as I loved her. I heard divorce over and over," Travis solemnly answered.

"Was that all?" Mike asked.

Travis shook his head. He drifted away while the last image repeated in his mind. Every vision was an experience except the last. The last image was a nightmare. A possibility he ran from every chance he could get. "No. I was in a courthouse with divorce papers. The crazy thing is that I wasn't upset about it either. Everything went black after that."

Mike processed what Travis told him and looked at his watch. He recognized it was still early in the day. He was confused by the timing. "You just had this dream? It wasn't last night?"

His wife's voice echoed in his mind. "Divorce" and "I hate you" filled his ears. He was numb. Travis noticed Mike was awaiting an answer. He remembered Mike's question and responded, "Yeah, it was a little while ago. I was eating an apple pie that Sensation sent over and I passed out. She probably put something in it."

Sensation's name made him curious. He tried to recount his thoughts. It sounded familiar, but he couldn't put his finger on it. "Sensation? The one who's been promoting the Free Love Initiative?" he asked.

Travis was surprised by Mike's curiosity. "Yeah, I didn't tell you about her?"

Mike threw his arms in the air and dumbfoundedly shook his head. "No, you didn't. The last time I saw you was when you dropped that poor girl off here. Which reminds me, I need to talk to you about that. But you've been in contact with Sensation?"

Travis remembered his last interaction with Mike. He believed they had spoken since. He realized that he was wrong. "There has been so much going on. I guess I didn't. I'm sorry," he exclaimed.

"Ummm, yeah! Tell me about her. There has to be a lot with her pushing this Free Love Initiative," said Mike. He hoped switching the subject from Travis' wife would lighten his mood.

"I met her when she unveiled the Free Love Initiative. She triggered my Divine Eyes. It was unlike anything I've experienced. We had dinner together afterwards. I learned she was the reason my eyes would activate whenever I saw a prostitute. She's like the Queenpin here. The women are her Diabolical Donnas. She's the evil I was brought here to stop," Travis answered.

Mike's mood didn't lighten upon hearing Travis' news. He became concerned. A lot had indeed occurred since their last meeting. Mike had a lot of questions. "Why did you have dinner with her?"

Travis sighed. His frustration surfaced. He knew it sounded crazy to have dinner with her. He hoped to have a sensible answer, but didn't. "I was hoping that I could learn something useful. Mike, I don't know what to do about this. Am I supposed to kill her? There are instructions for what I need to do. She said she wants to be the woman in my life. She knew things about me, too. How I feel… my wife… everything I've struggled with. At my house, she wanted me to hold her and kept saying we don't have to fight," he admitted.

Mike was taken aback by his revelation. He stood and slowly paced back and forth. He needed a moment to process what he heard. He didn't think Travis's interactions with Sensation were a coincidence. He believed her knowledge of Travis' misery was being strategically used against him. She knew what he desired. She was preying on his weakness. Then he realized something. His eyes widened as if a light bulb had been turned on. His mood saddened when he came to the realization. He walked near Travis and sat in the pew in front of him again.

"If Sensation is really one of Lucifer's demons, then she has tools to break you down. He is allowed to use anything against you. He will attack your heart and mind. He knows about you. And he's going to pass that knowledge to Sensation. You told me she sent you a pie and then you had the visions, right?" Mike solemnly asked.

"Yeah, so?" Travis shrugged.

Mike took a deep breath before he spoke. He was uncertain of how Travis would respond. "That pie was meant to open your eyes to the future if you never came here. The last vision was real," he revealed.

The revelation floored Travis. His worst fears were realized. There was nothing he could ever do to prevent his marriage from ending. He wept. Travis dropped to his knees and cupped his face. He was angry. His anger was soon replaced with heartache. The glimmer of hope he held onto was snuffed out and taken away. There in the house of God, his heart was broken.

Mike watched as Travis sobbed. He felt his pain. Mike placed his hand on Travis's shoulder. He tried to find the words to comfort him. Travis' body trembled. He clenched his fists and gritted his teeth. Mike didn't know what to make of his reaction. Something felt off.

"I know this has to be devastating for you. I'm sure that's why she sent the pie. Don't lean into that anger. You're in the house of God. You're never…" Mike empathized.

Travis cut off Mike by removing his hand from his shoulder. He stared at him with reddened eyes. Travis didn't want to hear what he had to say. There was nothing that could be said to rectify that moment. Nothing could be done to take away the truth. Travis stood and walked out without saying a word.

"Travis, wait…" Mike pleaded. Travis ignored his plea and left. Mike stood behind and prayed for him. He sensed his despair. He knew Travis was vulnerable and couldn't afford to be alone. Mike didn't want to fight him over it. He stayed back and hoped Travis wouldn't do something he would regret.

T.V. HOLIDAY

Travis drove straight home. He didn't want to focus on anything else. He didn't want to be The Iron Warrior. It was like a bomb had been dropped on him. He wanted God to talk to him. He parked his car and walked out to the beach. He looked out into the ocean. There was no one else on the beach. As he looked out into the ocean, no land was visible on the other side. Travis felt trapped.

"Talk to me, God. You wanted me to come here. You chose me to be your fighter. Why did you choose me? Why did my marriage have to end? I tried my best, God. I know it's not about my plan. I know it's about yours, but why couldn't I have this one?" he cried out.

"Maybe it wasn't meant for you to," a familiar voice chimed behind him and triggered his Divine Eyes.

He turned around and saw that it was Sensation behind him. She wore black capri pants with a long-sleeved red blouse. She held red heels in her hand while she walked along the sand. Her lipstick was a subtle red that looked almost natural. Her appearance was casual. It was in a way that Travis had not seen her before.

His blood boiled at the sight of her. The apple pie sent him into a tailspin. To harm her went against his core being. He wanted to break something. He shivered with electricity that he couldn't do anything with. Travis looked around for Sidious Craig and Coldred Black. He knew they had to be around.

"I see you're looking for my guys. I told them to stand back when I come here. This is your home. I don't want to fight you here," said Sensation. She stood back and tried to read him. His fury was slightly unsettling.

"You don't want to fight me!?! You gotta' lot of nerve coming here," Travis growled.

"Luc told me the pie would allow you to see the future. He said it would open your eyes and help you see things more… realistically," Sensation genuinely explained.

Travis scoffed at her explanation. He didn't believe her. He felt her sincerity was an act. He struggled to control himself. "You knew what he was going to show me, didn't you?"

"I didn't. Luc told me you would tell me," she answered.

"Bullshit!" Travis snapped, shaking his head as he took a step back from her. "Don't lie to me. I don't want to play any games. Just be honest."

"I really didn't know," she assured him. Sensation dropped her shoes and walked closer. She pulled her hair back and presented her cheek. "I'd like to, though. If you need to, you can hit me if you want."

Travis looked at her crazily. No matter how angry he was, he never thought of striking her. He wondered why she would offer herself like that. His anger was clouded with confusion. From her experience, Sensation knew men to handle their anger physically. She was willing to offer herself; however, she needed to prove her honesty.

He placed his fingers on her chin and made her face him. He stared into her hazel eyes. She didn't flinch. Travis could tell she was willing to let him hit her. "Why are you here?" he asked.

"I wanted to see you. I wanted to speak to you without all this heaven and hell stuff. Luc told me you're the man for me, but I need to know for myself. I know it was only one night, but I see how dedicated you are to your family. It doesn't seem like there is a place for me by your side. That spot is taken and you're not taking applications. Maybe I'm trying to figure this out too," she answered.

Travis sighed and looked back out into the ocean. He couldn't fight her response. They were trying to find a solution to being at odds with one another. He didn't want to figure out an answer right then. He had too much going on inside. He didn't want to be on the defensive with the enemy. Travis only wanted to breathe and deal with his pain. He sat and placed his arms around his knees.

"That spot was taken. It's vacant now," Travis sadly said while he gazed at the sea. "I still have your story in my mind about looking for God in the ocean. When I look at the ocean, it reminds me of God.

The water is everywhere. We don't know how deep it goes. It's filled with life. We can dive in and explore. But we can't go to the true depths of the ocean. It's not humanly possible. He allows us to float atop without any effort. The current can take us away. Take us to wherever. For years, I fought against the current. He was bringing me here the whole time. That pie showed me the end of my marriage. It was going to happen no matter what," he told her.

Sensation sat next to him and gazed into the ocean. She didn't want to push him again. "I'm sorry about your marriage. I know you may have a hard time believing that, but I really am. If you don't mind me asking, what was the story with you two? I understand if you don't want to talk about it. I'm just interested," inquired Sensation.

Travis looked at Sensation. She was the woman at the forefront of Lucifer's quest to rid God from Carnage Coast. Yet Travis found himself on the verge of opening up to her. It didn't make sense. He didn't care anymore either.

"We met in the Marine Corps. We joined boot camp on the same day and graduated on the same day. We were in the same platoon at Marine Combat Training and the same job school. We dated for a month, and I proposed to her. Then she got orders to Okinawa, Japan, and I got the same a month later," Travis revealed.

"Wow! Were you two from the same city?" asked Sensation.

Her reaction triggered a dejected grin. It was the same as everyone who had ever heard his story. A reminder of how special his marriage was. "No. It just so happened that was the way things played out," he responded.

"That sounds like it was meant to be," she grinned.

"Yeah… that's what we thought too. Anyway, we got married and had some bad arguments in the beginning. They struck a bad chord with her that never really went away. She would bring up divorce and one of us would move out or get ready to move out. It was a bad cycle. It continued after my son was born," Travis continued.

"Why did you keep going back?" Sensation asked.

Travis peered back at the sea. It was a question he asked himself multiple times. He knew the answer and didn't like it. "Because I loved her more than I loved myself. I didn't want to lose her. My parents divorced when I was seven. I lived with my father and he worked a lot. My mother got remarried and had a new family. She tried her best, but I got lost in the shuffle. So I grew up alone.

With my wife, I accepted a lot of things I shouldn't have. I was willing to be unhappy as long as we were together. I didn't want my son to grow up as I did. I didn't want to quit. I guess the reality is that she was always trying to leave, but I couldn't let go. Maybe it's for the best. God obviously has different plans for us. I hope she finds someone who can give her the love she needs. The love I couldn't," sighed Travis.

Sensation was astonished by his words. She appreciated his openness and was surprised by how he was handling everything. "I can't fathom that you were willing to be unhappy for her. I know you don't have much of a choice in the matter, but it's really big of you to let her go now. It sounds like you mean it."

Travis thought about his now ex-wife one more time. All the good and bad moments. All the tears from them both. The love and the pain. He processed saying goodbye to her for the last time. "Yeah… I do. Now what about you? You came here to learn about me. What's your story?"

Sensation wildly looked at him. She was surprised he asked about her. She had been focused on him. "My story!? It's not about my story. I'm here for you," she responded.

Travis felt loose around her. He put his ex-wife behind him and turned his attention to the woman next to him. "Umm, that's nice and all, but I'd like to know about you, too. You keep talking about loving me. Hell, pretty lady, I don't even know your real name."

Sensation felt flattered and grinned. Aside from Luc, it had been some time since someone took an interest in her. "Hmmm… should I tell you my name?" she asked playfully.

"I mean, unless there's nothing left of the real you, then I totally understand. However, I don't know what I'd call you for short. Sensation doesn't have a shortened form. What would I call you? Hey Saish, hey Sin… never mind on the Sin that's too on the nose," he joked.

"You're stupid! Don't call me any of those. They sound terrible," she laughed.

"Okay then! Can I get a name or what?" Travis retorted.

Sensation smiled and, disbelievingly, shook her head at the fun they began to have. She jokingly squinted like she was irritated and responded, "Ugh… my name is Lynda… Lynda Lynch."

Travis clapped and threw sand in the air. His over-the-top reaction made her blush. "Thank you! Sheesh! The other night, you were practically naked. I didn't have to work for that at all. Now, I'm asking for your name, and you're making me jump through hoops. What's up with that?" Travis playfully said.

Lynda laughed sheepishly and unknowingly brushed against his arm. She felt a spark, but it was jumbled with her giddiness. "You're a man. Good food and sex are the fast track to your heart. You can't tell me I'm wrong."

"No lies there," Travis jokingly assured her.

"And let's not forget you turned me down, too!" Lynda snapped.

"You had me shot at by God knows how many people! You can't have me shot and then expect me to smash right after. That's nuts!" he exclaimed.

Lynda was too embarrassed to answer. After learning more about him, she wished that she could take that one back. She sheepishly shrugged and looked away.

"Seriously… what's your story, Lynda? Where are you from? How in the blue hell did you end up here in Carnage Coast?" asked Travis.

She frustratingly sighed. Lynda was hesitant to say more. She felt good that he opened up to her. She didn't want to change that by revealing more of herself. "Ughhh…. You won't let this go," she grunted.

"No," Travis said, grinning.

"What's there to say? I grew up in Los Angeles with both of my parents. Big city with a lot going on. They worked hard and gave us a good life. I hate to say it, but I was spoiled. I actually became one of the mean girls you'd see in high school. I could have any guy I wanted. It was cool, you know," Lynda reminisced.

"Wait a minute, you were a mean girl! That's just terrible," Travis quipped.

Lynda embarrassingly hung her head. She didn't want to see his face. She could tell he wasn't serious, but it didn't ease her mortification. "Yeah, yeah… I was mean. No excuses. I got what I wanted. Everyone thought I was beautiful. Like, how could you blame me?"

"Okay, now you grew up in LA. Why the hell did you end up coming to Carnage Coast?" asked Travis.

"Sometimes I wonder the same thing. I could've gone to any school in California, but somehow the University of Carnage Coast popped up. They have an acting program that sounded like something worth diving into," said Lynda.

"You wanted to be an actress?" he surprisingly asked.

"Yeah! They live such a great life and everybody listens to them even when they say stupid things. I wanted to have fun and travel around the world. Besides, you don't have to be the greatest actress to get work. We can name a list of people with no acting ability whatsoever and they're getting paid millions," Lynda exclaimed.

He laughed at her comment. Learning about her excited him. He wanted to know more. "True. But you were practically born and raised in Hollywood. Yet you came here to do something you could've easily done there. Why?"

Lynda gazed into the sea. It was her turn to dig deep in her mind. It was a question she asked herself, but stopped. It only frustrated her. Being with him gave her the peace to speak about it.

"Everybody goes to Los Angeles to become an actress. I wanted to go somewhere where I would stand out and hone my skills. There was something about Carnage Coast. The school spoke to me in a way I can't describe. I was drawn here. It sounds weird when I say it now. Maybe I should've stayed in L.A. At the time, Carnage Coast was the only option on my mind," explained Lynda.

Lynda's answer reminded Travis of who lived in Carnage Coast. Everybody had a purpose for being there. He assumed Lynda didn't know why she was brought there. "What happened when you got here?" he asked.

"I got rejected. I wasn't pretty enough. I had no talent. I was nothing here. Then I failed out of college. Everything that came so easily was turned upside down. I got depressed and started drinking. As you know, drinking doesn't help anything. The drinking was the only thing that drowned out all the rejection," Lynda revealed solemnly.

"Why didn't you try to go home?" asked Travis.

The emotions Lynda buried bubbled to the surface. She placed her family in the distant past. It had been years since she was last home. The thoughts of her family saddened her.

"I couldn't go home like that. I was a failure and had a drinking problem. I couldn't let my parents see me like that. I tried to leave this city, but I couldn't. Every time I tried, something happened that forced me to stay here. Even when I wanted to, I couldn't get away from here," she disclosed.

Lynda's story cemented the notion that he was stuck in Carnage Coast. She was an outsider like him and couldn't leave. The realization momentarily sank him. "There was never a boyfriend or somebody who could've helped you through it?"

"No. I never had a meaningful relationship anyway. I never got the type of love you dream about. The love where someone loves you just as you are and doesn't want you to change. The love that can lift you off the ground and have your heart beating a thousand beats per minute. After a time, I gave up on it," said Lynda.

Lynda's feelings spoke to him. She spoke of a love he desired as well. "How did you end up in all of this?" he inquired.

"I got arrested one night. Lazarus paid my bond and owned me. I was locked into the street life from then on. The days blurred into the next. I became resentful and angry. People talk about God and how loving he is. Yet I was living this non-stop nightmare. I wasn't strong enough to leave on my own. I prayed for God to help me escape, but he never came. Like I told you, Luc came for me… not God," said Lynda.

Hearing Lynda's experiences made it easier for him to understand her. He didn't think it was unreasonable for her to have made the choices she did. "What do you really want, Lynda? Take the whole world going to hell out of the equation and everything. What do you want?"

She looked into his eyes and saw his interest in her. It warmed her heart. It was a feeling that she hadn't felt in a long time. She took a minute to think about his question. Aside from Luc, no man asked her what she wanted in life.

"I want to feel loved. The fame and fortune I dreamed of when I wanted to be an actress were all about love. But now, even if it's from one person, I only want to be loved," answered Lynda.

Travis gave Lynda a heartwarming smile, "Now that's one thing we can definitely agree on. I just want to be loved, too."

Lynda's eyes lit up. Luc hadn't led her astray. She felt they made a connection. The door to his heart had been opened. She desperately wanted to be with him. "I'm so glad we got to talk. I told you I don't want to fight. I know you're dealing with a lot of emotions right now. Do you think you could ever love me?" Lynda asked.

Travis was stunned at her question. It was a weighted inquiry. He blew off her requests when he believed he was still married. Things had changed in the last 24 hours. His life was open to new possibilities. He had the chance to experience the relationship he had always dreamed of. He wondered if it could be with Sensation. He wondered if he was lucky enough to find a woman who would be there for him. It was sudden, but his heart had been dried up for so long. The prospect of a new love excited him. It was something he was desperate to feel again.

"Y'know, if I believe in God, then I have to believe in hope. If I believe that, then I have to believe I can love another woman again. If you'd asked me this question about you a few days ago, my answer would've been no. But after talking to you now, I believe you're a woman I can love," Travis replied.

Lynda let out a sigh of relief. She was thrilled to hear his answer. She thought he could eventually join her. She felt invigorated. The love she desired was possible. Her dream was within reach. She was going to chase it.

"Love me like you loved your wife. I promise I can give you the love you always wanted. You'll never have to look anywhere else for love. I can be all the love you ever need," she pleaded.

Being married allowed Travis to express love for someone in all the ways he wanted. He believed God put him on earth to serve others and show love to those he met. Nothing was better than expressing love to his wife. He felt it was an extension of who he was meant to be. Loving Lynda would allow him to become the man he grew into.

"I would love that. But I can't let this world go to hell. My son is still in it. I can't let him inherit a world that is going to hell. I'll die before I let that happen," admitted Travis.

Disappointed in his answer, she asked, "What if I talk to Luc? We can make sure he is safe when the world falls?"

Travis closed his eyes and shook his head from side to side. "No, Lynda! That's not going to work either. I'm not letting him go to hell. But, what if you come with me?"

Lynda was caught off guard by Travis's question. She leaned back and looked in disbelief as she thought about his proposal. She never fathomed asking for it back. She promised to help Luc carry out his desire to rid this world of God. She wanted to be with him, but I couldn't see how unless he joined her. She didn't think crossing over was a possibility. It was too late for her.

"What you're asking is impossible?" she told him.

"Is it? You gave up on love, and I gave up on happiness. You said our love could save us both. You came here looking for a solution, and that's it. Maybe we can both finally get what we want," Travis responded.

Lynda didn't want to get swept away. For everything he said, the stark reality was that they were on two different sides. She thought his hope blinded him. She wanted to bring him back down. "I told you it's impossible. We both want love, but the truth is, one of us will have to choose. God left me to wallow. I don't want to go back to that. Just come with me. It's so much better," she argued.

He was undeterred by her argument. Travis was willing to fight for her. He was certain they had found the answer to their problem. He believed fear blanketed her judgment.

"The love you desire can only be experienced on my side. Love is a verb. It's patient and kind. It's not arrogant or rude. It's not irritable or resentful. It does not rejoice at wrongdoing but rejoices with the truth. It bears, believes, hopes, and endures everything. That's the love you really want. And I'll show it to you. Throw everything at me that you can. Do what you have to do. Try to stop me. I'll push through and show you love no matter what," said Travis.

Lynda thought he was crazy. She couldn't understand why he would willingly do something like that. She hated that they were on opposing sides. If it wasn't for the situation, she easily saw herself with him. She didn't want either one of them to choose. She wanted to experience the love he spoke about. She didn't want to hurt him.

"Are you sure this isn't a knee-jerk reaction to learning about your marriage? I admit that I got excited talking to you. I want this to be real. I don't want to break you. I..." said Lynda.

Travis moved closer to Lynda and leaned in near her ear, "My marriage was done quite some time ago. It's only official now. If you're willing to love me and let me have you, then I'll fight for you. And make no mistake, Lynda, one of us is going to break Lynda... it's just a matter of whose gonna' break first. No matter who breaks first, we end up together," he told her.

Travis wrapped his arm around her waist and gently kissed her cheek. Her skin was hot to the touch. She closed her eyes and lost herself in the moment. He stood and helped her up. She was willing to walk the path at his behest. His hope was infectious. She suddenly found herself hopeful about a future together.

"I better get going. I need to find ways to stop," said Lynda.

Travis smiled, "That's fine. I need to find ways to stop the Free Love Initiative."

Lynda laughed a little. "I'll see you soon," she said as she slowly let go of his hand and walked away.

T.V. HOLIDAY

Travis watched Lynda leave and walked toward his house when his cellphone rang. It was Mike. He informed Travis that Brittany was in the emergency room at Seventh City Memorial Hospital. Travis' heart dropped at the news. He felt a sinking feeling in his stomach that he was somehow responsible for her attempt. He told Mike he would be on his way and ran to his car. Travis arrived and found Mike near the door. Before he could say anything. Mike walked him outside to a place where no one was around.

"Mike, what's going on?" asked Travis.

"Sorry, I couldn't give you more information on the phone. I needed you to get here. Brittany tried to kill herself earlier," said Mike.

Travis' eyes widened in shock. "Why?" he asked sadly.

"It seems like this is all from that incident where you saved her. It sounds like she's been taking it hard since it hit the news," said Mike.

"Okay. How did you find out about all of this?" asked Travis.

"An officer came to see me earlier today. I didn't get a chance to tell you because you left. His name is Hicks. He's handling the investigation and was asking about how I knew Brittany and eventually about you," Mike told Travis.

"What did you tell him?"

"I told him the vigilante brought her in and asked me to help. He made it clear that he wants to speak to the vigilante. He thinks you did more harm to her with the video. He's the one who told me about her being here. He's outside of her room right now. I thought The Iron Warrior could speak to Brittany and help her if you catch my drift," Mike explained.

Travis nodded in agreement. His head filled with regret, but he pushed it aside to focus on Brittany. She needed his help. He followed Mike back in and was directed to her room. He noticed Hicks standing outside the room. Mike distracted him while Travis stepped behind a nearby curtain into an unoccupied bay. He transformed into The Iron

Warrior and stood by until he had his opening to enter the room. Once Hicks was distracted, The Warrior quickly entered Brittany's room.

He turned around and saw Brittany staring directly at him. Her eyes widened and slowly teared up. Her forehead and wrists were bandaged and she was handcuffed to the bed. The Warrior felt his strength and confidence pour out of him as he looked at her. He couldn't help but re-see that night while he looked at her. He pondered whether she would have been in her condition if he had only acted sooner. He only wanted to help people, but the sight of her proved he did the exact opposite.

"Hi, Brittany," The Warrior hesitantly opened.

He walked toward the side of her bed as she glared at him. She didn't say a word. Brittany followed him with her head as the rest of her body lay motionless.

"I was told about what happened. I wanted to come see how you were doing," The Warrior cautiously continued.

He felt like she didn't want him near. He was surprised Brittany didn't make a sound. There was no visible emotion aside from her tears. She could see the despair growing on his face. She could hear it in his voice. Her silence was deafening.

"I also wanted to tell you that I'm sorry. I'm sorry for not intervening sooner. I feel I'm the reason you're here. I should've taken the phone out of that guy's hand before any of this happened," The Warrior told her.

His last comment broke her stone-like expression. "Did you post it?" she asked.

The Warrior struggled to answer her question. He knew nothing good would come of it. "It's not that easy, Brittany. I..." he started.

"Did you do it?" she angrily interrupted.

"Yeah... it's my fault," he sighed.

He wanted to explain, but didn't think it would help. He shamefully hung his head while she wept. He looked at her handcuffs and his heart ached. He wanted to give her the opportunity to address her pain with him. He grabbed one of the handcuffs and snapped it in half. He reached over and did the same to the second pair. Brittany looked surprised. She didn't know what to make of his actions.

"If you want to take a swing at me… have at it. I deserve it," he said.

Brittany examined her handcuffs. She was amazed at his ability to snap the handcuffs. He stepped back to give her room to stand. Brittany gathered her strength and placed her feet on the floor. She was still weak from the blood loss. She painfully grunted as she faced him. He waited for her to strike him. Brittany spat in his face. The Warrior didn't flinch. He stood there as the moment sank in. Despite his intentions, he realized that he would not be able to make up for it.

"I'm sorry, Brittany… I'm truly sorry," said The Warrior.

He backed away and walked toward the door. He paused and wiped her spit off his face.

"You're going to pay for this," cried Brittany.

The Warrior looked back and saw her rage. He had a bad feeling. There was something simmering inside her, and he could feel it. He opened the door and left the room. He was troubled by his interaction with her. Before he could think any further, he heard yelling from the opposite end of the hallway.

"HEY!!! STOP!!!" the voice blared.

The Warrior saw Hicks running toward him, with Mike walking behind him. He decided not to run.

"What the hell were you doing in there?" Hicks asked as he reached the doorway.

"I apologized to her, but it seems like it's too late," The Warrior dejectedly answered. He looked at her door and lowered his head as her words echoed in his ears.

"You think!? That girl is damaged. Hopefully, the rest of her life isn't ruined because of what you did. What were you thinking?" Hicks snapped.

The Iron Warrior looked at Officer Hicks and could see the frustration in his face. He could tell Officer Hicks cared for Brittany's well-being.

"First of all, I didn't purposely do it. The guy threatened to post the video if I didn't back down. Either he or I pressed the button to post it when I squeezed his hand. I would never post something like that. I know what it could do. But it doesn't matter at this point. The damage is already done," The Warrior acknowledged.

Hicks was relieved to hear his response. It changed his perception of him. Hicks didn't care about the manhunt. He was thankful The Warrior intervened on Brittany's behalf. He wasn't going to arrest him. The Iron Warrior's Divine Eyes glitzed. Something was coming. Hicks saw the spark and was startled.

They looked down the hallway and saw Sensation, flanked by Sidious and Coldred, approach them. She wore an elegant pink-and-black dress with matching pink-and-black, red-bottom high heels. The Iron Warrior was mesmerized by her appearance. His attraction grew after their conversation. She walked up and looked him over. It was her first time seeing Travis as The Iron Warrior. She was astonished at the man he became. She placed her hand on his shoulder and softly ran it down his arm.

"You won't let me breathe, will you?" The Warrior coyly asked.

Sensation flashed a flirtatious smile, "Oh, I'm gracious. I'll give you a chance to come up for air… every now and then."

"What is going on here?" Hicks blurted out before The Warrior could respond. "Why are you here, lady? This is official police business!"

Sensation was focused on The Iron Warrior. Their eyes were locked onto one another as if they were in their own world. She refused to acknowledge Hicks' presence. "I heard the unfortunate news about the young lady and came to check on her," answered Sensation.

"Why is it any of your business?" Hicks asked rudely.

Sensation cut her eyes toward Officer Hicks' direction. Her face showed her irritation with him. "I'm the one who paid her medical bill, you ass clown! Don't you watch TV? Don't you know who I am?" Sensation snapped.

"I do," Mike interrupted sternly.

"Stop actin' all hard and shit," Sidious laughed. "We know you too, right, Red?"

"You bet we do. Ain't that right, Mike?" said Coldred.

Coldred's comment broke The Iron Warrior's gaze from Sensation. He looked at Sidious and Coldred in disbelief. He suspiciously turned toward Mike, who glanced back at him. Questions filled his mind after their revelation.

"Yo, I Dub! I guess your man over there didn't give you the full rundown of the shit you're in, huh?" Sidious mockingly asked.

"Yeah, Playboy… we got that red pill waiting for you whenever you need it. How about you stop playin' around and roll wit' our girl here?" Coldred suggested.

Hicks stepped into the center of the conversation. He was the only one with authority present. "Obviously, you all have some kind of connection that I have no clue about. Lady, I don't give a damn about the TV. I don't know who you are. It's nice that you paid the girl's bills. We'll let you know when you can see her. Now take these dipshits and go wait in the lobby."

"Ugh! You're rude and annoying. Why don't you just go home?" Sensation snapped.

Her frustration amused Hicks. He wasn't going to let her boss him around. "I can't. No wife at home."

"I'm not surprised. Let me guess… no woman could ever settle for an asshole like you?" Sensation remarked.

"WRONG!!! Had three of 'em. I just wore 'em out," Hicks retorted.

"Okay, enough already!!!" The Warrior shouted. He took a second to make sure he had everyone's attention and lowered his tone. "This is getting stupid. I'm getting out of here."

Sensation stopped him by placing her hand on his arm. "Not so fast. You see, I had Sidious call the police and let them know you were here…" Sensation started.

The Iron Warrior was surprised by her news. "How could you have known I was…"

Sensation gently placed her finger on his lips to stop him from talking. "Remember, I get a certain feeling when I know you're going to be around. Needless to say, there are cops outside waiting for you. Not to mention, I have a few of my own friends scattered around the building, too." She removed her finger from his lips and caressed his cheek. She moved close enough for him to smell the perfume radiating off her skin. "You're a wanted man, remember. Wanted by the city. But most importantly, wanted by me. Now you can either come with me and we walk out of here together… or you fight your way out of here. The choice is yours."

The Iron Warrior became lost in her eyes. She was captivating. He shook his head to snap out of her gaze. He told her to throw everything at him and she took the steps to do just that.

"You're really going to make this hard for me, huh?" he smiled.

"You told me to remember. I can keep a promise," she said softly.

He grabbed her hand and gently kissed the back of it. "Me too."

He walked past Sidious and Coldred to look through the emergency room doors. He saw the reflection of red and blue lights bouncing off the walls. There were multiple officers outside. The Iron Warrior didn't want to fight his way through them. He didn't want to make the officers shoot him. He had to find another way out.

The Iron Warrior looked around for another exit. He glanced at Sensation, who grinned while he tried to figure a way out. He found a doorway to a stairwell that had an exit sign above it. He went through the door and two large men wearing brass knuckles were waiting on the other side. The door behind them had another exit sign above it.

"You won the jackpot, dipshit! Let's play!" said one of them.

Before the man could raise his arm to throw a punch, The Iron Warrior charged at him headfirst into his chest. He grabbed the man's legs and launched him into the wall next to the exit. The impact knocked the wind out of the man. He followed up the throw with a knee to the face that knocked him out.

The other male clubbed The Warrior in the back of the neck with his forearm. Fighting more than one person at a time irritated him. He didn't want to waste time with him. The male grabbed The Warrior's left arm and swung him face-first into the bottom of the stairwell. The blow slightly fazed the Warrior. His pain from earlier slowly returned. The pain made him anxious to end the fight. Before the male could do another move, The Warrior grabbed his collar and punched him with a hard right cross to his face that knocked him out too.

The Iron Warrior cracked open the door and saw police cars outside the building. They had set up a perimeter and surrounded the exits. He had to figure another way out. He closed the door and ran up to the third floor. He thought about changing back into Travis, but he didn't want to risk someone seeing him.

"Ahem, ahem… hey Warrior!" a voice boomed over the public announcement system. "Round three, baby. Before you run off this time, we wanted to keep you playing with us because you're so much fun! You know we're here, but you don't know where. Lord knows who we can be with right now. They all have the potential to be Free Lovers. Are you sure you want to leave all these people with us before you go?"

The Iron Warrior recognized the voice. It was Cassidy. He didn't want to leave anyone at the mercy of others. He didn't want to repeat the mistake he made with Brittany. There was also no way for him to change back into Travis now. The Iron Warrior had to show his face and let people know he didn't abandon them.

He stepped out onto the third floor. Nurses in the hallway were stunned. One of the nurses saw him and dropped her tray in shock. Another nurse ran back into a patient's room. He went to the nurses' station, where four women sat. They nervously slid away from the counter as he approached. He did his best to assure them that he wouldn't hurt them. A nurse named Kimberly was the only one willing to help him.

She told The Warrior that the P.A. system was near the main hospital entrance. He felt the main entrance would surely be a trap. The hospital had seven floors and he had already skipped the first two. Sensation trapped him in a maze. He asked whether she had seen anyone who seemed suspicious. Nurse Kimberly directed him to Mr. Simon's room. Before leaving, he instructed her to contact the nursing stations on the other floors to see if a suspicious person was present. If not, he wanted them to lock the floor and not let anybody in.

Nurse Kimberly rapidly called the other floors while he went to Mr. Simon's room. He opened the door and saw an elderly male lying in bed. The Warrior surveyed the room. Before he could look behind the door, a woman jumped on his back and wrapped her arm around his neck and her legs around his waist. He tried to shake her off, but she hung on and choked him. He reached back and tried to pull her off. She used her free hand and gouged his right eye. A surge of anger erupted in him. As he became angrier, The Warrior felt pain in his eye and the oxygen escaped from his lungs. He backed her into a wall. The impact made her momentarily loosen her grip, but she quickly repositioned on his back.

He tried to back her into the wall again. She unwrapped her legs from his waist and placed her feet on the wall. She pushed off the wall and back onto him. He grabbed her legs and used the momentum to turn sideways and fall back-first to the floor. He dropped all of his body weight to pancake her. The impact forced her to let go. The Warrior quickly rolled away from her.

     T. V. HOLIDAY

She writhed in pain and rolled onto her stomach. Nurse Kimberly opened the door and found them on the floor. She ran toward the woman and stuck a needle in her right arm. It was a sedative. The woman shoved Nurse Kimberly away and tried to get up. She stumbled to her feet but suddenly fell back to the floor. She lay there motionless.

He sat and tried to regroup. The pain settled into other parts of his body. He tried to remain calm. He couldn't afford to panic. There were still people who needed his help. Nurse Kimberly told him there was a suspicious person on every floor. The Iron Warrior hung his head and sighed. The news was what he expected, which didn't make him feel any better. He had his work cut out for him.

He asked for another way out of the hospital. She informed him of a laundry chute on the fifth floor that led to the basement parking structure. The Iron Warrior instructed her to lock the floor door behind him once he left. He planned to use the fire alarm as a signal to let them know the building was clear. He thanked Nurse Kimberly for her help and went back down to the first floor. He took out two men. He went floor by floor, saving the fifth for last. With each fight, he became angrier at the sight of those willing to harm others. They fought him viciously and did what they could to stop him. As his anger increased, he experienced more pain from each fight. It slowed him down but didn't lower his resolve.

This was Sensation's game. He reminded himself that she wasn't the one holding guns to the heads of injured and sick people. He gave her the invitation and she answered. It was what he asked for. Although he asked for it, he didn't like it one bit. He tried to keep his feelings for her separate from those he fought.

The Iron Warrior made his way to the fifth floor. His right eye was bloodshot after it was gouged. He felt a sharp pain with every breath. His ribs felt like they were fractured. His hands were numb from the punches he threw. Whoever was on the fifth floor was his final hurdle.

He walked around and noticed it was a children's floor. The nurses knew he was coming because of Nurse Kimberly's phone call. They directed him to the suspicious person. The Iron Warrior found the room where the person was located. The door was closed. He prepared for one more battle and entered.

He saw a woman sitting in a chair next to a girl lying in the bed. The girl was awake and smiling. She looked like a teenager. Her hair was almost thinned out. She was frail, with heavy bags under her eyes. Tubes and needles were connected to her. He recognized the woman next to the girl. It was Domino.

"Hey Lover! I've been waiting for you. I have a special person I want you to meet. This is Ashley, my daughter," Domino smiled. She motioned for him to come closer. He immediately felt conflicted. He didn't want to fight her, especially in front of her daughter. He wasn't sure what to do. He walked over and stood with them.

"Hey Sugar Plum! This is my special friend I told you about. He saved me a few weeks ago. His name is The Iron Warrior," Domino told her.

"Iron Warrior? What's that supposed to mean?" Ashley asked.

Her curiosity broke him from his seriousness and made him chuckle a little. "The one who is strong, hardened, and dedicated to serving others," he answered.

Ashley mused over his words. "I thought warriors were just angry fighters."

He was careful about what he chose to say. Speaking to her made him remember who he was. It made him remember the man he strived to be.

"Warriors have to be fighters. A fighter has a more personal goal. Warriors fight for something bigger than themselves. They focus on being better so they can be strong enough for others. Serving others with love is the greatest honor a warrior can have," The Iron Warrior explained.

"That's pretty cool. I'm a fighter right now. Maybe I can be a warrior someday," she confidently told him.

"What are you fighting, Ashley?" The Iron Warrior asked.

"Leukemia. I know I'm going to get better. I'm not going to let this end my life. My Mom gets scared, but I keep telling her I'm going to be okay," Ashley answered.

He could feel her strength. It was inspiring and rejuvenating. He held his fist out and she weakly fist-bumped him. "It sounds like you have the beginning of a warrior spirit yourself. Kick ass, Ashley," The Iron Warrior told her. "I need to talk to your Mom for a second. Is that cool?"

Ashley nodded her head and waved, "It was nice to meet you. I'll see you later. And thanks for saving my Mom."

"You don't have to thank me. That's what I'm supposed to do," he responded before walking near the door with Domino behind him.

Domino wiped the tears from her face and tried to get her emotions under control. "Thank you for that. She's my world."

"You don't have to thank me for that either. I like her. She's gonna be a badass on the other side of this. Get ready," he said.

Domino glanced back at her with a prideful smile. "You don't have to tell me that. I'm well aware. She's 16 and ready to tackle the world. She keeps me grounded."

"What happens now? You're not really about to fight me, are you?" he asked. He hated to switch the conversation, but needed to address the elephant in the room.

"Of course not. I knew you were going to be here. I wasn't going to let someone else be on the same floor with Ashley. I told the nurses to send you to me. Besides, I owe you a favor," responded Domino.

The Iron Warrior was confused. His mind had been preoccupied with his sudden pain and getting out of the hospital. He couldn't remember what she was referring to.

"You saved my life, remember? I figured this'll be the only way you let me pay back that favor. Anyway, there's a chute that leads to the basement-" Domino started.

"I know… that's my way out of here," he interrupted.

Domino looked surprised at his knowledge of it. "Okay… well, what you don't know is that someone is waiting for you down there."

At that point, he didn't care who was down there. Everyone else in the hospital was okay. He still had enough strength for another fight. In his mind, whoever was unlucky enough to be in his way had it coming.

The Iron Warrior headed to the chute before Domino could say another word. He found it at the end of the hallway. The opening was big enough for him to slide into it. He couldn't see the bottom. He jumped in without giving it another thought. He slid down faster than he anticipated and bent his knees to brace for the landing. He looked down and saw what appeared to be water. He slid out and fell on his back in a pool. The pool wasn't deep. The Warrior sat up and groaned from lower back pain. He recognized it was the size of a kid's pool. The liquid also smelled weird. It was gasoline.

"It's about damn time! A girl was wonderin' how long it was gonna' take for you to come," a female's voice sarcastically exclaimed.

The Iron Warrior looked around as his eyes adjusted to the darkness in the room. There were no windows. He noticed multiple washers and dryers. He kept looking but couldn't see anything more.

"Can't see? Here, let me give you a light," said the voice slyly.

The Iron Warrior saw the flicker of a flame hurled his way. Before he could react, the flame ignited the pool and him. He became furious, and the fire became intense. The burning grew too intense and began to overwhelm him. He rolled out to get away from the fire.

"Stop, drop, and roll, huh? Not this time, baby!" said the voice again. A figure stepped into the room. It was Lovelyn with a crowbar in hand and a gas mask on her face. "I've been hot for you. I finally got you hot for me."

Lovelyn struck his back with the crowbar. The Warrior wailed in pain. He hadn't lost his faith, but he felt everything. She struck his back again, and then his arms and legs to flatten him on the floor. The smoke filled his lungs. He was losing strength. Lovelyn placed the crowbar beneath his chin and raised him to his knees. She wound up and struck him across his face. Blood spat out of his mouth as The Warrior fell back unconscious.

The billowing smoke set off a nearby smoke detector. The alarm sounded, activating the sprinkler system. The sprinklers rained down, slowly putting out the fire. The flames died down on The Warrior as well. His skin was terribly burned.

Lovelyn mounted him. "I did this to you. It wasn't Sensation. It was me." She kissed him, but there was no reaction. He remained unconscious. "I wish I didn't have to give you to her; we could have so much fun together."

"Save the fun for someone else, Lovelyn. He belongs to me," another voice echoed from around the corner.

Sensation walked in with an umbrella, flanked by Sidious and Coldred. Lovelyn stepped off The Iron Warrior and bitterly glared at Sensation. Coldred picked The Iron Warrior up and threw him over his shoulder. Sensation noticed Lovelyn's bitterness and approached her.

"I know you want him. But don't be mistaken, I did this to him. Not you. He is mine, not yours," Sensation told her.

"Can't you share? Sharing is caring, y'know," Lovelyn madly exclaimed.

Sensation's eyes widened in displeasure. She ran her fingers through Lovelyn's hair. She tightened her grip and wrenched her head back. Sensation licked Lovelyn from her neck to her cheek. Her tongue burned, Lovelyn, making her cringe.

"I've shared so much with you all already. I'm not sharing him. If you don't like it, I can always share a kiss with you," threatened Sensation.

Lovelyn's expression changed to one of utter terror. She knew what Sensation was capable of with a kiss. She didn't want that fate.

"You don't have to do that," Sidious interjected. "I can give her what she needs. She won't want him after she has me. The Iron Warrior is yours… I'll make her mine," he leered.

Sensation mused over his proposal. "Make sure you show him your appreciation for this moment," said Sensation. She flung Lovelyn at him, and he grabbed hold of her. Lovelyn exhaled before they left.

Meanwhile, the police officers stormed the hospital and arrested the defeated Donnas. Everyone was arrested except for Domino. She never hurt or held anyone hostage. Sensation, Sidious, Coldred, and Lovelyn snuck out without difficulty.

T.V. HOLIDAY

The Iron Warrior's eyes fluttered as he awakened. While his eyes adjusted to the light in the room, he looked around and saw windows that overlooked the city. He was lying in a large bed under blankets. The opposite wall was covered with mirrors that reflected the cityscape. The Warrior realized he was in a bedroom and not a hospital. He recognized he was still in his armor. His exposed arms were bandaged. He touched his chin and felt his skin. It felt warped due to the burns. As he came to his senses, his body was ravaged with excruciating pain. The last thing he remembered was Lovelyn setting him on fire. Being severely beaten made him feel defeated. He questioned whether he was capable of being The Iron Warrior.

Sensation entered the room, shocked to see him awake. He eyed his surroundings and realized he was in her bedroom. The Iron Warrior tried to sit up but had trouble moving. Sensation ran over and motioned for him to lie back down while she sat beside him.

"What's going on? How did I get here?" The Warrior asked, still confused and amazed.

"I put you through hell as you told me to. You've been out for two days. I brought you to my place, and I've been taking care of you. Granted, I don't know anything about first aid, but I think I did okay. You got burned really bad, which surprised me. I didn't think you could get hurt like that. When I saw the condition you were in, I couldn't leave you there," she explained.

The Iron Warrior was floored by her explanation. He was thankful for her willingness to care for him. She made him feel special. He reached forward and held her hand. Sensation felt a rush different than the ecstasy that flowed through her. He humbly thanked her, and she blushingly accepted. Despite how special he felt, to know that he was unconscious for two days worried him. He needed help that she couldn't give.

"I need to go. I need to find out how I got hurt like this," The Warrior told her.

She was disappointed to hear that he had to go. She had a request and was almost too embarrassed to ask for it. But she didn't want to stay quiet. "Can I see Travis before you go? The Iron Warrior is cool and impressive, but I was really hoping to see the real you, y'know. I've been waiting for you to wake up and… I'd like to spend some time with you if that's okay?"

Her request warmed his heart. Deep down, he wanted to spend time with her, too. He was happy to know she wanted the same. "One condition. You can get Travis if I can get Lynda," said The Iron Warrior.

"Now that I can definitely do," Sensation gleefully responded.

Sensation helped him out of bed. He went into the bathroom while she went inside her walk-in closet. She changed into a comfortable tank top and boy shorts. Lynda wanted him to see her naturally. She hoped it would be enough for him. She was nervous and excited. Lynda ordered sushi from one of the restaurants downstairs while she waited for Travis.

In the bathroom, he changed back into Travis and noticed the burns Lynda couldn't bandage. He was still impressed with how she took care of him. She was quickly becoming someone he wanted to be with. The thought of her brought a sense of joy. As joy filled him, his scars and bruises faded away. Travis scanned his arms and examined his face in the mirror. He couldn't believe what was happening. The pain he felt from before suddenly went away. His strength returned as well. He was re-energized.

He shouted for Lynda and walked out to show her how much he had healed. She was bewildered. Lynda walked over and touched where he was burned. He wrapped his arms around her waist and hugged her. His embrace caught her off guard. She gladly responded in kind and wrapped her arms around him, too. He lifted and held her tightly. She closed her eyes and didn't want to let go. The doorbell snapped them out of their embrace. It was their dinner. They sat on her bed together and ate.

"Do you always look this cute when you go to sleep?" smirked Travis.

His question thrilled her. It erased her fear of not being pretty enough. "Aww, thank you. You really call this cute, though? It's just a shirt and shorts," Lynda bashfully responded.

He thought her bashfulness was cute. "Absolutely! Beautiful women don't have to do much to look beautiful. And you are beautiful as it is, so…" complimented Travis.

"Okay, now keep this up, and I'm going to expect compliments like this regularly," she giggled.

"Since you're willing to be honest, I have a question for you. Have you ever been with a white woman?" asked Lynda.

Travis almost choked on his food upon hearing her question. It caught him off guard. A wave of anxiety hit her after seeing his reaction.

"WOW!!! You don't pull any punches," exclaimed Travis. He noticed her trepidation and realized his response might have triggered it. "No, I've never been with a white woman. Or any other woman for that matter," he admitted.

His answer didn't soothe her concerns. "Why not?"

"There really wasn't much diversity where I'm from. I liked white girls, but I was too afraid to date them. My father used to say white girls were trouble, and I'd end up like O.J. Simpson," Travis opened up.

Lynda laughingly fell forward on the bed. She was overtaken with laughter. Her concerns immediately disappeared. "Oh my God, are you serious?"

"Yeah! He could've been joking, but I thought he was for real. The sad part is that white girls liked me. I couldn't get a black girl to save my life. I was never black enough for them," Travis embarrassingly answered.

Lynda sat up and was baffled. "Wait a minute, not black enough? What the heck does that mean?"

"I wasn't a thug. My pants were worn around my waist. I wasn't a stereotype. I spoke properly, listened to more than hip-hop music, and didn't play basketball or football. I was called a chocolate-covered white boy because of it. Nobody accepted me for me," revealed Travis.

She was saddened to hear his experience. "Does race matter to you at all?" asked Lynda.

"My race is my skin color. I know people may feel that they are better than me or others because of it. But at the end of the day, we are all human. We all bleed the same. We hurt the same and experience joy the same," explained Travis.

Lynda wasn't sure what to say next. She was surprised to hear Travis' explanation. She heard strength and conviction in his voice. It was something she admired.

"What about you? Does race matter to you? Have you ever been with a black guy?"

Lynda looked at him foolishly. Travis felt like he had stuck his foot in his mouth and was embarrassed. He shrugged his shoulders and threw his hands up apologetically.

Lynda recognized the look on his face. "I get it. It's okay. No, I've never been in a relationship with a black guy. It just never happened. I don't care about race either. I don't think I'm better than anyone because of my skin color. That's just stupid. I want a guy who'll treat me right and accept me for who I am, too," she answered.

"What else do you want to know? Ask me anything," he encouraged.

His invitation excited her. She was thankful to have another deep and honest conversation with him. It was refreshing. "Hmmm, okay… be careful what you ask for. Here's one… have you ever been with a man before?" Lynda asked.

Travis almost choked on his food again. He was flabbergasted by her inquiry but valued her frankness. She apologetically looked away and tilted her head. She was embarrassed and worried that she was being too forward with him. He motioned that he was okay.

"No, I've never been with a man, nor do I have a desire to be with one. I love women. From your shape to the softness and gentleness that you bring to life. That can never be replaced. That's what I want. People can do whatever they want. Or prefer to be with whomever they want. I want a woman. That's all there is to it," explained Travis.

"I hope that didn't offend you," said Lynda.

"It's okay, I'm not offended. I said you could ask me anything, and I meant it," Travis smiled. "Now… same question for you. Have you ever been with a woman?"

Lynda looked at him foolishly again. Travis continually forgot about the life she lived. Being a prostitute meant she could've been with a litany of people. After learning more about her, he found it hard to envision her on the street.

"You might think I'm weird for saying this, but I can understand," Travis assured her.

"Seriously!" Lynda said in amazement. "Come on now! I would've thought the man chosen by God would be all over me about how wrong I am."

"It's not my place to judge you. I only want to serve others and show love to those I meet. At least I try to, y'know," stated Travis.

"That's fine and all, but aren't there beliefs and commandments you have to go by? Somebody like me would burn in hell in the eyes of someone like you," said Lynda.

"There is some truth to that. But Jesus didn't judge others. And God uses us all. I'd rather have a relationship with God. My father and I didn't go to church when I was younger. I didn't really become a Christian until I got older. I've read the Bible multiple times. But like all people, I sinned too. I believe God gives us storms for a reason. Our storms are meant to guide us back to our relationship with him. They're reminders that we can't live without him," stated Travis.

"You say it doesn't matter, and to your credit, you haven't judged me. But there is one more thing I haven't told you. I'm a little scared to tell you. I didn't expect to feel nervous right now," Lynda said.

Lynda looked at Travis, unsure whether she should continue. She didn't want to ruin the mood between them. They were having a deep conversation, and she wanted to be honest. She didn't want him to reject her. He could hear the uneasiness in her voice and felt her mood change.

"We've been open about a lot of things tonight. You might as well hit me with it. I'll find out sooner or later anyway, right?" he told her.

"Travis, I've killed people," Lynda blurted.

Travis' jaw dropped. Her revelation took him by surprise. He didn't expect to hear that. The image he created of her didn't add up to a murderer. He believed there was an explanation for her actions. He didn't want his burgeoning feelings to cloud his judgment. Before Travis reached a conclusion, he decided to approach the revelation logically.

"Okay. A few things. How? How many? And why?" he asked frankly.

Tears slowly fell down her cheeks. "When I kiss them, I absorb their soul and they burn to death. I've killed five people. They were responsible for the worst times in my life. The things they did to me..." said Lynda before she trailed off.

Travis saw the pain etched in her face. He could feel her sorrow and anger. Travis felt some relief when he heard her explanation. He motioned for her to come near him. Travis spread his feet and opened a space for her to sit in front of him with her back against his chest. He softly held her. Although he would never condone killing someone, he tried to remember where he was. If there was any place or time where someone needed grace, it was there with Lynda.

"I'm sorry you experienced all those horrible times in your life. If I were in your shoes, it'd be hard to say I would've done things differently. I'm not saying you were right. But I'm not going to hold it against you either. I can tell you've been through a lot. I'm not going to judge you for that, Lynda. You're safe with me," Travis told her reassuringly.

     T. V. H O L I D A Y

Lynda felt an easiness return and she became comfortable in his arms. She snuggled up against him. "Thank you. You don't know how much that means to me. I don't have any desire to kill another person. At least, not unless I absolutely have to."

Travis didn't expect her to be perfect. She was a woman who gave her soul to Luc. She experienced trauma throughout her time in Carnage Coast. He had a yearning to help her more than anything. He hoped to be a light in her life. He thought about her and her ability to kill people with a kiss, which brought up a question.

"I remembered something. If you can kill people with a kiss, why were you so desperate to kiss me that night at my house?" he asked.

Travis's question made Lynda nervous. After everything they spoke about, she didn't want anything to change his feelings about her. "I was hoping you would give in and be with me. We can be together if we're on the same side. As long as you remain a Man of God, I can take your soul," she answered.

He wondered if it was true. "I don't think you'll be able to take my soul. I think there's more to it than that. For a regular person, yeah, I can see that. But I can't help but think that I'll be different," said Travis.

She sat up and looked into his eyes. "Yeah, just like your inability to get hurt?" Lynda said sarcastically. "I don't want to chance it. I'm catching some serious feelings for you. I don't want to lose this. It feels good, and I know it can only get better. I wish you would stop holding on and come with me. I promise you it'll be okay."

Lynda's plea was a stark reminder of the divide between them. One of them needed to break away from their commitment. They wanted to be together, but neither seemed willing to budge.

"I can say the same to you. I'm not giving up hope. Listen, I have to find out how I was able to get hurt. I don't want to leave, but I do need to find out how it happened. If you want, you can spend the night at my house whenever you want," Travis told her confidently.

Lynda wondered if trying to hurt him would make things awkward when she spent the night. Travis reminded him of their current moment and assured her it would be okay. Lynda bought him clothing while she nursed him back to health. He put on the clothes and left for Last Hope.

T.V. HOLIDAY

The evening approached. The time Travis spent with Lynda flew by. He drove to Last Hope to find Mike. It was getting late, but he didn't know where else to look for him. He ran inside and looked around. He shouted for Mike, who met him in the sanctuary. Travis followed him down a hallway and entered a living area. It had a living room set with a TV and a coffee table. There was a kitchen area to the left of it that had another table for eating. The other side of the room had a desk with a computer that appeared to be a workstation. He was surprised to learn Mike lived in the church.

Travis sat at the kitchen table while Mike prepared the coffee. There was a door a few feet away where he heard a ruffling in the other room. He questionably looked at Mike and pointed.

"Company?" Travis asked slyly.

"No, that's my wife. She was really tired today, so she's going down a little early," Mike answered.

"You're married?" Travis asked, shockingly.

"Well, yeah! You'd know that if you stuck around long enough. She's been dying to meet you, but you're never around when she's here," Mike laughed. "What's going on?"

"Everybody is full of surprises today. I was with Sensation the last two days."

Mike was befuddled. "How did you end up with her?" he curiously asked.

"I've started feeling pain as The Iron Warrior. I felt it after the ambush. In the hospital, it got worse with each fight. Then I was set on fire and knocked out. Sensation took me back to her place and nursed me over the last two days. I woke up earlier and was covered in burns. I thought I was supposed to be invincible if I had my faith. Mike, what's going on?" Travis asked.

Mike went to get their coffee and processed what Travis told him. He returned to the table and took a sip. "Let's go back to the ambush. Tell me what you were feeling when it happened," Mike instructed.

Travis recalled the night's events. His dinner with Sensation irritated him. His irritation transformed into rage after Lovelyn shot him multiple times. It ultimately turned into fury when she goaded him into changing. There was no going back after that.

"I snapped. I was so angry that I lost myself. There's a part of me I tap into when it's time to fight. I go to a dark place when I'm pushed too far. It's like I become someone else. My voice changes and everything," Travis embarrassingly admitted.

"And the hospital?"

Travis remembered his anger rising throughout each fight. The thought of innocent people being hurt enraged him. He wasn't going to allow someone to get hurt again. Every form of resistance sent him back to that dark place.

"And just to make sure I completely understand everything, you were set on fire, knocked unconscious, and woke up covered in burns. Burns that are no longer present, right?" Mike clarified.

Travis answered with a nod. Before he could ask another question, Mike went across the room and grabbed his Bible. He returned and flipped through the pages. "Ahh, here! Ephesians 6:10 to 6:17. This explains your armor."

He slid it to Travis and pointed out key areas. The passage covered the Armor of God. Mike pointed out The Belt of Truth, the Breastplate of Righteousness, the Readiness of the Gospel for his shoes, the Shield of Faith, the Helmet of Salvation, and the Sword of the Spirit. The passage struck a chord with Travis. He saw it as the foundation behind The Iron Warrior. He was encouraged by the knowledge, but didn't understand why he felt hurt.

"You have to be powered by love for you to reach the full potential of your power. Love activates your armor and fully empowers your abilities. When you stray from that, you become weakened and susceptible to attacks. The power of love can also heal you. If you continue to act in ways that don't reflect God's love, your faith will diminish as well. You have to live your life in a Godly manner. If not, your soul will become corrupted. It'll reflect in your armor. You'll retain your strength and abilities, but you'll lose your invincibility. You'll be able to die," Mike clarified.

Travis was despondent. He knew what it meant to live a Godly life. He wasn't a monk and didn't have the gift of celibacy. He was unsure whether he could live the way he needed to be The Iron Warrior. Holding on to his faith was hard enough. To be fueled by love in Carnage Coast seemed like the goal post had been moved too far. His invincibility had been thrown out the window. Death felt like an immediate reality rather than a far-gone future.

"Mike, that's impossible!!" Travis exhaled. "I'm human, man. We have a range of emotions. How am I supposed to only operate on love and fight at the same time?"

"Yes, we're human, and you don't have to ignore your other emotions. You have to control them. They can't control you. You'll go down the wrong path and then you'll be in a world of trouble. A minute ago, you mentioned a dark place inside. You need to find a resolution for that. It's not healthy," urged Mike.

Travis paused to make sure he found the right words to respond. He felt the urgency and desperation in Mike's voice and respected his concern. He didn't want to be dismissive of his pleas but was unwilling to give up the darkness. He wasn't afraid of it. He saw people die. He had people die in his hands. Things he couldn't unsee stayed with him. He operated in light and thrived in the dark. He always tapped into it when he needed to. He was at peace with it. He believed it was part of what made him who he was.

"Mike, when I got baptized, I felt something. I didn't feel completely anew. I felt a struggle in my soul. I don't think it wanted to leave me then. I did find a resolution. I made peace with it. It's a part of me and it's going anywhere," Travis passionately stated.

Travis's explanation did not alleviate Mike's concern. He could see Travis was firm in his belief. Mike wished he could change his mind. He feared what would become of Travis if he didn't change course.

"I know you think it may be of some benefit to you, but it's not. You're leaving yourself susceptible to something bad if you let it take root in your soul. Nothing good can come from holding on to that darkness. You have to let it go," urged Mike.

Travis stoically shook his head. His defiance disheartened Mike. He decided to focus on another topic. He hoped to return to Travis' darkness at a different time when he would be more open to listening.

"You told me that you were burned earlier? How did you heal?" asked Mike.

As Travis attempted to retrace his thoughts, he remembered being in Lynda's bathroom. He thought about how she cared for him. Thinking about her made him smile. He wanted to hold her and feel the warmth of her body against his. He wanted to smell the sweetness of her perfume again.

Mike observed Travis' smile and became curious. "What are you thinking about?" asked Mike.

Mike's words snapped Travis out of his train of thought and brought him back to the room. "Sorry, I was thinking about Sensation," Travis admitted.

"I noticed you, too, were very cozy with one another in the hospital. How did that come about?" asked Mike.

"She came to visit me after I left last time. We had a really nice conversation. It felt like we connected on another level. She was there for me. She was there when I needed someone…," said Travis. His voice trailed off as he reminisced about how she was there for him.

Mike was hesitant to speak. He sensed Travis' growing attachment to her in his voice.

"Travis… I think you need to be careful here. I can see you're getting close to her. Hear me out for a second. You two meet for dinner and learn she is aligned with Luc. She has you ambushed. Then she tries to seduce you. You get the pie that reveals the family and marriage you were holding on to are gone. She meets you afterward to simply "talk." Lastly, she sets up the thing at the hospital where you're set on fire and then takes you back to her home. Doesn't it sound a little too coincidental that she's always popping right up after you've been hit with something? Do you really think she is being genuine? Or could this be all part of a plan to weaken you?" Mike cautiously described.

Travis took Mike's words to heart. He knew Mike was trying to look out for him. His description of events opened a different perspective. Upon hearing it out loud, it sounded like a perfect plan. It made sense. But Travis didn't want to listen to logic.

"Maybe I'm just a sucker right now. I've been desperate for that one-on-one human connection. She's the only woman who knows what's going on with me. Maybe I should take more time to grieve my marriage. Maybe I should sit alone and be in pain. All of this is happening so fast. Maybe it's so fast that I can't see what's happening. Or maybe, I just don't give a damn anymore," Travis told him.

"This is a dangerous line you're walking. Are you sure you're not just chasing a feeling? You and I both know feelings can change. Following our feelings can lead us to places where we don't need to be," Mike replied.

Travis knew it was a dangerous line. He regularly listened to his feelings. He believed they were signals that let him know when something was right or wrong. He didn't think he was chasing a feeling. He was trying to hold on to who he was. He believed loving his family brought out the best in him. Travis felt that love allowed me to push farther and harder, endure when he wanted to give up, and hold on to hope. He believed it gave him strength that he didn't have.

"You and I both know loving others is not the same as having someone close to love. Sensation isn't asking me to save her. She isn't trying to change me. She only wants us to love each other. Obviously, the feelings I have for her have already healed me. I don't want to let that go, Mike. I'm literally going to go through hell for this love. And as stupid as this may sound, I wouldn't have it any other way," Travis retorted.

Mike leaned back and realized he wouldn't be able to change Travis's mind about Sensation. His feelings for her were worrisome. The more Mike listened, the more concerned he became about Travis' emotional stability. It was clear to Mike that he couldn't see the warning signs.

"Where do you think this is going? If this is a trap, you aren't stopping yourself from falling into it. If she has made her choice, loving her won't matter. The fate of the world is at stake here. I understand how you feel, but your feelings can't come before the world. This is the ultimate test of putting others before yourself. The love that you're craving might have to be sacrificed. If not, we all die," Mike argued.

"Then I have to figure that out, Mike. I'll find a way to stop this Free Love Initiative. But I'm not letting her go. How can I fight for this world if I have to give up a love that's giving me the strength to fight for it?" countered Travis.

"Others have tried to walk this line and they failed. Please don't try to do this. I know you probably think you're strong enough to overcome what's in front of you. But you are making yourself extremely vulnerable," Mike desperately warned him.

"Others? Like who?" Travis suspiciously asked.

He sensed the suspicion in Travis's question. He didn't want to make Travis think that he was untrustworthy. "Well, this was going to come up at some point. I might as well tell you now," Mike opened. "I'm old Travis. I'm really old. I've served in this role as a watcher for God's champions. I was once a champion. I fought for a long time. You're part of a long line of champions who've fought on behalf of God. There have been different stakes for every champion. Unfortunately, so many of us feel that the world is on the brink of falling into Lucifer's hands."

     T. V. HOLIDAY

Travis was surprised to learn Mike was a champion. It gave him credibility, adding weight to his words. "Did you all have to show God is still alive in this world?" asked Travis.

"Not exactly. If you look throughout history, you can see our failures. The Holocaust, the rise and prominence of slavery, and the drug epidemic in the United States during the late 1980s are just examples. When you look back at the rise of evil and the damning effects it has had on our world, it's evidence of a warrior's fall. Our failures gave way to the devastation those historical events generated. God's presence slowly dissipated over time," Mike explained.

"When did this begin?"

"Job…"

Travis threw his hands up and motioned for Mike to stop. His revelation was a bombshell. His heart dropped into his stomach. His hands became cold and clammy. Travis read the Book of Job multiple times. The revelations made Travis feel like he drank water from a fire hose. He muttered, "No way," under his breath. He wrestled with the notion that he was connected to the Bible. Travis sank into his chair as Mike continued.

"If you remember the Book of Job, he was chosen to be tested. He not only survived but also kept his faith, and he was greatly rewarded. Job was the first, but the game between God and Luc continued. Many men and women have been chosen. There are seven battlefields around the world. Carnage Coast was the seventh battleground created for this war. Hence, the Seventh City.

Now it's down to this. Because we have lost so much, Carnage Coast is the last stand between heaven and hell. The city isn't large compared to the other major battlegrounds. This population is prone to being easily influenced. Lucifer has the advantage here," Mike sadly explained.

Mike spoke with a sense of grief. It made Travis wonder about his past. Mike was a failed champion. Travis hated that a question came to mind. But he had to ask, "Mike, what was failure?"

Mike closed his eyes and took a deep breath. He had hoped to convey the importance of the situation without using his story. Travis' defiance made it necessary for him to tell it. He didn't want to. But for the sake of opening his eyes, he felt there was no other way.

"World War II. My failure allowed Luc to influence Hitler to almost wipe out a race of people. My wife was Jewish. Her life was in jeopardy. I didn't want to lose her. I gave up. I gave up without knowing the true consequences of what I did. The lives of millions of people were lost because I chose my will over God's. That's on me. I accept that. I wish I could get another chance to do it over, though. I want to think I would've found a way," Mike grimly stated.

"Then you see that's what I'm trying to do," Travis responded.

"I know. And that's why I'm telling you not to. It can't be done. Look back through time. Men, to our credit and fault, have chosen the love of a woman over everything else more often than not. Adam chose Eve over the word of God. King David sacrificed his own warriors for Bathsheba. When a woman touches a man, it's either love or lust that we feel. A woman's love can be one of our greatest strengths or most damning weaknesses.

"Sensation has gotten to you. You know it. I know it. Unfortunately for you, this isn't like mine or anybody else's stake. The fate of the world is on your shoulders. Those of us before you, our failures didn't end the world. Your failure will literally condemn us to hell. It doesn't matter how strong you think you are or how strong you really are; the risk is too great. You're already falling. You've been hurt, you've already been weakened.

"After me, warriors were sent to an isolated place so they couldn't be easily influenced. My wife influenced me. I love her greatly and will to my dying breath. I was given the opportunity to serve in this role for future champions. To try and guide you all from making the same mistakes I did. I failed with Sidious Craig and Coldred Black. I don't want to fail you. Travis, I know you're lonely. I know your family has been ripped away from you. The pain you feel is real. Sensation's affection feels great, but you can't let it cloud your heart. You have to ask yourself if she really loves you or if she is playing the role Luc wants her to play. She is a pawn to weaken you. You can't allow him to do it. You can't give him the opportunity to take this world. Please, Travis, you have to be stronger than all of us who came before you. Be stronger than me. This world needs your strength," pleaded Mike.

Travis couldn't ignore Mike's pleas. He didn't want to think of Lynda's words as a mere ploy to destroy him. He didn't want to hurt her. Their time together was genuine. He believed what she told him. Her feelings for him felt real. Travis didn't want to question it. He didn't want to fail Mike or end up like the champions before.

"What made Sidious and Coldred fall? What historical events are they responsible for?" Travis asked. He hoped their stories would give him guidance on the pitfalls to avoid.

"They weren't very noble men to begin with. They were easily swayed. Coldred was a championship-level boxer. He had a desire to hurt others and was very selfish. I hoped he would grow to love others. He had a darkness inside of him that couldn't be extinguished. He lost his battle with it. Luc promised him peace to be the punisher he felt that he truly was. Coldred's fall led to the rise in school shootings across the United States.

"Sidious was worse. He was a very smart man with a great ability to influence others. But he was crazy. Luc exploited it. He fought a fierce inner battle but failed. Luc promised him the freedom to express his manic influence without guilt or shame. Sidious' fall led to the worldwide pandemic, violent protests that followed," Mike sadly revealed.

Travis exhaled heavily. His shoulders slumped forward. He hung his head low. Mike's words rang in his head. It felt as if a foot was crushing his chest. The weight of the world was on his shoulders in every way. It took his breath away.

"Mike, I'm a weak man. I'm not strong enough to do this on my own. I know. I know that the way this is set up is probably for the best. But it's not the best for me. I can't fail. But I can't do it the way you're asking me to. I'm not giving her up. This isn't simply lust between us. I'm going to find a way to win this battle. I'm going to walk this line. I'll take all of the pain that comes with this road, but this is my road to take. All I can do is my best," Travis asserted.

Mike was showered with disappointment. He hoped his story would help. As he looked at him, Mike felt Travis would be another champion lost to Luc. He was nervous. He was afraid it was too late for him to turn back.

"If you take this path, your best may not be enough. Are you willing to risk this world for that? Are you willing to risk your son's life?" Mike questioned

Travis raised his head and looked Mike in his eyes. Shaken and nervously, Travis told him, "To save his life, I'm going to have to."

Travis left while Mike remained crestfallen in his chair. There was a rumbling in the other room. The door cracked open and a head poked out. It was his wife, Shannah. She asked if she had missed Travis and noticed Mike's glum demeanor. There were only certain times when Mike was down in such a manner. Shannah asked if they were about to lose another. He glanced at her and replied, "I think so, sweetie… I think so."

T.V. HOLIDAY

Travis drove home and walked out to the beach. He loved the openness of the ocean. The solitude allowed him to feel closer to God. He had to find a way to overcome The Free Love Initiative. He also had to figure out how to keep his feelings from leading him astray. Travis also thought about Brittany. He couldn't overlook the damage the video brought to her. Everything started with it; he decided to do one himself. He hoped a new video would have a greater impact. Travis invoked The Iron Warrior and activated the camera on his phone. He placed it on one of the nearby rocks. He sat on the sand and looked out to the sea.

"My name is The Iron Warrior. I've been the subject of a lot of news. I wanted to speak directly to all of you. You might be wondering why I'm here. There is a darkness that lives in the underbelly of this city. It's infectious and poisonous. I'm here to be the light in that darkness. I stand in it to provide the light, which leads the way out. I am God's instrument. I'm the support he sends to help when you're down. I'm the strength he sends to help when you can't find it on your own. I'm the ear he provides if you need someone to speak to. I can carry the weight of your pain when it's too much. Not because I have to, but because I choose to. That's how I'm made. I'm not here for me. I'm here for you. My purpose is to serve you. I don't fight for me, I fight for you.

"Granted, I don't make the best decisions at times. I make mistakes. I hurt people. I hurt someone already and I can't make up for it. The last video brought a lot of pain to someone. Pain that could've been avoided. For that, I am sorry. To the young lady in that video, I apologize. I should've acted sooner. I'm sorry for all the hurt and suffering you've endured because of my inaction. I own it and am truly sorry.

"I want to address the Free Love Initiative. On the surface, there are many things anyone would be on board with. I believe being accepted and loved is a universal desire. It's not for us to judge people. I believe we should leave that to God. Racism is a set of beliefs not based on facts. We have the freedom to think, feel and act in any manner we choose. As long as we have free will, I don't believe racism will ever go away. But I do believe that if we treat each other with love, respect and kindness, the racism that we know can dissipate. It doesn't matter what we sign into law; everyone has to make the active choice to love one another to overcome that hatred.

"Prostitution may be the oldest profession. Sex is one of the greatest experiences one can have. Especially when you truly love the person you're becoming one with. But when that's missing, it's not everything it can be.

"I understand people have strong feelings about abortion. As a man who lost a child prematurely, I don't stand with it. I wish I could've met that child. I still feel that lost to this day.

"I know there are health benefits to certain drugs. I've seen people use drugs to escape their reality. Drugs are highly addictive. The problem is that drugs mask the pain and alter our ability to face reality and accept what is. It destroys us from the inside out. Drugs put us on a freeway to death. I don't think we need to provide safe places for people to travel on this road.

"There are more things to the Initiative, but I'll only address two more. One is the elimination of formalized religion. I admit there has been a lot of division amongst us because of it. What is diversity without tolerance of thought and belief? We get caught up in traditions instead of focusing on a relationship with God. I don't have the answer to this. It's not like you're asking me either. Even with the different religions, I believe we're closer than we are apart.

"The second issue is the Initiative's registration. Not registering for it will create the same oppression we desire to escape. It's another form of control. Either think like us or suffer the consequences. We'll imprison and punish a different group of people. People who simply want the desire to live their lives in the way they choose. The Free Love

Initiative will be another form of power for all of those in a position to inherit it.

"Lastly, love is already free. We say it comes at a cost. Rejection hurts. We can't run from it. But do we ever think to remember that rejection may be the other person's honest way of saying you aren't the person for them? We're perfectly human. If we aren't open to lives of growth and love, then we limit our life experience. We don't need to vote on the issues the Free Love Initiative addresses. We can address that freely and now. We don't need to sign anything. To know love is to know God, and to know God is to know love. If we share that, we can get closer to the peace we all truly desire. That's real love. No cost, no vote, and no waiting. What are you going to choose?"

Three weeks passed, and The Iron Warrior's second video, titled "I Declare," went viral. Public opinion of him swayed in a positive direction. Citizens took his post and created The Real Love Movement to counter The Free Love Initiative. Content was created in the form of videos, posts, and blogs that captured people genuinely caring for others. Every post and video was given a #RealLove tag. It developed a groundswell of support. Those opposed to the Free Love Initiative had a platform to voice their views.

Hicks became The Iron Warrior's ally. Mike told him the truth about Carnage Coast. Hicks worked the streets and arrested The Double Ds whenever he could. He knew it wouldn't stop her organization. He only hoped to slow their progress. He informed The Iron Warrior whenever he spotted The Donnas on the hunt for a recruit. Aside from helping Mike and The Iron Warrior, he spent his spare time assisting Brittany recover.

Brittany was released from her mental illness hold. Hicks checked on her daily. He took her to Last Hope on Sundays for service. During that time, Brittany developed a friendship with him. Local news outlets followed up with her to see how she was doing since the attack. Despite his protests, Brittany spoke to the newspapers and TV reporters. She found her voice and spoke out against the Free Love Initiative. Brittany thanked Sensation for paying for her medical bills, but denounced everything she stood for. She found a new sense of purpose.

The Iron Warrior found his footing within Carnage Coast. Aside from working with Hicks to stop The Donnas, he spoke to those whom he was able to save. He spent significant time with them and learned about their situations. He directed them to Last Hope, where Mike offered them services and resources. Travis paid for Ashley's medical treatment to help Domino. She showed vast signs of improvement. He found positive ways to assert himself throughout the city.

Despite The Real Love Movement's growth, The Free Love Initiative still had a core group of supporters. Sensation's organization continued to rake in exorbitant amounts of money. The influential players ensured the Free Love Movement received promotion everywhere. Legal rights were obtained to create a pornography film company titled Sensual Eruptions.

Sensation's Fatal Four handled the day-to-day aspects of the organization. Vivian focused on their financial growth while Domino wrote screenplays for future films. Cassidy tried to recruit new Donnas but continually ran into opposition from The Iron Warrior. Cassidy's recruitment numbers were plummeting. Sensation maintained a daily presence at The Pit. She remained involved in day-to-day operations and met regularly with her business partners. She committed to the promotional requirements and approved Cassidy's plans to stop The Iron Warrior. She allowed Sidious to keep Lovelyn busy and tasked Coldred to be her enforcer for anyone who dared to challenge her authority. Sensation kept a grip on her organization and ensured things ran smoothly.

Meanwhile, Travis and Lynda grew remarkably close. Their budding romance blossomed into a full-blown love affair. She stayed with him every night. They walked along the beach hand-in-hand and shared their hopes and dreams. When together, they felt an escape from the world they were locked in. They weren't The Iron Warrior and Sensation. They were only Travis and Lynda. She provided him with the companionship and acceptance he craved. He gave her the love she dreamed about.

Travis studied Lynda in short order. He listened and learned what made her happy and what made her sad. He validated her and spoke with care and compassion. He regularly brought her flowers. He gave her the opportunity to fulfill her acting dream. He allowed her to make an appearance in a storyline for his wrestling promotion. He was her safe haven where she could open up and be herself. Lynda's love gave him strength. He didn't suffer another injury. Once again, he became impervious to physical pain.

Lynda developed a hope for her future. She hoped her soul could be saved. She kept up her appearances as Sensation, but only in appearance. Her heart was with Travis. She no longer cared if The Free Love Initiative passed. She no longer wanted the life she had. Every day was a reminder of the hell she was trapped in. Going home to Travis intensified her hope for a better future. They were unable to express their love physically, aside from hugs. They hoped to fully experience each other one day. It was another desire that kept them focused on a future together.

T.V. HOLIDAY

Sensation met with her Fatal Four, along with Sidious and Coldred, in her office. Sidious and Coldred stood by in the room as they always did. As she looked out of the window, her mind was focused on Travis. She wished the day would hurry so she could spend more time with him. Cassidy asked what she wanted them to do. Her question snapped Sensation out of her daze. She turned her chair around and all eyes were on her.

Sensation shook her head and tried to refocus, "What's the question again?"

"We're getting hit from all sides. This Real Love Movement is gaining a lot of momentum and taking votes away from us. The Iron Warrior's influence is growing and he's slowing our recruitment. I thought you were working on weakening him," explained Vivian.

"I am, and you know that…" Sensation quickly responded.

"Seems like he's been working you," Lovelyn quipped.

Lovelyn's disrespect sparked Sensation. She was astounded by it. She scooted her chair back and stood. Sidious raised his hand and motioned for her to pause. He walked toward Lovelyn, who cut him a look. He flashed a sickening smile and backhanded her out of the chair. He picked Lovelyn up by her hair and forcibly sat her back in the seat.

"What did you say?" Sidious eerily asked her.

"What I meant to say was that… we don't see the killer in you anymore. These cunts won't say it, but I will. Where's the soulless bitch who came in here setting assholes on fire whenever she wanted?" Lovelyn answered and asked angrily. Her lip was busted and she spat blood at Sidious' feet. She defiantly wiped her mouth as she waited for Sensation's response.

Sensation eyed the room. Everyone was anxious to hear what she had to say. She wondered if Lovelyn's words reflected everyone's feelings. The vibe in the room was different. Lovelyn was the only one to challenge her openly. Sensation had difficulty reading everyone.

"Don't get it twisted. I'm still that bitch and will take your life whenever I feel like it. I've been feeling that way about you, Lovelyn. Keep running your mouth and I'll make you hotter than you've ever been," Sensation threatened.

Lovelyn delightfully laughed at her threat. "Oh yeah… make me hot bitch!"

Sensation glared at her intensely. She kicked her chair back and aggressively stood.

"Shut up, Lovelyn!" Cassidy irritably interrupted. "Look, Sensation, we're not trying to piss you off. We've been down with you. Since you took over, things have been better. You ain't like Lazarus. This is yours, but you've made it feel like ours, too. We don't wanna' see it fall. But things are slippin'. You're gone every night and, while you let us do whatever we need to do, it ain't workin' anymore. Vivian's doin' her thing, I'm fightin' The Iron Warrior and can't get a new Donna because of this Real Love bullshit. I can't count on Lovelyn because you let Sidious lock her up most of the time. I know she messed up, but I need her back. We gotta' get this back on track. We gotta' turn this back around."

"She's right, Sensation," Vivian added. "Things aren't running as well as they did a few weeks ago. The vote for the initiative is on June 1st. Thankfully, we were able to get this special election because of our business partners. Our numbers are still good, but they aren't what they were. They're not overwhelming anymore. We need to recapture support."

Cassidy and Vivian's pleas calmed Sensation down. Coldred picked up her chair and moved it back so she could sit. She took a moment to take in what they had to say. Despite how she truly felt, she had to maintain her image and reputation. She noticed Domino sat quietly. Domino watched the interaction amongst them but did not intervene.

"Why have you been so quiet, Domino?" asked Sensation.

"Sorry. I don't feel like I have anything to add because you put me in charge of the movies. There's nothing wrong on my end. Porn doesn't require much of a script, so that's not an issue. We have enough Donnas to film and provide content for the website. Porn will generate enough money for us, no matter what we do. The Free Love Initiative is good and all, but I feel like we've already made it. We can ride this out and live the lives we've always wanted on this alone," explained Domino.

"Of course, you would want us to focus on porn. You don't want any part of the dirt we do. We can take over this world with the Free Love Initiative. All you want to do is make money and be a mommy. You ain't cut for this Domino," said Lovelyn. She didn't respect Domino. Lovelyn felt she did not deserve a spot in the Fatal Four.

Domino scoffed at her comment and rolled her eyes. She didn't feel the need to explain herself to Lovelyn. Domino didn't want to sell her body anymore. She wasn't ashamed to be a mother. She wanted to be by Ashley's side. Sensation's direction took her off the street. She was no longer in constant danger or at the mercy of someone.

"What do you think we should do about all of this, Domino?" Sensation asked.

"Let's do a rally," Domino suggested. "This is political stuff, right? Politicians do rallies. Hold it a few days out from the final day to vote. That way, you can get whoever else is not on board by that point. Do it in the heart of downtown in front of City Hall."

Their eyes lit up at Domino's idea. It was the perfect solution to secure the support they needed for the Free Love Initiative to pass. They could involve all their business associates. They believed it would give them an opportunity to be seen positively in the public's view. The Real Love Movement had support, but there wasn't anything formal for it. A rally would allow them to get back in front of the city.

"What about The Iron Warrior?" Cassidy interjected. "What if he shows up?" The Iron Warrior remained at the forefront of her thoughts. She was assured he would show up. She didn't want to leave anything to chance.

"Then let's have something for him," said Coldred as he approached the table. "There's a demon where we're from. It has an insatiable appetite for human life. Whether man, woman, or child, it'll kill and revel in the bloodlust. All it needs is the freedom to roam. Its name is Abaddon. Abaddon will destroy the city. It will take everything for The Iron Warrior to beat it. Lives will be lost. If Abaddon does what it can do, The Iron Warrior will fall."

Vivian, Cassidy, Lovelyn, and Coldred nodded their heads. They loved the idea. Domino remained quiet. She didn't want to hurt The Iron Warrior. He saved her life and met Ashley. He wasn't her enemy. He proved to be a good man.

"Then it's settled. Plan the rally. And at the rally, we release Abaddon," Sensation ordered.

The Fatal Four, along with Sidious and Coldred, left Sensation's office while she remained at the table. Sensation contemplated their plan and how it would affect Travis.

"A penny for your thoughts," a familiar voice echoed.

The voice startled her. She stood and looked to see where it came from. It was Luc. He sat at her desk with a warm smile on his face. She was unsure why he was there. In the past, Sensation was always happy to see Luc. Things had changed since she last saw him. Her heart rate elevated. She finished a conversation with her Fatal Four, who were worried. Now Luc was in front of her before she could comprehend everything that had unfolded moments earlier. He recognized her uneasiness.

"Let me put you at ease. I know you've fallen for Travis. If you can remember, that was part of the plan. I wanted you to take hold of his heart. The Free Love Initiative is moving forward as planned. You've done well, Lynda. I'm pleased," Luc told her.

He stood from the chair and slowly approached her. Luc took her into his arms and hugged Sensation softly. Her heart continued to race. Sensation had difficulty breathing and was short of breath.

"I feel like I've failed you," Sensation said nervously.

"Failed? Absolutely not," Luc laughed. Luc kissed Sensation on her forehead and continued, "You're doing everything like I hoped you would. Remember, Lynda, I chose you for a reason. You have him right where I want him. Now go to him."

Sensation looked nervously, but Luc gave her a reassuring smile. She backed away and left to see Travis. As Luc watched her go, his smile faded away. He removed a cell phone from his pocket and made a phone call.

"Yes, sir," a voice answered.

"Release Abaddon," Luc ordered.

T.V. HOLIDAY

Hicks got up earlier than usual before his shift. He went to a donut shop to get a cup of coffee and donuts before he visited Brittany. He never developed a friendship with someone he met while working. He felt sad when he met Brittany. He felt she had a bright future and wanted to help her reach it. Hicks arrived and Brittany cracked the door open. She went to the bathroom, tying up her hair, while he walked in and sat at the kitchen table. Hicks bought four donuts, and one was a bear claw. He sat back and bit into the bear claw as he got settled.

"Did you get me a bear claw?"

"Sure, kid. I know that's your favorite," Hicks responded as he placed the bear claw back in the donut box. "What's the plan for today?" he asked.

"I have another interview on Good Morning Carnage Coast, and then I'm speaking to a women's group tonight," Brittany answered.

"What's the topic?"

"What else?" she replied.

"Iron Warrior and Free Love?"

"You know it," Brittany answered sarcastically.

She stepped out wearing business pants and a white blouse. Her hair was tied up in a bun. Brittany stood in front of her dresser mirror and put on makeup. The stitches on her forehead left a visible scar. She put on enough makeup to make it barely visible. She wore a nice watch over the scar where her wrist was slit.

"I'm proud of you, kid. I'm glad you're using this experience to help others. Everybody can't bounce back as you have. It says a lot about who you are," Hicks complimented.

Brittany faintly smiled. He regularly complimented her resilience. He had become the big brother she never had. She continued to get dressed while he ate more donuts.

"Thanks, Jimmy. That means a lot coming from you. The Iron Warrior's position against The Free Love Initiative will help it fall. But once this election has passed, I'm done praising him. He still pressed the button, Jimmy. I wouldn't have gone through any of this if it wasn't for him," she responded.

Hicks sighed. He wanted to tell her the truth about Carnage Coast. He hoped it would help her understand the gravity of the situation. Hicks promised Mike and The Iron Warrior that he would help keep their secret safe. She was still holding onto her pain. He struggled to remain silent. They had many conversations about The Iron Warrior and how he didn't purposely post the video. Brittany's stance remained unchanged. She still held him responsible for it.

Brittany stopped putting on her makeup and looked at Hicks through the mirror. She could see his concern. She walked over to Hicks and sat with him. "I appreciate you looking out for me. I really do. You don't have to, though. I still don't understand why you do. I'm not anyone special."

"I used to only clock in and clock out work. I had a sister who would tell me I had a lot more to give. She would push me to give back more. I ignored her when she said stuff like that. She passed away not too long ago. She was robbed at gunpoint and killed. The cops who showed up were pretty cold. After that, I promised myself that I would do more like she said. Then I met you. I'm keeping my promise to her. Besides, you look a lot like her, too. I don't mean to make you my project," explained Hicks.

His explanation helped her understand him better. She was grateful that he cared. Brittany leaned across the table and hugged him. As she sat back, she oversaw the open box of donuts and noticed the half-eaten bear claw. She suspiciously eyed him while he mischievously glanced away.

"Umm …what happened to my bear claw?" she asked teasingly.

Hicks paused as he tried to think of a suitable response. "Don't you have an interview to go to?"

T.V. HOLIDAY

Sensation went to see Travis at The Pavilion. She knew he would be in his office for the morning. The Pavilion employees became familiar with her because of Travis and warmly greeted her. She got on the elevator to the top floor of the building, where his office was located. Cheryl met her in the hallway and walked her in. Once the doors closed, she hugged Travis tightly and closed her eyes. She was no longer Sensation. She was simply Lynda. Travis held her gently and soothingly ran his hand across her back. He could tell something was wrong.

"Luc came to see me this morning. He said I've done well for him, but knows my heart is with you. He knows I don't want this life anymore. I can feel it and I know he can too," Lynda fearfully revealed. She loosened her hug and took a step back. He walked her over to a couch he had and they sat. She took a deep breath and tried to keep her composure.

Travis stood and paced the room while he tried to wrap his thoughts around the situation.

"If he truly knows how you feel, does it matter what you do next? If he already knows you want out, then don't go back. What difference does it make?"

Lynda's eyes widened like a light bulb went on in her mind. She took his words to heart. She wondered if it would make a difference if she continued her public life as Sensation. She didn't want to be on the opposite side of Travis anymore. She was tired of fighting her feelings. She was tired of the line between them. She was ready to make a decision.

"It doesn't matter what I say. He knows me and knows how I feel. I should just draw the line here. I want my soul. I don't want to go to hell. I don't want to be a demon. I want to be with you. If that means giving my life to God, then I'll do it," Lynda exclaimed. The fear in her voice was replaced with a newfound strength and fervor.

Travis was surprised to hear her declaration. It was the moment he hoped and prayed for. He couldn't believe it was real. Her decision meant they could finally be together. It meant they didn't have to fight each other. She walked over to him, brimming with confidence.

"I love that you want your soul. Don't do it simply for me, though. Do it because you want to. Are you sure this is what you want?" Travis asked.

Lynda shook her head and placed both of her hands on Travis's face. "Absolutely. Being with you has given me hope for a life I thought I'd never experience. I have that life with you and I hope it lasts. I want to live life with you. I want to enjoy everything life has to offer with you. I want to meet your son one day. I don't want this love to ever go away."

Travis grabbed one of her hands from his face and kissed the back of it. He pulled her closer and smiled, "I'll be with you for as long as you allow me to be." His face shifted to one of concern as he continued, "Now that you've said it out loud, should you even go back? I don't want anything to happen to you."

"I don't have to go back anytime soon. We're going to do a rally for the Free Love Initiative. If you can keep things going with your Real Love Movement, the rally won't matter. The most important thing, though, is that there is something called Abaddon. Coldred mentioned it. It's some kind of demon from hell that may have the ability to kill you. They're going to release it at the rally," stated Lynda.

"As long as you're loving me, there's nothing that will be able to stop me," said Travis. "In the meantime, maybe we can reach out to Mike. He can help us try to figure out how to get your soul back."

Before they could happily settle on their plan, the sound of an explosion could be heard from down the street. Screams flooded the city. Smoke filled the sky. Travis' Divine Eyes lit up. Something was wrong. He ran to the window and saw three cars on fire down the street while people frantically ran away. He couldn't see much more beyond the smoke. His Divine Eyes electrified once more, with even

   T. V. HOLIDAY

greater intensity. He opened the window and removed the screen. The Pavilion was seven stories high.

"I am the light in the dark, God's fist in the war, the man powered by faith, make me The Iron Warrior once more," exclaimed Travis.

The Helmet of Salvation covered his head. The Breastplate of Righteousness appeared and covered his chest and shoulders. Metal gauntlets wrapped around his forearms. The Belt of Truth wrapped around his waist and the Boots of Readiness enveloped his feet. White metal covered the rest of his body. The Iron Warrior illuminated in front of Lynda. He stepped onto the windowpane ledge as Lynda walked over and reached out for his hand.

"Be careful," said Lynda.

He held Lynda's hand and gently pulled her closer to him. He smiled, "I'll do my best."

The door burst open and Cheryl ran into the room, "Travis, are you…" Cheryl stopped in shock at the sight of The Iron Warrior. She quickly looked around the room for Travis but didn't see him. He made eye contact with her before he leaped to the street and headed toward the fire.

The ground shook every other second like something was walking. Another explosion occurred further down the street. The impact flung those nearby through the store windows. The Iron Warrior ran toward the screaming. A car suddenly became visible and flew toward him. He dove out of the way as it crashed into another vehicle.

The Warrior quickly got up and ran to the car. He looked inside, but no one was in it. He looked out of the corner of his eye and noticed a fireball crash into a store directly to his right. The blast propelled him across the street. Window fragments rippled in the air as bricks crumbled onto the sidewalk. The people who were inside ran out of the remaining stores and fled. The ground-shaking tremors grew closer and suddenly stopped. The Iron Warrior looked up and saw a sight unlike any other he had ever seen.

A 10-foot-tall figure that weighed more than 500 pounds stood in front of him. It was surrounded from head to toe by a dark red fire. Its body was black and covered in bright red scars. Ivory blades protruded from its forearms and extended two feet beyond its fists. Curved ivory blades bulged from its back like hooks. Fire flamed from its eyes. Beastly teeth obtruded from its mouth. Ivory horns came out of its head like a ram. It was Abaddon.

"Son… of…. a…. bitch," The Warrior muttered to himself in amazement.

Abaddon fixed its eyes on The Warrior and charged at him. The Warrior jumped to his feet, but it was too late. Abaddon lowered his level and rammed his chest. The impact lifted The Warrior into the air and flung him into a metal traffic pole. His impact severely dented it.

The Warrior didn't feel any anger. His love for Lynda and faith in God were strong, which solidified his armor. He felt the impact, but it had little effect. Abaddon charged at him again and swiped at his head with one of the ivory blades from its forearms. The Warrior ducked and Abaddon cut the pole in half. It fell forward as The Warrior rolled out of the way. It crashed into Abaddon but split upon contact. The pole did not affect Abaddon.

The Warrior ran toward Abaddon with both of his fists forward. He tried to shoot himself into its abdomen but was struck with a standing sidekick that knocked him into a nearby car. Abaddon roared as the Iron Warrior tried to catch his breath. He stood and tried to shake off the blow. Abaddon leaped and tried to land on him feetfirst. The Warrior dove forward and barely missed contact with it. He ran back at Abaddon and hit it with a diving shoulder tackle into the back of its right leg. The force made Abaddon drop to one knee. The Warrior stayed focused and followed up with a standing sidekick of his own to Abaddon's ribs.

Abaddon swung his right arm back to knock The Warrior away, but missed. The Warrior ducked it but was clotheslined to the ground.

The heat that emanated from Abaddon made The Warrior sweat and sapped the oxygen from him. Abaddon picked him up and slammed The Warrior across his knee for a vicious backbreaker before flinging him further down the street.

Meanwhile, back at The Pavilion, Cheryl remained in shock at the sight of The Iron Warrior. Before she could say a word, a hand reached from behind and grabbed her collar. She was pulled out of the office as a group of people entered ahead of her. The person spun Cheryl around and got in her face. It was Lovelyn.

"Do me a favor. Get the outta' here. Take whoever else you can 'cause this bitch is about to go up in flames," Lovelyn told her.

Cheryl didn't argue. She looked around and saw the group that had entered Travis' office. She left and warned whoever she could to do the same. Sidious, Coldred, Vivian, Domino, Cassidy, and Lovelyn entered the office and approached Sensation.

"What are you doing? This wasn't the plan. This was supposed to be at the rally!!!" Sensation angrily shouted.

"I loved the plan. So, I thought… why wait for the rally?" a familiar voice echoed throughout the room.

Luc walked through the doors and entered behind the group. A cold chill raced through Sensation's spine. He approached and pulled her toward him for another hug. He held her face and peered into her eyes.

"We aren't waiting for the rally. We're going to break The Iron Warrior now," Luc told her.

Sensation remained quiet, fearfully looking at him. She thought about Travis and her desire for her soul. She didn't want to shrink in the face of her fight. The newfound strength she had found earlier returned.

"We're not going to break him. He may be too strong at this point," Sensation countered.

"Oh yes, he's strong, but we're about to break him. I promise," Luc eerily told her. "Coldred!"

"Yes, sir!" Coldred responded.

"I want you and Sidious to kill everyone you see. Ladies, set the explosives. We're going to bring this place to ashes. And Sensation… my sweet, sweet Sensation, you're going to stand with me and watch the show," Luc ordered.

Smiles spread across all their faces except for Sensation and Domino. Sidious and Coldred left and went office to office. They killed everyone they saw. Cassidy, Lovelyn, and Vivian scattered throughout The Pavilion and planted explosives. Screams echoed throughout the halls while Luc and Sensation watched the battle on the street.

Back on the street, The Iron Warrior had his hands full with Abaddon. He was unable to hurt it. He still felt strong, but fatigue was starting to set in. Abaddon pummeled him up and down the street. They fought their way to the front of The Pavilion. Abaddon released a fireball from its mouth and The Warrior dove out of the way. Abaddon sent rapid fireballs his way and forced him to run for cover. He continued evasive maneuvers until he could find an opening to attack.

Police cars swarmed the area. Hicks arrived on the scene as well. The Iron Warrior shouted for them to make sure the area was evacuated. Hicks led the evacuation. As more officers arrived, they shot at Abaddon, but their bullets did not have any effect. The Carnage Coast Police Department's SWAT Team arrived with its armored vehicle, The Battlecat. Abaddon absorbed the bullets and sent fireballs at the patrol vehicles and Battlecat. The vehicles flew into the nearby buildings, but The Battlecat withstood the attack. The officers fled from it for safety.

The Warrior hopped into it and drove straight into Abaddon. The collision knocked Abaddon back a few feet. He backed up to gain more ground. He revved the engine and floored it to ram Abaddon again. Abaddon saw it coming and rammed it head-on. The collision pushed The Battlecat back. Abaddon lifted The Battlecat and slammed it on the ground multiple times while The Warrior was still inside. All four tires popped off of it. Abaddon flipped The Battlecat in the air and it landed upside down. The Warrior was dizzy from the constant flips and slams. He had trouble regaining his composure.

Back in the building, Domino hid her explosives. She went to every person she could see and told them to flee the building. She warned them that the building was going to explode. They thought she was a crazy person who snuck inside. The screams had not reached her area of the building. Domino tried to think of a way to warn everyone. She found a fire alarm and pulled it.

The alarm boomed throughout the building and people stepped out into the hallway.

"Get the hell out of here!!! There is a fire!!! The building is going to blow!!!" she shouted.

Domino found an exit sign and went to the door. She opened it and pulled those nearby through it. Lovelyn exited a stairwell into the same hallway. She saw Domino push people out of the building. She slid into a corner and watched in disgust. Her blood boiled at Domino's betrayal.

People rushed out of The Pavilion and filled the parking lot and street. The people caught Abaddon's attention. Abaddon charged at the group and stabbed everyone it saw. The Warrior crawled out of The Battlecat and saw Abaddon killing people. A surge of adrenaline powered him to protect his people.

A woman tripped and had difficulty getting up. Abaddon saw her on the ground and its flames grew higher. It lasered a fire beam in her direction. The Iron Warrior dove in front of her. A shield was released from his left gauntlet and enlarged to protect them from its flame. The flame bounced off the shield. The Warrior ordered the woman to leave and covered her as she ran away. He found a nearby rock and threw it at Abaddon to distract it. The rock struck Abaddon's head, which caused it to stop using its fire beam.

The Warrior looked at his shield in shock. It was shaped like a law enforcement badge. An eagle with extended wings was embedded along the top of the shield. A red cross was in the center that was placed over a circular sun. The shape of sunrays extended to the edges of the shield. Banners were above and below the cross. The top of the banner read Iron and the bottom read Warrior. Another banner was underneath Warrior with the numbers 714. It was the Shield of Truth, specialized for The Iron Warrior.

Meanwhile, above the fray, Sensation and Luc viewed the chaos. Sensation felt hope as she watched The Iron Warrior fight Abaddon.

"Luc, I told you he isn't going to break. He's too strong. I don't see where this is going to help us. It's destruction for the sake of destruction," urged Sensation.

"There is never anything wrong with destruction. But you're about to witness his demise, my dear," Luc smiled.

Luc's confidence made Sensation uneasy. She was hopeful that The Iron Warrior could keep up the fight, but unsure what Luc had in store for him.

Back on the street, Abaddon bombarded The Warrior with fireballs. One of the fireballs destroyed a fire hydrant. Water shot from it into the air. Water rained down and landed on Abaddon. Its flames dwindled while Abaddon tried to escape the water. The Warrior noticed how the water affected it.

He ran over to the hydrant and placed the Shield of Faith in the water stream. He guided the water onto Abaddon and tried to drown out its flames. His confidence and faith rose. As Abaddon backed down, the street flooded from the excess water. The police officers backed away and cleared the area, which only left The Iron Warrior and Juggernaut amid the growing flood.

The Warrior's right gauntlet opened as he approached Abaddon. A flaming sword extended into his hand. It was the Sword of the Spirit. He accessed the full Armor of God. He ran toward Abaddon and hit

     T. V. HOLIDAY

it with a jumping knee in the face that knocked Abaddon underneath the water. He used the shield to pummel Abaddon and broke the horns on its head. He used the Sword of the Spirit and sliced one of the ivory blades off its forearm. He stood over Abaddon and raised the Sword of the Spirit over his head. He was ready to end the battle and destroy Abaddon. Before he could stab it, he heard a woman scream behind him.

He looked back toward The Pavilion entrance and saw Domino, who had been pushed into the water that had built up. Cassidy, Vivian, and Lovelyn were behind her. Domino's lips were busted and she bled from her nose. Her clothes were torn. It looked like she had been in a fight. Lovelyn grabbed Domino by her hair and stood her up. She wrapped her arm around Domino's throat and held a gun to her head. Domino cried out in pain. Her distress angered him.

"Shut up, you traitorous bitch!" Lovelyn shouted as she pushed the gun into Domino's temple.

"Hey, Iron Dipshit!! We got your favorite here. We found this cunt trying to be all righteous. Drop the sword and shield," Cassidy told him.

"Let her go, Cassidy!!!" The Iron Warrior shouted as he dropped the sword and shield.

"That's not up to us. It's up to the boss," Cassidy responded as she looked up toward Sensation, who was in the window.

Sensation watched in shock. She was unaware of what they were doing. She looked for Luc, but he was nowhere to be found. Sidious and Coldred flanked her on either side. She looked down and made eye contact with The Iron Warrior. Anger rose on her face, but she didn't know what they were going to do.

"Sensation, don't do this!!! Let her go!!!" The Iron Warrior desperately shouted.

"Renounce your faith or I drive a bullet through this bitch's skull," Lovelyn threatened.

Fear for Domino's life overtook him. He looked at Domino and thought of her daughter, Ashley. The Iron Warrior glanced at Sensation and doubt crept into his heart. He wondered if everything they shared was a ploy just for that moment. He thought about the consequences of giving up his faith. He had to find another option. He had to find another way to save Domino. Anger began to fill his heart.

"Choose! Warrior!!!!" Vivian shouted. "Your faith or her life. Think about her daughter. Are you really going to let Ashley grow up without her Mom?"

The Iron Warrior looked up toward Sensation. He was desperate. He pleaded, "Sensation, please don't let this happen. Call them off."

Sensation wanted to help. She didn't want them to kill Domino. She said that she wanted her soul. The moment arrived to try and earn it back. She decided to call them off. She would deal with whatever the consequences would be for her.

Lovelyn shoved Domino ahead of her. Domino looked toward the Iron Warrior as her eyes filled with tears.

"Promise to take care of Ashley. Don't let my girl fall into any of this. Please…" Domino cried.

The Iron Warrior became teary-eyed as well. "I promise… but…"

"Kill her," Sensation's voice echoed from The Pavilion.

A loud BANG reverberated throughout the parking lot and street. Blood splattered forward. Lovelyn shot Domino in the head and cackled loudly.

"NOOOOOOO!!!!" The Iron Warrior wailed.

Domino began to fall forward as The Iron Warrior ran to catch her. He didn't make it in time. Domino fell into the water. He knelt and cradled her in his arms. "Domino!!! Domino!!!" he shouted while he shook her, but she was nonresponsive. Her eyes rolled into the back of her head. She died in his arms. The Iron Warrior cried as he held her lifeless body.

Lovelyn, Cassidy, and Vivian laughed as they ran away. The Iron Warrior looked up toward Sensation. She stared back at him. The anger he felt turned to rage. His love for Sensation began to vanish. Sensation, Sidious, and Coldred moved from the window and back into The Pavilion. He looked around at the bodies of the people who worked in his building. He looked at Domino and rage flooded his soul.

As the rage and sadness filled him, his body began to ache. The pain ravaged his body. He was getting weaker. He was aware of his feelings but couldn't fight against the rage. The Warrior felt another burst of pain. He looked down and saw an ivory blade protruding through his abdomen. Abaddon was back!

He howled in pain as Abaddon lifted him off the ground. It hurled him back into the growing flood. It leaped in the air and landed feet first onto his upper body. The Iron Warrior felt multiple ribs crack as blood spurted out of his mouth. The water rushed in and made him choke.

Abaddon lifted him out of the water and bearhugged him. The Warrior rapidly lost oxygen. More ribs cracked. Without the oxygen, he couldn't yell. He was losing consciousness. The Warrior began to fade.

Explosions from within The Pavilion rattled the street. The explosives Vivian, Cassidy, and Lovelyn placed throughout the building went off. Multiple bombs exploded at the entrance. The impact broke Abaddon's bearhug and propelled them into separate directions. Parts of The Pavilion began to cave in. Debris and rubble filled the street. Downtown Carnage Coast became a full-blown disaster area.

The Iron Warrior crashed through a glass window into a hardware store. The water quickly flooded the store. He regained consciousness as blood poured from his stab wound. His face was cut from the glass shards. The Iron Warrior was tired and weak. His heart was empty. There was no more love inside. His faith was present, but he was overcome with rage. The smell of smoke became closer. Abaddon was coming.

He looked around for a weapon to defend himself. He found a chainsaw nearby. He grabbed it and pulled the cord, but it didn't start. The smell of smoke filled his nose and he could hear Abaddon breathing. He pulled the cord again and it started. He struggled to get to his feet and turned around.

Abaddon swung his ivory blade at The Warrior but he blocked it with the chainsaw. He tried to cut the blade; however, it was too strong. Abaddon reached back and wildly swung the blade again. The Warrior tried to block it again, but Abaddon's strength knocked the chainsaw out of his hands and he fell into the water.

A light illuminated nearby underneath the water. It was the Sword of the Spirit. He reached for it, but Abaddon choked him. The Warrior inched for the sword. He was quickly losing oxygen. His lungs were starting to fill with water. He got his fingertips on the sword and grabbed it. He swung the sword at Abaddon's neck and chopped off its head.

Its grip immediately loosened and it keeled over. The Iron Warrior sat up and gasped for air. He scooted away and stumbled to his feet and staggered out of the store. He looked across the street and saw The Pavilion was in shambles. He surveyed the damage. The bodies and destruction sank him. Although Abaddon had been defeated, he felt like he lost too. Carnage Coast looked like the war zone he had imagined upon his arrival. He heard yelling in the distance but couldn't make out what it was. His vision blurred. He did not have any strength. The Iron Warrior collapsed into the water.

Chapter
31

Sidious and Coldred took Sensation back to The Pit. Coldred threw her over his shoulder and carried her to the living quarters on the top floor. She tried to fight her way out of his grip, but he was too strong. Sidious followed behind and grinned maniacally as she struggled. They entered the apartment and Coldred threw her on a nearby couch.

"What the hell are you two? I thought you were with me. Why are you doing this?" Sensation snapped at them. She stood and tried to shove Coldred, but he didn't move.

Coldred leaned over and removed his sunglasses, which revealed flames in his eyes. She gasped. She had never seen his eyes before.

"We were with you. You stopped being with us. Our loyalty has always been with Luc, not you. You betrayed us for the dumbass who just got his ass whooped by Abaddon. This is on you," Coldred told her.

"You were supposed to bring him on our side. You flipped instead. Now, you're going to stay here until the rally. You're going to get a chance to redeem yourself to Luc and all of us there," Sidious chimed in.

"But that is a week away, you expect me to stay locked up in this room. Like on house arrest?" Sensation asked angrily.

Lovelyn sauntered into the room and stepped around Sidious and Coldred. She arrogantly slapped Sensation, who became enraged. She stepped toward Lovelyn but was blocked by Sidious. He inserted his finger in front of her and waved it.

"Nuh uh," said Sidious. "She gets to do what she wants."

Lovelyn turned and kissed Sidious aggressively. They developed a wicked relationship filled with lust. Her love for aggression matched his maniacal drive. Lovelyn looked back at Sensation, who was confused.

"I can thank you for this here," said Lovelyn as she leaned against Sidious' chest. "You thought you were punishing me, but we've had nothing but fun. You can have your punk ass Warrior if he's still alive. We knew you went soft. You're not that bitch anymore. I'm that bitch now. You're lucky house arrest is all that's going to happen. Luc won't let us do more than that."

"Why did you kill Domino? I didn't give that order. That was never something I would tell you to do," demanded Sensation.

A sadistic smile spread across Lovelyn's face. "Oh, really, because I'm pretty sure I heard your voice; now, didn't I?" she said sarcastically.

Sensation's eyes watered, "I never said that. That was somebody else… I never gave that order. She had a kid, Lovelyn. Domino didn't deserve that."

"Deserve!!!" Lovelyn interjected loudly. "I can give two shit about her kid. The little bitch is going to die soon anyway. Domino was letting people out of the building. She was weak and had no place for what we're doing."

The pain and anguish of Domino's death bubbled within Sensation. Tears of anger rolled down her cheek. "You're going to pay for Domino. I'm going to make sure of it."

Lovelyn and Sidious laughed. "You're going to pay for this," she said mockingly. "Let me tell you somethin'. Cash in on it! I'll be waitin'. It'll be you and me. You're not gonna' have anybody standing with you. I'm gonna' tax that ass for as long as I want before I blow your brains out too."

"I won't be alone," Sensation told them defiantly.

"Oh really!" Coldred exclaimed. "Don't tell me you're talking about The Iron Warrior. What was the last thing he heard from you?"

"Yeah, Sensation, think about it," said Sidious. "The last thing he heard from you was that you gave the order to kill Domino."

"I didn't say it. It wasn't me," Sensation indignantly retorted.

"It doesn't matter if you did or didn't," Lovelyn sarcastically told her. "Your boyfriend begged for help and you weren't there. He heard your voice and that's all that matters. I saw the look in his eyes. Whatever love you think you two had, it's gone."

Sensation furiously shook her head, "He knows me. He knows I wouldn't say yes."

"Does he, though? Think about everything you've put him through. This seems like something you'd do. All of this just to break him…. Tsk, tsk, tsk, I don't know Sensation. If he survived Abaddon, maybe we'll find out," Sidious insinuated.

"And if there is anything left, Sid and I are going to make sure we finish him. No more pussyfooting. And quite frankly, I can't wait," said Coldred.

Lovelyn removed a cellphone from her pocket and dropped it on the floor. "Why don't you give him a call? I'm sure he'll be thrilled to hear from you."

Sidious, Coldred, and Lovelyn left Sensation and locked the door from the outside. She fell to her knees and cried. Everything fell apart so quickly. She had to let Travis know that she didn't give the order to kill Domino. She wasn't sure if he would believe her. Sensation decided she had to take the chance. It was the only thing she could do.

Sensation called his phone, and her heartbeat raced with every ring. There was no answer, and it went straight to voicemail. She left a message:

"Travis, I hope you're okay. I'm locked in The Pit. They all turned on me. I didn't plan that. I didn't give the order to kill Domino. I know you heard my voice, but, baby, I swear I didn't say it. I was going to say no and take whatever consequences that would've come from it. Somebody said it in my voice. Please believe me. I love you. I really love you. Being together with you has been the most special I've ever felt in my life. I want my soul. I want a life with you. That wasn't a lie. I'm choosing God. I'm choosing you. Please believe me."

Meanwhile, Cassidy left The Pit and was satisfied with the course of events from the day. She didn't have feelings for Domino. Her death wouldn't put a hamper on their plans moving forward. Cassidy approached her car, which was parked in the corner of the lot. As Cassidy opened the door, she heard footsteps behind her. Before she could turn around, her head was rammed into the door frame. The impact knocked her dizzy. A white cloth filled with ammonia covered her mouth. Cassidy tried to fight back but quickly passed out. The person shoved Cassidy into the car and slid in next to her. The person searched Cassidy's pockets and found the keys. She started the car and sped out of the lot.

T. V. HOLIDAY

The Iron Warrior was out for five days after his encounter with Abaddon. Hicks found him after he passed out. Despite his immediate need for medical attention, Hicks took him to Last Hope. He believed Mike could give him the best care. Mike treated The Warrior's wounds and prayed over him daily. He slowly healed and his abdomen wound closed but was still battered and bruised.

Beads of cold-water droplets ran down his forehead and into his eye sockets. The Iron Warrior's eyes fluttered. He opened them but could barely see. His vision was blurred. The room was dimly lit. He felt a cold, wet rag on his forehead, with minimal pressure applied. His body was hot to the touch. As his eyesight returned, he saw a figure standing beside him.

He blinked his eyes more and focused his vision. As his eyesight returned, he could tell the figure was an older woman with a slim build. Her brunette hair was highlighted with strands of gray. She wore a purple blouse with flowers imprinted on it—a pearl necklace draped her neck. Large gold earrings hung from her ears. She wore gold, square-shaped glasses that accentuated her brown eyes.

"Who are you?" The Iron Warrior asked groggily.

"That's a good question. You're always out of here before we can get a chance to meet. My name is Shannah. I'm Mike's wife," said Shannah.

The Iron Warrior was surprised at her revelation. He felt comforted knowing Shannah was there. He knew he was in a safe place. He wished he had met her under better circumstances. He tried to sit up but felt jolts of pain throughout his body. He was wracked with pain and felt weak. He lay back down, taking heavy breaths.

"Now, now, now, you stay still. You're in really bad shape. Even though it's been a few days, you still have a long way to go," said Shannah as she tried to make him comfortable.

Shannah's comments made The Warrior pause. "A few days? How long have I been out?" he asked in shock.

"Five days," answered Shannah.

The Iron Warrior had a hard time wrapping his head around the news. He had been out for only two days after his fight in the hospital. His recovery times were getting longer. He worried about what could've happened while he was out.

"You were near death. It's a miracle your wound closed. God has his hands on you, my boy," said Shannah.

Shannah's comments struck a chord with him. The mere thought of God's presence made him question his existence in Carnage Coast. The thought that God oversaw all the chaos in his life angered him. To think of all the hurt God allowed him to be subjected to made him depressed.

"God has his hands on me? This has been hell. I've been stabbed, shot, beaten with a crowbar, set on fire, almost drowned, loved, and dumped all within a matter of almost two months. Like... why?" The Iron Warrior desperately asked.

"Why is that a question? God has a distinct path for all of us. All walks are not the same," Shannah answered. There was a wisdom in her voice that gave her an air of credibility.

"I know, but everyone who came before me didn't have the stakes I have. I'm trying to hold on, but it's getting difficult. This is the second time I woke up to a woman taking care of me. I can't stay strong enough to fight how I'm supposed to, so I don't get hurt. I'm human. All I wanted was my family and that was ripped away from me. I wanted a woman to love, and I fought for it. Yet here I am busted up. Another person I should've looked out for is dead. I'm not good at this. God was wrong. I can't fight this battle," The Iron Warrior cried out.

Shannah wanted to fully understand everything he said before she responded. He cupped his face in his hands and tried to keep himself from breaking down. He was overcome with emotion. She gently placed her hand over his heart. She could feel his pain.

"God was not wrong. He's never wrong. We can never become the person we're meant to be if we never go through the trials he places before us. Everything you've faced has brought you here. You're going to have to bear losses. The ones before you had their crosses to bear. You were chosen for this fight. Take pride in knowing God believes you can fight this battle for all of us. You have to realize you're not alone. When you don't feel strong, there are those of us around to help keep you strong. You can quit if you want. But if you were going to quit so easily, God wouldn't have chosen you," explained Shannah.

The Iron Warrior broke down. He didn't have anything more left in him. Shannah's words echoed in his ears. He couldn't comprehend being chosen for the life he was living. He wanted his time in Carnage Coast to be over. He didn't want to fight anymore.

A vibrating noise could be heard across the room. It kept repeating. It was his cellphone. Hicks retrieved it while he was unconscious. Shannah picked up the phone and gave it to him. The caller was Sensation. Upon seeing her name, he tossed his phone to the floor.

"She has called a lot the last few days. Why don't you want to speak to her?" asked Shannah.

"I can't speak to her right now. I don't know what to think about her," The Warrior frustratingly admitted.

"Isn't she the one you were willing to put us all at risk for?" Shannah asked.

The Iron Warrior cut his eyes toward Shannah and noticed an indignant look on her face.

"Oh, don't look at me like that. Mike's my husband. I know what's going on with you. You've gotten exactly what you asked for, so what's the problem?" Shannah told him frankly.

Shannah's disclosure humbled him. "I don't know if she's genuine or not. One minute, she's telling me how much she wants me and giving me all this love and affection. But she is also the one who has put me through a lot. I thought I had a good understanding of who she is. Maybe I don't."

"What changed?" asked Shannah.

"She gave the order to have Domino killed. I still can't believe she did that. Before all of that happened, she was in my arms, telling me how much she wanted her soul. No sooner than she said that, the city went to hell," The Warrior explained.

"Did you see her give the order?"

"No. But what difference does it make? I heard it. I heard her voice, and I'll never forget it," said The Warrior.

"How can you be so sure it was her? Yes, you heard her, but you have to remember what we are dealing with. There are monsters and magic in our world. How can you be so sure unless you saw it with your own eyes?" asked Shannah.

The Iron Warrior paused and thought about Shannah's words. He didn't see Sensation mouth the words. He recognized her voice, though. The Warrior remained silent. He had been so angry about Domino's death that his feelings about Sensation started to become an afterthought.

"How much do you like this woman? It has to be love, right? If not love, then why feel this way? Why so angry? Why so upset?" Shannah continued.

"I started to feel love for her. Loving her made me feel like me again," The Iron Warrior admitted solemnly.

"Ahhh, and there it is!" Shannah exclaimed. "Are you upset because she isn't who you thought she was? Or not being able to be who you've been?"

"I don't know," he stammered. "I've spent my adult life loving someone. It feels like that's all I know. Sensation was a chance to do that again. A chance to be the me I know."

"Yes, but who are you without someone to love?"

Shannah's question struck him to his core. He didn't have a response for her. He pondered her words and re-asked himself the question multiple times in his head.

"You are a warrior. Warriors serve and give themselves for the good of others. Service is a sacrifice. God's heart is that of a servant. Servants love the deepest. A warrior's greatest power is love. It's their greatest power. They're boosted by it. The marks of a warrior are the wounds of love, service, and fighting the great fight. You are a warrior. You were made for this. You've wanted someone to love. But now is the time to love without having someone. Show real love by truly giving it to everyone you see. Maybe this is what God wants you to see," said Shannah.

The Iron Warrior still didn't have any words for a response. He only listened.

"Loving someone will happen again. You have to have faith. Faith is invisible. It allows us to hope confidently. Faith reminds us of our humanity. It reminds us that we can't do this on our own. We were never designed to operate outside of it. The faith we search for is hidden in our fears. Faith and Love go hand in hand. You need to find who you are without anyone else. Until then, it's up to you to love without restriction because you are a warrior. Doing that solidifies your faith. It only makes you stronger. Whether Sensation is with you or not, love her," Shannah told him.

Mike and Hicks entered the room. Mike kissed Shannah's forehead while Hicks stood beside The Warrior. They were surprised to see him awake and grew anxious while he was out. They asked how he was doing. He had difficulty responding. His conversation with Shannah weighed on him. He struggled to sit up and grimaced as Mike stepped over to assist.

"As my uncle used to say, I've seen better days," The Iron Warrior said.

"I hate to say it, but we need better right now. You woke up just in time," Mike opened.

"We only have another day before the Free Love Rally. Downtown is still in shambles after your fight with that monster. The rally has been moved to outside of The Pit. We've got to figure out something. Sensation's people have been saying the fight with the monster has been all your fault. They're making you the fall guy for all of this," said Hicks

"It looks like it's working too. People seem like they're getting back on board with it. We have to do something about this rally," added Mike.

"Yeah, that and not to mention, we've found something on social media. We don't know if it's part of the Free Love Rally, but something called the Love Countdown is set to happen that day. Our Criminal Intelligence Unit has been trying to get to the bottom of it, but nothing so far," Hicks chimed in.

The Iron Warrior's mind wasn't present. He heard Hicks and Mike, but his thoughts were still on Shannah's words. He asked for his phone and Hicks gave it to him. The Iron Warrior forced himself to stand. Mike rushed over to help, but The Warrior waved him off. He wanted to stand on his own.

"You okay?" asked Mike.

"No, but I'll be fine eventually. I really appreciate all of you taking care of me. I know there's a lot to talk about, but I can't right now. I need to go. I need to be alone," The Warrior told them.

He looked at Shannah and flashed her a broken smile. The Warrior hobbled out, leaving Hicks and Mike flabbergasted. They only had one day before the rally and five days before the actual vote. They were running out of time. He returned home and changed back into Travis. He listened to Lynda's voicemail. He felt a flurry of emotions and threw his phone. He settled into the emptiness of the room. As he stood in silence, Travis could hear nothing but his thoughts. Lynda made her decision. He had to make his.

Chapter
33

The day of the rally arrived. Downtown Carnage Coast had multiple construction vehicles and cones littered throughout the streets. The area surrounding The Pavilion was blocked off from traffic. The water receded, allowing construction crews to begin rebuilding. The streets were left in rubble from The Iron Warrior's battle with Abaddon.

The area surrounding The Pit remained intact. Digital billboards stood tall and The Pit was illuminated with various digital screens. Sensation's face and Free Love Initiative propaganda were all over The Pit. A stage was erected in front of it for the rally. Speakers were on the outskirts of the stage and an area was designated for a live band. Vivian and Lovelyn set up the event to function like a large party.

The rally was set to kick off at 2 p.m. Sensation remained locked in her room. She watched helplessly as The Donnas set up the rally. They planned for her to give a speech as the face of the Free Love Initiative. Lovelyn, Coldred, and Sidious threatened to kill her if she went against them. Vivian took control of the news and promised it would be a safe haven from The Iron Warrior and his destructive ways. She accused him of being selfish and not present when it was time to help people after the battle. With Vivian's narrative, public opinion shifted back in favor of the Initiative. She set up early registration booths for citizens. Police Officers, including Hicks, were present for crowd control and safety. She and Lovelyn hoped it would close the deal on the Initiative before the vote two days later.

Music bounced off the buildings. The live band brought a vibrant energy to the atmosphere. Donnas danced on stage and walked through the crowd in scantily clad clothing. It was reminiscent of a walk down the Las Vegas Strip. Mayor James was present along with many others. Vivian kicked off the event with an opening address and promised a Sensational appearance.

Lovelyn and Sidious went to get Sensation. She wore black jeans, a black tank top, and a purple leather jacket. The jacket matched her purple high-heeled boots. She walked by them without saying a word.

She felt The Donnas' hatred for her as she walked through the crowd. Sensation made eye contact with Coldred, who stood at the opposite end of the stage. He glared at her with a stone-like expression. Sensation looked back and saw Lovelyn and Coldred, who devilishly grinned. Vivian introduced her to a raucous ovation. Before she could take a step, Lovelyn grabbed her arm and told her not to mess up. Sensation snatched her arm away and went to grab the microphone from Vivian. Vivian held onto it and leaned toward her ear.

"Watch your mouth," Vivian warned her.

Sensation snatched the microphone out of her hand and faced the crowd. She looked at everyone and saw children present as well. The noise died down, giving her a chance to speak.

"Thank you for that introduction," Sensation opened. "I've literally thought about this all week. I'm amazed so many of you are here. When I look at you, I see people who want to be loved and accepted at any cost. I've felt that way. I'd have given anything to be loved. I had been hurt so much that I stopped believing it was possible. I felt like it shouldn't be hard to love somebody. Just love whoever you want and do whatever you want. That sounds like ultimate freedom. And with ultimate freedom should come true love. But I didn't get that. I got pain. And when I looked around, I saw people who were in pain like me. All I wanted to do was get away from it. To do whatever I could to make sure I didn't wake up with it anymore. But then something happened… I met a guy.

"He came to me when I was at my lowest. I was broken in every way. He healed me and promised me all the love I ever wanted. It would only cost my soul. I gave it to him in a heartbeat. But soon after, things weren't what he promised. He said that he'd be the guy for me. But then he said there was someone else for me. He used my voice without my permission. It cost someone her life. He betrayed me and turned everyone against me. And yet I gave him my soul.

"Then I met another guy. He was the one the other guy said was for me. I pushed too hard at first. When I slowed things down, I got to know him. He's one of the good guys, y'know. He got really excited at the thought of loving me. He never asked me for anything. He was willing to go through hell just to be with me. He asked me to throw everything at him. He loved me through it all. Now all I want is to be with him. That may not be possible anymore. The man to whom I gave my soul manipulated us. He drove a wedge between us. I've been crying all week. Hoping the guy I love is still alive. Hoping there may still be a future for us. Hoping he believes me. But that may not happen now. And it's all because of the man who deceived me.

"Why am I telling you this? I'm telling you because the man who deceived and fooled me is the same man behind this Initiative. The Free Love Initiative was my idea. We have so much lust in us. All we want to do is please ourselves. Lust has a price; love doesn't. I'm paying for my decision. Don't sign for this Initiative. Don't vote for it. If you do, you'll condemn all of us to hell. That's exactly what the man I gave my soul to wants. He wants you to reject God. He wants you to give in to your desires at any cost. He's counting on it.

"If you're wondering about the man I love, you already know him. He's The Iron Warrior. He isn't the man you've heard about lately. The Iron Warrior is…" said Sensation before she was cut off.

Lovelyn ran across the stage and dropkicked her. Coldred and Sidious approached while the crowd watched in shock. They didn't know what to make of Sensation's speech. As she sat up, she felt the ecstasy rise throughout her body. It was a feeling she hadn't felt in a while.

"I told you not to screw this up, didn't I?" Lovelyn said as she stood over Sensation.

The ecstasy energized Sensation. "Like I give a damn!" she responded.

Sidious, Coldred, and Lovelyn laughed at her response. Lovelyn leaned over and laughed in Sensation's face. Before she could speak, a folded metal chair was thrown from behind the stage. It struck Lovelyn's face and knocked her into the crowd. Sidious, Coldred, and Sensation looked at where the chair came from. Sensation was in utter disbelief as a figure stepped onto the stage. Sidious and Coldred stared in anger. It was The Iron Warrior. He was still wounded from his battle with Abaddon and had a noticeable limp.

"Don't tell me you thought I was going to miss this party," The Iron Warrior joked. He looked at Sensation and winked. "Hi, baby," he said softly.

"It's about time," said Coldred as he clenched his fists.

"Party time!" Sidious exclaimed. "Looks like Abaddon left just enough for us to stomp out. Plus, you threw a chair at my girl. Who does that?"

"She had it coming," The Warrior frankly stated. "Punch your tickets, it's showtime."

Before they could engage, a large number 10 flashed on The Pit's digital screen. The number 9 flashed as the countdown proceeded. It was The Love Countdown. It grabbed everyone's attention. None of them knew what it was in reference to.

The screen flashed an image of a woman strapped in a rolling chair on a rooftop. The camera zoomed in and revealed it was Cassidy. Her hands and ankles were tied to the chair. She bled from her mouth and her eyes were blackened. Her clothes were torn, and she sat slumped over as a snickering voice came through the speaker.

"Such a moving speech, Sensation! I didn't see that coming. And here it is, I was planning to run down the Free Love Initiative. You did it for me," an angry voice blared.

A woman stepped in front of the camera. It was Brittany. She held a knife and waved it back and forth.

"Although I have to disagree with you about The Iron Warrior. For all the good he has done, he's responsible for so much pain. Look at what he did to the city. Look at what he did to me!!! No, no, no, no, no, no. Don't vote for the Free Love Initiative. Don't support The Real Love Movement. Fuck all of it! Some of you may recognize me, but do you recognize who is with me?" Brittany angrily shouted.

She walked toward Cassidy and slapped her. She placed the knife underneath her chin and yanked her hair back. Cassidy whimpered while Brittany reveled in her terror. She played with the knife and tapped it against her throat.

"This is the other star in my video. This is the coldhearted bitch who wanted to make me a Diabolical Donna. I'm making my own video now and I'm going to break her. So, this is for The Iron Warrior. If you're not here in 20 minutes, I'm going to gut this sleazy slut from taint to sternum," Brittany threatened.

Upon seeing the video, Hicks decided to go after Brittany. He looked at the video and examined the surrounding imagery. He scanned the nearby buildings and noticed one with a possible view similar to the one in the video. It was the Ford Building. The Ford Building was seven stories high. Hicks raced to the building to stop Brittany.

On the stage, The Warrior was torn. He needed to get to the rooftop to stop Brittany, but couldn't leave Sensation with Sidious and Coldred. Sidious lunged at him but was caught in mid-air. The Warrior placed his hand on Sidious' chest and shoved him through the stage. He faced Coldred, who wildly swung at him. The Warrior ducked a flurry of punches and kicked him square in his chest. The kick rattled Coldred's ribcage and forced him back. Warrior tried to keep up with him in his weakened state.

Coldred ran toward The Warrior and tried to clothesline him. The Warrior ducked and jabbed his ribs. Coldred winced as he spun around. The Warrior wanted to punch him again but was blocked. Coldred drove his knee into The Warrior's abdomen and knocked the wind out of him, as he bent over in pain. Coldred elbowed the center of his back, knocking him down.

Coldred went to kick him in his ribs, but The Warrior caught his leg and backdropped him. The Warrior staggered to his feet and created distance between them. Coldred got back up and charged at him again. The Warrior tried to move, but the floorboard broke beneath him. Sidious's hands came up and pulled his foot through the stage. The Warrior looked up and Coldred kicked his face.

Meanwhile, Sensation tried to stand, but her leg was pulled out from under her. Lovelyn climbed atop Sensation.

"We're gonna' beat you and your boyfriend for the whole city to see. And then I'm gonna' go kill that ho who got Cass," laughed Lovelyn.

Lovelyn punched Sensation, cutting her eye. She rained down a succession of forearms to open up the wound. Blood poured and covered the lower half of Sensation's face. She wasn't a fighter, but she tried to defend herself and clawed Lovelyn's face. The scratch burned Lovelyn, who shrieked in agony. Lovelyn crawled away and held her face.

The crowd continued to watch in amazement. They weren't sure if a real fight was happening in front of them, or if a woman's life was in serious jeopardy. Vivian took the microphone and told the crowd that Sensation's words were lies. She stated that The Iron Warrior and Sensation would be taken care of shortly and they could get back to the rally soon enough.

Meanwhile, Hicks found the right rooftop and kicked open the door. He made eye contact with Brittany, who stood over Cassidy. He noticed a cameraman standing nearby recording the entire incident. He was saddened to see the state she was in. She seemed to be in a healthy state of mind. Hicks was disappointed to see what she was doing. He wanted to believe the situation could end well, but was very hesitant. He ran toward her. She stood behind Cassidy and placed the knife underneath her neck again.

She exhaled heavily upon seeing him. He was the last person she wanted to see. She didn't want him involved. Her actions were meant only for The Iron Warrior. Cassidy tried to speak, but Brittany covered her mouth. Brittany sliced her cheek and told her to keep her mouth shut. Cassidy squirmed in misery.

"Jesus, Jimmy, what are you doing here?" she frustratingly shouted.

"Dammit, kid, stop it! Don't do this. Don't do something you can't come back from," Hicks begged.

"Stop trying to protect me, Jimmy. This has nothing to do with you. The Iron Warrior and this cunt are going to pay for what they did," Brittany snapped.

Hicks took small steps toward her. Her outrage worried him. "Brittany put the knife down. The Iron Warrior apologized. This isn't the way. Please drop the knife. I don't want anybody to get hurt. Please put it down," he urged.

Brittany lowered the knife and spat at Cassidy's face. She stepped around her and walked toward Hicks. He was hesitant to reach for his gun. He was conflicted. Brittany dropped the knife to his relief and cried. She hugged him and broke down.

"I'm sorry, Jimmy," Brittany cried.

"It's okay, kid. I get it. We can make this right. I'm going to untie her. It'll be fine," he assured.

Hicks went over and began untying the rope around Cassidy's ankles. Cassidy pleaded for him to hurry. Brittany walked up behind him and removed the gun from his holster. Hicks reached for his gun, but it was too late. He dreadfully looked back at Brittany as she aimed his gun at him. He was frozen in disbelief. He raised his hand to motion for Brittany. She shot him in the leg and he crumpled in pain. Brittany shot Cassidy in her legs as well and wiped the tears from her face.

"I'm sorry, Jimmy. I didn't want to hurt you, but you got in my way. Now you're a part of this. If you try to get in my way any further, I'm going to have to kill you. Go over there and stay put," said Brittany.

She turned toward the camera and smiled, "Tick tock, Warrior, tick tock!"

Sidious came up from underneath the stage to help Coldred fight The Iron Warrior. They overwhelmed and battered him. They mercilessly punched and kicked him. The Warrior was losing strength. He had enough faith to stay alive but was too weak to fight them off. He needed to stop them and Brittany.

Sensation saw The Iron Warrior was in trouble. She ran over to help, but Coldred removed a handgun from underneath his jacket and shot her twice. She fell while the crowd panicked and fled. The police officers tried to get control, but they were overpowered. The Warrior shouted in rage. He stood to go after Coldred and Sidious, but Lovelyn fired ten shots at his upper body and legs that dropped him to the floor.

The Iron Warrior wailed in pain. He bled profusely while Sensation's wounds slowly healed. Sidious and Coldred propped The Iron Warrior on his knees and held his arms. He struggled to remain conscious as the crowd turned into a sea of pandemonium. Hicks and Cassidy were being held hostage on the roof, and there was no way he could get to them.

Brittany appeared on the video screen again. She stood near the ledge with Cassidy, who was untied from the chair. Cassidy could barely stand. She screamed for help while Brittany heckled her.

"Time's up, Warrior. Now she gets to earn her red wings," said Brittany.

Brittany stabbed Cassidy in her chest and pulled the knife down through her abdomen. Cassidy squealed in agony. Brittany pushed her from the rooftop. Cassidy's body exploded onto the ground to Brittany's delight. Hicks screamed at Brittany, but it was to no avail. He was unable to protect Cassidy as he had sworn to do.

"We're not done yet, Warrior! The cameraman is next. Fifteen minutes this time," she warned.

Back on the stage, The Iron Warrior was in jeopardy. He remembered Shannah's words about bearing losses. He understood that would be a reality. He couldn't stomach what Brittany did. Lovelyn watched Brittany kill Cassidy and wanted vengeance for her friend. She felt a tinge of sadness before refocusing on The Iron Warrior and Sensation.

"Let him go," cried Sensation.

Lovelyn laughingly walked up to her, "Aww, how cute. He's gonna' die right now. Either from you… or from us."

Sensation was confused, "What are you talking about?"

"Either you kiss him, or we're gonna' put a bullet in his head," Lovelyn threatened.

Sensation's heart sank as she looked at him. His head was hung low. He was bleeding out and at the mercy of Coldred and Sidious. She walked toward him and knelt. She held his head up and looked into his eyes. Tears spilled from their eyes. She pressed her forehead against his and closed her eyes. She pleaded, "Please don't make me do this."

Lovelyn knelt across from them. "The choice is yours. We'll happily put a bullet in his head," she cackled.

The Warrior tried to speak but coughed up more blood. He struggled to talk but fought to get words out. "I can take it. You're not going to hurt me. I believe you. I love you," he said.

Sensation opened her eyes and looked at him one last time. He gave her a faint smile as he struggled to keep his head up. "I love you too, baby," she cried.

Sensation leaned forward and kissed The Iron Warrior. She pulled him closer and pressed her body against his. She held him tightly and kissed him with all the love she had. She didn't want to let him go. Coldred and Sidious let him go, and The Warrior embraced her with both arms. Smoke rose from his body. Sidious, Coldred, and Lovelyn backed away as the smoke grew thicker. His body ignited in flames. Sensation slowly backed away and watched him become enflamed. The Warrior bellowed while the flames grew and changed from orange to blue. Electricity sparked from his eyes. Fire flamed from his mouth. What was left of the crowd shouted in terror while Sidious, Coldred, and Lovelyn grinned in delight.

Sensation felt another rush of ecstasy. She closed her eyes and cupped her face. She couldn't handle seeing him set on fire. She heard gasps from Sidious, Coldred, and Lovelyn nearby. She looked up and couldn't believe what she saw.

The blue flame that engulfed The Iron Warrior simmered. His screams lowered to utter silence, and he inhaled the flames. His white armor changed and half of it turned black. His gunshot wounds closed. There were no more traces of blood. He opened his eyes and they sparked with electricity and white flames. He stood as everyone gazed in astonishment.

"It's not possible! You're supposed to be dead," said Coldred.

"Baby!!!" Sensation shouted. She jumped up and leaped into his arms.

The Warrior hugged her and whispered, "I told you I could take it. Now let's finish this," he happily told her.

Sensation faced Lovelyn while Vivian ran away. The Warrior turned around and faced Sidious and Coldred. His right gauntlet opened and the Sword of the Spirit extended into his hand. He charged at Coldred and wildly swung it but missed. Sidious kicked The Warrior's back, but he barely budged. Sidious removed a crystal pellet from his pocket and smashed it on the ground. Smoke exploded and blinded The Warrior's vision. Coldred kicked the Sword of the Spirit out of his hand and it slid near Lovelyn and Sensation.

Sidious and Coldred tried to tag-team The Warrior again, but to no avail. Their punches and kicks had no effect. Coldred fired more shots at him, but the bullets bounced off The Warrior's back. They began to doubt their chances against him. The smoke cleared and The Warrior could see the Sword of the Spirit. He fought them back and went to pick it up. He saw Sidious in mid-air, leaping toward him. He swiped the Sword of the Spirit and sliced Sidious in half. His body fell in two as The Warrior flicked the blood off his sword.

On the other side of the stage, Sensation faced off with Lovelyn. She wildly swung her arms to scratch her, but missed. Lovelyn grabbed

     T. V. HOLIDAY

her jacket and used Sensation's momentum to flip her. She grabbed Sensation's head and rammed it against the floor multiple times. The force made Sensation dizzy and unable to fight back. Sensation was surprised that she felt any pain. It was the first time she felt any since she sold her soul.

"You fight like a bitch," Lovelyn laughed.

Lovelyn stood and stomped on Sensation's fingers. Sensation screamed and held her hands close to her chest. Lovelyn gleefully stomped on her stomach and repeatedly kicked her. Blood trickled down Sensation's forehead as she tried to cover up from Lovelyn's assault.

Back on the other side of the stage, Coldred and The Iron Warrior squared off.

"You can't take me one-on-one, can you?" Coldred arrogantly claimed.

The Iron Warrior withdrew the Sword of the Spirit back into his gauntlet. "Let's rock!"

Coldred opened up with a hard right to his face that turned The Warrior's head. He connected with more lefts and rights, but none of them had an effect. Coldred skeptically glared at him.

"My turn," smiled The Iron Warrior.

He leapt and hit Coldred with a jumping knee to his face. He unloaded with a series of punches to Coldred's face. He bludgeoned Coldred and rendered him defenseless. He sat up, Coldred, who had fallen, and clasped his head. The Warrior swiftly cranked Coldred's head and broke his neck. Although he felt like a strength unlike anything he had ever felt, he was relieved to be done with Sidious and Coldred.

On the other side of the stage, Lovelyn grabbed her gun and climbed on top of Sensation, who was battered and bloodied. She pointed the gun at her face and laughed, "You were supposed to make me hot bitch. You ain't hot enough for me."

Sensation swiped the gun away and reached for Lovelyn's face. She kissed her for one last gasp to save herself. Lovelyn shoved her off and aimed the gun back at her face. She felt a slight burning sensation pulsate throughout her body. She lifted her head and exhaled a breath of smoke. Sensation became dejected. She couldn't understand what was happening. The Iron Warrior didn't die from her kiss, and neither did Lovelyn.

"You're really not hot enough for me. Bye bye bitch!" Lovelyn hooted.

Before she could pull the trigger, another chair was hurled at her. The impact knocked her off her feet and the gun out of her hand. She held her head as she tried to recuperate.

"Okay, you really need to stop throwing chairs at me. I'm gonna' kill your slut, and then you're next," Lovelyn stated dizzily.

Sensation quickly grabbed the gun and shot Lovelyn multiple times. The blasts knocked her off the stage and onto the ground. The Iron Warrior ran over and held Sensation, who fell limp in his arms. She was relieved to know that her fight was over. He helped Sensation to her feet and hugged her tightly.

The video screen came back, showing them hugging from a distance.

"Hey Warrior!! I see you. How cute! You and your lady are together. Welp, I told you that you had fifteen minutes. And guess what, time is up! I want you to meet Brad. Say hi, Brad," Brittany's voice blared.

The camera shifted to the man she called Brad, who was very nervous. She aimed the gun at him. He tried to reason with her, but his words were ignored. He pleaded with Brittany, who took pleasure in his begging. She shot him in the chest, instantly killing him. She turned the camera toward Hicks as he struggled to his feet. He couldn't sit while she continued to kill people. He hobbled toward her, but she shot his other leg. Hicks fell and hollered in anguish. She turned the camera toward herself and gazed into the lens.

"You've got ten minutes for this one. And I'm begging you to get here. I don't want to do this one. Jimmy's a good guy, but he picked the wrong girl to try to save. You got ten minutes for him. If you don't

     T. V. HOLIDAY

make it for Jimmy, there will be one more that you won't be able to walk away from. I'll even give you a hint: we're at the Ford building. See you soon," Brittany yelled.

The Iron Warrior watched in horror. He had to save Hicks.

"Go get her baby. I'll see you when you get back," encouraged Sensation.

The Iron Warrior raced to the Ford Building. He reached the rooftop and found Brittany sitting in the chair where Cassidy sat. She was near the edge of the building. Hicks sat nearby, and his pants were covered in blood as sweat covered his face. He grimaced while she nonchalantly held him at gunpoint.

"You finally came. As usual, you're late. Still watching people suffer before you decide to step in, huh?" Brittany said.

"Why are you doing this?" The Iron Warrior asked. He stood across from Brittany and did not try to get closer.

"Why, why, why? That's the million-dollar question, isn't it?" responded Brittany. She stood and paced back and forth while carelessly pointing the firearm at Hicks. She smacked her head like she was trying to knock some sense into herself. "Come on, hero, you don't have any idea?"

"Brittany, please, why have you done this? I thought you were over this. He apologized. He didn't purposely press the button," Hicks chimed in, amid taking heavy breaths.

His words enraged her. She walked over to him and shook him by his collar. "Stop defending him, Jimmy! You're better than that. There's no defense for what he did."

"What do you want from me, Brittany? I apologized to you in the hospital. It's my fault that guy pressed the button. I truly wish I could take that one back. I only wanted to help you. I know there will never be enough apologies for it. I'm sorry," pleaded The Warrior.

"To hell with your sorry!" she shouted. "You have absolutely no idea what that night did to me. I believed in the Free Love Initiative.

I believed in Sensation. I wanted to be a Donna. My thoughts of the world were destroyed that night. But it wasn't enough, you showed up and blasted it for the world to see. They destroyed me, but you put the nail in my coffin, you self-righteous prick!!

"The woman I was died that night. Brittany died that night. Nobody saw me anymore. Everyone knew me as a victim. It didn't matter what I did before. It was all flushed away. My life has been all about that night. If there was any chance to heal and have some type of life, you took it from me. You robbed me of a future where I could've been happy. You forced this on me. You killed me!!! I hate you!!!" Brittany revealed.

The Iron Warrior hesitated before he gave her a response. He understood the gravity of her pain. There truly were no more apologies he could give.

"If Brittany is dead, then who are you now?" asked The Warrior solemnly.

"You and Sensation have spoken so much about love. All you need is love, love is free, love is all there is, blah, blah, blah, blah, blah. Fuck love! I don't have any more love to give. I am a soulless, loveless woman because of you. From here on out, you can call me Candace Loveless. And I'm going to do the opposite of love. My heart has nothing but hate now. I'm going to kill everything this world loves. Whenever I see happiness, I'm going to take it away. I'm going to make people feel just as miserable as I do before I kill them... like you killed me," declared Candace Loveless.

The Iron Warrior and Hicks' hearts dropped. They both felt like they failed her. The Warrior felt responsible for her downfall. Hicks tried to give back, but it was for nothing. A once innocent woman stood before them as a psychotic woman. She had blood on her hands. The woman they hoped to save was gone.

"Brittany, please kid…" Hicks begged.

Candace shot him in his abdomen. "My name is not Brittany anymore!!! Brittany is dead!!! My name is Candace Loveless!!! Let that go, Jimmy!"

The Iron Warrior deployed The Shield of Faith and charged toward her. She fired multiple rounds at him, but he blocked them with the shield. He knocked the gun out of her hand and shoulder tackled her down. He went to check on Hicks while Candace searched for the gun.

"Hang in there, Hicks," The Warrior told him as he applied pressure to the gunshot wound in his abdomen. He placed Hicks' hands on it and helped him apply pressure. He grabbed Hicks' police radio and pressed the emergency button for assistance.

"Help her, Warrior. I hoped I could've made it easier for her. There has to be something still good inside of her," Hicks pleaded.

They looked over and saw Candace standing on the roof's edge. She held the gun to her head with a sadistic smile. "I hate you, Iron Warrior! This is my gift to you. You killed me once, now you get to watch me die again," Candace stated.

"DON'T!!!" shouted The Iron Warrior and Hicks.

Candace pulled the trigger, but the handgun did not fire. It merely clicked. She pulled the trigger again and again, but there was still no action. It was out of ammo. She threw the gun out of frustration.

"Welp, that's not the only way to go," said Candace.

She raised both middle fingers toward The Iron Warrior and threw herself off the roof. He sprang to his feet and launched himself after her. She kept her middle fingers raised with a smile on her face. He prayed for God to allow him to catch her and protect them when they hit the ground. He closed the distance and grabbed her. He quickly rotated his body so he could take the brunt of the impact. A slight shield enveloped them before they hit the concrete.

The velocity of their fall shattered the concrete. The impact knocked Candace unconscious and took the wind out of him. He checked her pulse and was relieved to learn that she was still alive.

He thanked God that he was able to catch her. He sat up and rolled her onto the sidewalk. He regretfully glanced at her. He tried to live without regret, but couldn't help it when he saw her. Brittany was gone and that was on him.

Police Officers arrived with medics to treat Candace and take her into custody. Officers made it to the rooftop and gave aid to Hicks before he bled out. The Iron Warrior looked around and took in the aftermath of the chaos.

"Hey, handsome, you ready to get out of here?" said the woman who turned out to be Sensation.

The Warrior smiled at the mere sight of her. He picked her up and gave her a big hug. They were ecstatic seeing each other.

"Let's go home," The Warrior told her. They left together as officers and medics took control of the scene.

T.V. HOLIDAY

The following day, Travis and Lynda met with Mike and Shannah. They needed help to understand what happened at the rally. Mike revealed Travis's love for Lynda, and his faith in God gave him the strength to reach his full potential as The Iron Warrior. Although during the kiss, Travis absorbed the darkness in Lynda's soul, which resulted in parts of The Warrior's armor turning black. As long as he had faith in God and enough love, Travis could keep the darkness at bay.

While Travis absorbed Lynda's darkness, some of his light was transferred to her soul. Upon taking in the light, Lynda lost her ability to take someone's soul. Her connection to Luc dampened. She wanted to get baptized and wash away any remaining evil in her soul. Mike was unsure if it would work. He had never baptized anyone who had given their soul away.

Mike performed the baptism inside Last Hope. Mike and Travis stood on both sides of Lynda before she went under. The water bubbled and smoked once she stepped in. Her heart raced and her blood temperature rose. Her body tingled and the ecstasy pulsated throughout her. She accepted Jesus Christ into her life and was dipped into the water. Her body went into shock and seized under the water. The ecstasy momentarily enflamed her, but quickly extinguished. The power Luc gave her was no longer there. Lynda felt like she was reborn into a new person with a future she hadn't thought possible.

Travis and Lynda visited Domino's daughter, Ashley, at Seventh City Memorial Hospital. They promised to take care of her as her mother wished. They promised Ashley a home once she beat her cancer.

June 1st arrived. The vote for the Free Love Initiative was the primary focus of every news outlet. Travis and Lynda watched the coverage nervously. The polls closed as evening approached. They sat in and she cuddled next to him as he wrapped his arms around her.

"I really hope this thing doesn't pass," said Lynda earnestly.

"I'd like to think people listened to you at the rally, but you never know," Travis told her.

The news came on with the result of the vote. The news anchor, Ken Plaster, made the announcement. "Breaking news, ladies and gentlemen! The results are in. With a final tally of 55 to 50… The Free Love Initiative will not pass."

They shouted with joy. The Free Love Initiative failed. Travis rolled out of bed and pumped his fists into the air. Lynda jumped up and down on the bed like a kid in celebration. She leaped into Travis' arms and they danced around the room. They shared a passionate kiss to celebrate their victory. The failure of the Free Love Initiative meant the citizens of Carnage Coast still believed in God. His influence was still present. The world was not going to descend into hell. They pressed their foreheads together with their eyes closed and reveled in the moment.

"Where do you want to go from here, baby?" Travis asked. "We can finally get the hell out of here. I can go back and see my son. We can do whatever we want to do."

"I don't care. I just want to be with you," Lynda responded. She focused his eyes toward hers and caressed his face. "I accept you, Travis. You're the man I chose to be with. I don't want anyone else but you. You are IT for me. I can't wait to live life with you and share all of the ups and downs that come with it. I hope you never get tired of me. You're my man. And I'll be your girl forever. I love you."

Travis smiled with joy. His heart was overwhelmed by her love. He could feel the sincerity in her words. For everything he had been through, having Lynda in his arms was one of the best gifts he could've received.

"I'm going to love you for as long as I live. I'll do everything I can to be the man you need me to be. Your love is a blessing. I don't want to go on without it. I'm going to give you all of me. I'm yours for as long as you're willing to have me. I love you, Lynda," Travis stated.

They kissed again. Their hearts raced as their passion for each other rushed to the service. They were happy and overjoyed to be together.

"Do you like whipped cream?" Lynda asked.

"Whipped cream? Who cares about whipped cream right now?" Travis started before he recognized the look on Lynda's face. Her seductive smile and eyes hinted at much more than simply liking whipped cream. "Yes, yes, I do, but I don't think we have…"

She placed her finger on his lips in a shushing manner. "I bought some. Get it, and when you get back, I'll be your cherry on top," Lynda told him as she gently kissed his cheek.

Travis set her down and headed to the kitchen. Before leaving the bedroom, he turned and told Lynda, "I love you."

"I love you too," Lynda happily responded.

Travis raced downstairs and searched for the whipped cream. He was able to rise to the challenge and overcome the Initiative. Travis was thankful that God helped him stand when he needed it most. He believed he could be The Iron Warrior, as God planned. His confidence was at an all-time high. His faith had never been stronger. He held the line between heaven and hell. He was the light in the dark, God's fist in the war, the man powered by faith; he wasn't going to question God anymore.

Travis finally had the relationship he had always dreamed of. He had settled for a life of unhappiness for a long time. Everyone sensed his unhappiness but him. Lynda was everything he hoped for. There was no other woman for him. He risked the world to love her and was able to have both. Travis envisioned their future together. He thought about vacations with his son. Traveling to foreign countries, baseball games and sharing a home filled his mind. He wasn't worried about his time in Carnage Coast. As long as he had Lynda, he happily embraced what was to come.

He found the whipped cream but heard an unusual, heavy thud come from the bedroom. His Divine Eyes were activated, which alarmed him. Travis ran back to the bedroom and froze at the door. His body went numb and the whipped cream oozed out of his hands.

Lynda lay face down on the floor next to the bed. He shockingly stared at her and was overtaken with panic. Travis rushed toward Lynda and cradled her in his arms. He checked her pulse, but she was unresponsive.

"LYNDA!!! LYNDA!!!" he shouted as he shook her to wake her.

Lynda lay motionless in his arms. She was gone. The joy he had was suddenly washed away with agony and grief. He didn't want to believe it. He was heartbroken. He couldn't understand what happened. She was alive moments earlier and was of perfect health. Her eyes were closed and there were no visible signs of trauma. It didn't make sense.

"Sad, isn't it?" asked a voice from within the room.

Travis quickly turned and saw a man standing in the doorway. His skin complexion was light. His ethnicity couldn't be determined just by looking at him. A black, clean-cut goatee surrounded his mouth and was the only hair on his head. He wore an all-red suit with a black shirt and red tie topped off with sunglasses. He had an eerie smile that felt familiar.

"Who the hell are you?" Travis angrily asked.

"Ohhh, sooo angry," he cooed. "I'm the one who should be angry. If she did what she was supposed to do, The Free Love Initiative would've given me the world. You would've fallen and she'd be alive and happy."

While Travis listened, he recognized what he was talking about. He recognized the man standing in his doorway. It was Luc. A wave of rage and fury accompanied his pain and grief. Luc was the reason Travis had to go to Carnage Coast. He was the evil Travis needed to stop. There was no fear in Travis' heart. It was filled with animosity.

Luc shook his head and chuckled, "You realize this is all your fault, right?"

"Fuck you! Bring her back!" Travis barked.

"My, my, my, my, my, such hostility. No! She and I made a deal. I don't care how much she wanted to go back on it. She can pledge to live a life for the man in the penthouse, but her soul will always belong to me. You got her thinking that she could live a different life. You gave her hope. You failed her, not me," Luc told him nonchalantly. Travis' anger amused him.

"She rejected you! This city rejected your initiative. You lost!" Travis snapped.

"No!" Luc interjected. "You simply won a battle. This is a war!! We're just getting started. You're not going anywhere. You think you can be the light for others? You openly accepted my darkness. It won't be long before it overtakes you. Then you'll fall, just like this world. You can't stop me. I'm going to win this city. And before it's all over, you're going to beg me for mercy."

Travis eyed Luc while he held Lynda. His eyes were sparked and enflamed. He gritted his teeth. He wanted to fight Luc. He wanted to end the war right then. Travis didn't care who he was. He wanted to hurt him. He wanted to make him pay.

"I know you've been wanting someone to hold. So, I'll do you a favor. You can keep her body, but her soul is mine. Then get ready because round two is coming," Luc declared.

Luc faded away into the darkness of the hallway. Travis's hope of leaving Carnage Coast was ripped away. His future with Lynda was dead. The chance to see his son again was pushed aside. He was alone again. No one to care for. No one to love. No one to stop the darkness from growing within him.

...

Gladiators, Warriors and Survivors

Doors open
The crowd waits,
Cheering for my death
For that is which I fight,
I fight my death.

The arena chants
The roar trickles my ears,
Fight my battles for you to see
For I am a Gladiator
Struggle defines me.

Blind to my war
The one with myself,
Internal conflict deadly
Opposition always at the ready.

Spiritual battle for my soul
Emotional volcano
Trying not to explode
Can't lose my mind
Can't lose self-control,
Prepped for combat
Working to save my life
For a Warrior I am
You can't extinguish my light.

Through hell, fire and brimstone
I seek the safety of home,
Even if it's empty
I find peace when I'm alone
For I am a Survivor
My will is cast in stone.

So don't make plans
Don't buy tickets to my demise,
I am a Gladiator, Warrior and Survivor
I always rise.

The Iron Warrior
will return in...

Cataclysm:
Legend of The Iron Warrior Vol. 2